DANCING ON FIELDS OF

Sorrow

AND

Blessing

DANCING ON FIELDS OF
Sorrow AND *Blessing*

A NOVEL

P. MULLINS ELSON

REDEMPTION
PRESS

Dancing on Fields of Sorrow and Blessing, Copyright © 2021 P. Mullins Elson
Published by Redemption Press, PO Box 427, Enumclaw, WA 98022.
Toll-Free (844) 2REDEEM (273-3336)

Redemption Press is honored to present this title in partnership with the author. Redemption Press provides our imprint seal representing design excellence, creative content, and high quality production.

All Scripture used in text is taken from the King James Version of the Bible, public domain.

Page 266, C-SPAN, "Eleanor Roosevelt. Pearl Harbor Radio Address. Dec. 7, 1941," YouTube video, 2:56, October 21, 2013, https://youtu.be/4unsg4W0JTM.

Page 268-269, War Archives, "President Franklin D. Roosevelt Declares War on Japan (Full Speech)." YouTube video, 4:47, August 26, 2011, https://www.youtube.com/watch?v=lK8gYGg0dkE .

This book is a work of fiction. While this book is set in a historical context, non-historical names, characters, places and incidents are products of the author's imagination or are used fictitiously. Any resemblance to actual events or locales or persons, living or dead, is entirely coincidental.

ISBN 13: 978-1-64645-410-5
978-1-64645-409-9 (ePub)
978-1-64645-411-2 (Mobi)

Library of Congress Catalog Number 2021915879

It was God who placed the words on my heart,
but all of you who broke them free.
—PME—

Wallace's Wish

Reach for me, sweet child of time, and take my wearied hand.
Follow you must, down cobblestoned roads, past listless moss and rubble.
Come hear my tale of love long lost, of steadfast hope despite the cost.
Mid huckster's cries and bondaged hope, from bless-ed grounds I call.
Rebuild, I whisper; refine, I beg! Let not your heart be troubled.
The grasp of sin has lost its hold, God's grace has overcome.
Take heed, sweet child, glean hope in all, our souls have been set free.

—PATTY MULLINS-ELSON—

Prologue

But they that wait upon the LORD shall renew their strength;
they shall mount up with wings as eagles; they shall run,
and not be weary; and they shall walk, and not faint.
ISAIAH 40:31

September 1920

Wallace rose that Sunday morning as he did every day, before the sunrise and the rooster's crow. It was unusually damp in Charleston County. The air was already swelteringly oppressive.

He dressed himself, kissed his sleeping wife and daughter, and went outside. The roar of the Ashley River thundering just within its banks reached his ears, and he sighed. The heavy rains and flooding they'd been experiencing the last two weeks were threatening to devastate the crops, but something else was bothering him this morning. A vague sense that something was amiss. . . . He shook his head and pushed aside his growing anxiety. It was time to tend to the needs of the day.

The sun pushed its first faint rays of daylight over the horizon as Wallace walked the long line of ancient oaks. He stopped to look back at the home where he'd been born. An image of his grandmother, sweeping the yard as she often had when he was a boy, brought a warm feeling to his heart. He was proud to live among his ancestors on this land that held many secrets, sorrow, and pain. But there was blessing here too, he knew.

His birthplace, built in the early 1840s, was a small structure, pine-framed and meant to house two or three families. Behind it was a row of dilapidated cabins, made of rough brick and long left abandoned. Slave homes, they'd been. He closed his eyes, picturing himself alongside his forefathers, working the fields and overseeing the land. His father and grandfather had been caretakers of this property, and they were never far from his thoughts.

In his father's day, this had been a rice plantation, but its main crop now was tobacco. This year would have been better for rice, he thought wryly. He took a moment to survey the soggy crop waiting to be harvested. Maybe things would dry up this week. He continued his stroll past large plots of equally sodden tomato, melon, and cabbage plants. Despite the weather, everything seemed to be in order.

He counted the small herd of livestock grazing peacefully in the pasture nearby. When he realized what he was doing, he shook his head. "I don't know what's got me worried today, Lord, but I know You're faithful and You make all things right in Your good time. You got it all under control." He looked up at the morning sky, now painted with brilliant reds, oranges, purples, and yellows. His smile was sure as he continued. "I do thank You for these fields of sorrow and blessing, God. Yessuh, that's what they are. Fields of sorrow and blessing."

He considered himself blessed indeed, as many farmers in the area were feeling the crush of an agricultural depression. Foreclosures, crop destruction, and collapsing sale prices had folks abandoning their farms and moving to the cities, hoping to find jobs and security there. Wallace, however, was determined to continue what the good Lord had given him to do.

Almost back to the homestead now, he stopped to observe the hand-carved stones that graced what had previously been the unmarked graves of his forefathers. Wallace remembered helping his father place those stones as a child. Stories of the past, centered on the many traditions carried over from Africa, flooded his mind. He pictured the women preparing food in the brick fireplaces and taking care of children as their men dug graves, often by torchlight, after a long day's work. They'd made wooden caskets and sometimes fashioned simple grave markers. "The dead can only find rest at home with the ancestors," he muttered. The Lowcountry saying was firmly rooted in African tradition.

Humming an old, remembered tune, he stood up from the gravesite, brushed a bit of dirt off his trousers, and made his way past what was left of the plantation house.

General Sherman and the Union army had missed Summerton Place as they pushed their way through Charleston, but the mansion hadn't survived the great earthquake of 1886. Walls tumbled, fire raged, and lives changed. More sorrow, more blessing that day. Loss and redemption. . . it all seemed to go hand in hand on Summerton land. All that remained now of the once grandiose mansion were a few scattered stone columns and an old brick fireplace, partially obscured by the vines and rubble that had overtaken what had been the grand foyer.

People talked about the old house and what had happened there, but Wallace paid them no mind. Gossip was a favorite pastime of nosey Charlestonians. Though he was a generation away from the enslavement of his ancestors, he often felt the cool sting of an entitled Southern society that still held certain racial divides.

Wallace had been born into freedom; he'd not experienced the bondage of his forefathers, but their heritage was his own. Farming the hallowed land was in his blood, and the past had given him a right to these fields. They were, indeed, now his.

He supposed that he could rebuild over the old home—and some day he might—but for now, he'd allowed it to remain in its devastated state to remind him of an era gone forever. His life would be measured, not so much by the past or by the suffering of his people, but by the blessings he believed would come. The mansion reminded him of his purpose. Time had a way of righting wrong, of adjusting the ramifications of human sin which came from understanding the greatness of his Lord.

The broken walls of this house had seen unspeakable atrocities; that he knew. A shudder ran through him as he heard the echo in the wind. Secrets and whispers of another time swirled around him. Visions of his grandmother, dancing and singing; of drunken eyes, watching. He shook his head, returning to the present.

The foreboding in the air remained. He couldn't put his finger on it, couldn't explain, but the fields seemed alive with the voices of the past. He headed home. Something didn't feel right with this day.

"'Bout time you got back. We need to head on up to the church." Ida was sitting in a wooden rocker on the front porch, weaving a sweetgrass basket as she waited. She stopped and looked at her husband. "How's the crop?"

"Doin' good, considering. . . the rains haven't hurt us too much, leas' not yet." He looked around. "Where's Bessany?"

"Gittin' her dress on." Ida got up and strode to the front door. "Bessany! You better be ready—your daddy's here, and we gotta go." She looked back and winked at her husband as he took off his hat and shook his head. "Watch, we gon' be late again. Bess, you better be puttin' on that white dress I made you!" Ida had made Bessany's Sunday clothes of delicate lace, truly a gift of great care.

Bessany ran down the stairs and did a pirouette on the wooden floor. The morning light caught the carefully stitched lilies strewn across her dress as she twirled like a ballerina for her audience of two.

Ida held out her hand. "Come on, child. The Lord's awaitin'."

They left the house and headed down the long path to the church house. Built well before the War, the small structure had been used by generations of Summerton slaves. Now, it was used by anyone who worked on the plantation or lived in the nearby villages. The doors were always open. His father had called the church the praise house, and Wallace liked to do the same. A giant oak stood watch over the building, steady and with fortitude, as if it held secrets of its own. Everything about the place felt sacred.

They approached a narrow footbridge that spanned a short portion of the river. Bessany ran ahead as she always did.

"Look, Daddy! I beat you again," she called as she passed her parents. She was a precocious child, always running, always asking. "Daddy, I wanna go fishing today. You said you'd take me."

She had been asking relentlessly to go fishing with him, but the river had been ferocious, even overflowing its banks in some places. "Maybe after we get our chores done. The water looks a mite calmer today." He held up his hand. "Wait, child."

She obeyed while Wallace did a quick check that the bridge was secure. Satisfied, he grinned and pointed up into the trees. "Look!" He exclaimed. As Bessany's eyes followed his finger, he took off running across the bridge.

"Daddy!" Bessany squealed and chased him as fast as she could. Ida just laughed at the sight of their antics.

But the child wasn't deterred. "I'll even make my own pole, with a stick and string, jus' like you showed me, Daddy. Please?" She bounced up the church steps. She was a vision in white.

Wallace wrapped his arm around his daughter. The truth was, he couldn't help himself. He'd give her all the fish in the sea if he could. He'd cast the nets for her, gather up all that life had blessed him with, and hand it to her. She was everything, and in his heart, he thanked the Lord for her.

"We'll see. We have things to do first." He looked at Ida, who scowled slightly as they walked into the praise house. Sundays were for worship first, she always said.

After church, they shared dinner at the table. Bessany, barely finishing dessert, gave her father a mischievous look, then ran outside. Wallace stayed behind to help Ida clean up, then headed to the barns. Days were long on the farm and chores were numerous, but he did only what was necessary on Sundays. It was the Lord's day. The field hands had the day off, and family time took precedence over the needs of the farm. He finished up as quickly as possible and headed home to look for Bessany. She usually helped him feed the chickens, but she was nowhere to be found. *Probably up to no good.*

He opened the door to his home. "Bessany! Let's go! Sun's goin' down!" He heard nothing. He walked out of the house and out to the chicken coop, but she wasn't there. He walked further, past the barn and the old plantation ruins, calling out her name. He went back to the house, where Ida had returned from gathering grasses for her baskets.

"Where's Bessany?" That strange aching from the morning had returned. "Have you seen her?"

Ida piled the gathered grass near her worktable. "I thought she was with you. She went off to find a good stick to use for a pole. She took some string from my basket. . . said you were gon' take her fishing." She looked up at the sun. "She's been gone since you left. I thought she went to find you."

"I haven't seen her all day." He thought for a moment, then suddenly it dawned on him. A wash of panic rushed over him and an alarm went off in his heart. He knew where she was.

"Get the field hands. Tell them to meet me by the river," he said frantically.

He ran across the fields, barely able to breathe, pressing forward toward the bridge. *If I can just get there, Lord!* They'd crossed it many times before, holding hands, running, racing together on their way to church. But today was different. He'd felt it as soon as he awoke.

He got to the bridge and looked over the wooden rails to the swollen Ashley River below. He didn't see her.

He looked along the base of the bridge and spotted a makeshift fishing pole at the edge of the river. And then he saw her. Her white lace dress was tangled in a fallen tree, and she was face down in the raging, unforgiving river.

As he ran to her, the sound of his people filled his heart and mind. African drums and a faint, solemn hum of song. . . torturous singing, sorrowful reverence. Tradition swirled around him as the wind moaned through the trees. The hallowed fields had taken her to a place where he could not follow.

⁓

Twelve months had passed. He stood at the graveside, fresh lilies in his hand. The flowers tumbled to the ground as he fell to his knees, his heart hard against the God he'd loved. He questioned now every belief system and every lesson his father and his father's father had taught him.

Why had God taken one so young and innocent? And her mother, swiftly after. It would be unbearable for the mightiest of believers, and Wallace was weak. With a sob, he picked up the scattered lilies and arranged them neatly on the graves.

He traced their names in the stone with his fingertips, first Bessany, then Ida.

He about jumped out of his skin when a hand touched his shoulder. He turned to find his father and a well-dressed gentleman behind him, a stack of papers in his hand.

"Son. We must move past our grief. Ida. . . Bessany. . . they's gone. They with the others now, waitin' for you in that place prepared for all o' us one day. Let the light take them; we must move on."

"He needs to know, Moses." The gentleman interrupted.

His father nodded. A wistful smile touched his lips. "Son, a miracle has happened—we've found her. The last of our kin. Sweet Jesus, she is alive."

Chapter 1

And now abideth faith, hope, charity,
these three; but the greatest of these is charity.
1 CORINTHIANS 13:13

June 1939

The Great Depression had taken its toll on families across the country, and South Carolina was no exception. Even now, years after the economy had crashed, much of Charleston was on the brink of bankruptcy. Orphanages in the area had filled at an alarming rate. Local agencies had difficulty coping; obtaining the needed funds was difficult—but you would never know it by looking at Livy Marigold.

Livy was a strong, perpetually happy woman. She was the director of Palmetto Manor, a large orphanage in Charleston, and she was quite good at her job. Of course, there was a reason for that—she was an orphan herself. The few bits of information she knew about her mother only left her with more questions. The nuns who'd raised her had assured her of her mother's love, though she had not survived Livy's birth.

According to legend, her mother had been searching for her own family at the time, though even that information was questionable. She had arrived at the convent door, injured, weak, and pregnant, with no memory of who she was or where she was from but a desperate drive to find out. Her clothing and bearing indicated a life of comfort, but despite a fervent search for information, neither the nuns nor the local police had been able to identify her. Not more than three weeks after her arrival, she'd died in childbirth. By that time, they were sure her name was Hope Marigold and that she loved her baby very much, but further questions had led to inexplicable sadness and hours of weeping.

Sometimes in her quiet moments, Livy pictured her mother wandering the streets of Charleston, pregnant with nowhere to go. She often wondered who and where her father was. How her mother had ended up alone at a convent. The only mementos Livy had of her mother were a plain gold wedding band and a lovely locket. Etched on the outside of the locket was an oak tree. The inside contained a tiny etching of the Lord's Prayer. The nuns had told her how her mother would clasp the locket and cry. Sometimes it would make her happy, they said, and other times, she would be angry as she tried to remember why it was so important.

And that's all Livy knew about who she was.

For years, she'd tried to solve the mystery of her existence, but now she simply refused to dwell there. It didn't matter where she'd come from, she told herself. She'd worked and studied hard to become who she was, and that's all that mattered.

And that made it easy for Livy to understand and empathize with the distressing journeys the children in her care endured. Her experience made her determined to shield them as much as possible from the insecurities of the day and of the future. At thirty-nine, she had never married, and she was just fine with that. The orphanage had become her home and her life's ambition; she didn't need a man to make her complete or to take care of her. The children gave her purpose. They filled the void of never having children of her own. And in return for the blessing their lives extended to her, she gave them hope. She loved them, they knew it, and it showed.

She knew how to survive with her head held high and a smile on her face. Under no circumstances did Livy allow the children under her care to know how difficult it was to make ends meet. Most of the children she housed came from varying degrees of poverty. Many had been left on her doorstep with nothing. Others had come with a few belongings, brought by parents who could no longer support them. Some would return but others, Livy knew, would not be back.

Mr. Whitfield was one of those. He was different. She would not forget the day he'd brought his daughter, Hattie, to her. He was well-dressed, and his mannerisms spoke of wealth and prosperity, yet something in his demeanor raised her hackles. He presented his daughter with a chest of her belongings, told Livy that his wife had passed away with pneumonia, and left without a backward look. The thirteen-year-old was beautiful, but her chestnut hair, worn across her face, hid an alarming, barely healed scar that ran from the bottom of her ear to the corner of her perfect mouth.

In the three years since Hattie Whitfield had arrived, she'd become quite special to Livy. Hattie didn't talk about her scar or her father much, but she frequently spoke of her love for her mother. The information she had shared was limited, just that she had obtained the scar while playing with her mother's garden tools. Livy was sure there was more to the story because, along with the physical mark, the girl carried other scars too—deep emotional ones that kept her withdrawn and often silent.

Livy couldn't explain the immediate draw she'd felt toward the girl, but it was there. It had taken a while for Hattie to fit smoothly into life at Palmetto Manor. The first few months had required adjustments for everyone. The older children had teased her, while the younger ones shied away due to her scar, but Hattie seemed to take it all in stride. Shunning her peers, she immersed herself in books, her school studies, and gardening. She began to write regularly in a diary she kept beside her bed and spent hours by the tree behind the orphanage. As the years passed and she became a young lady, she proved to be a godsend for Livy. She helped willingly around the house, and the children fell in love with her—as did anyone who took the time to get to know her.

Livy brushed aside her thoughts and walked into the kitchen, looking for the girl. There were pressing matters at hand.

"Where's Hattie?" she asked one of the boys sitting at the kitchen table.

"Where do you think, Miss Livy?"

"Is she out in the garden already? Oh my, that girl! I need her to get ready—some folks are coming by to meet her." She wasn't sure how she felt about this new prospect. Hattie was sixteen, and it was unusual for a family to request a child so old.

She looked out the kitchen window and found Hattie nestled up near the oak tree with her ever-present book. She twirled a strand of her long brown hair around a finger as she read. Livy stepped outside.

"Hattie? You must come inside. I've got some good news." Livy wasn't sure if it was good news, but she'd present it that way. "There's a couple on their way to meet you. They're from the city, and they seem real nice." It took an effort to keep her tone positive.

Hattie closed her book. Then she stood, straightened up, and brushed the dust off her skirt. "Oh," she said. "I didn't know."

Whatever hero she was enjoying today would have to wait, Livy thought as she watched her move. Always so compliant. . . she wished desperately to read the girl's mind. "Come on, now. Let's see what dress we can find. Tell you what—I'll let you borrow one of mine. I can help you get ready if you'd like. Not that you need it or anything."

Livy forced a smile. They had been down this road before, and each potential adoption had ended in disappointment. She put her arm around Hattie's waist, and they strolled back to the house in silence. Maybe this time would be different, but ultimately, the scar changed people's minds. Every time. But Livy would remain positive.

"Go upstairs, sweetheart. Pick out something you like from my closet."

"But, Miss Livy, why? Aren't I too old? *I* wouldn't adopt me! Besides, you need me here," she said, setting her book on the kitchen counter. "There's no point in getting all fussed up over it, they'll just take one look at me—"

"Okay, you stop right there," Livy said firmly. The girl's words ripped at her core. How could she not know her worth to this world? She grabbed Hattie's arm and pulled her to a mirror. "D'you see that girl?"

Hattie tried to cover her scar, but Livy caught her hand and held it.

"Look at that beautiful, perfect girl. Oh, honey, you know nothing of what you are! Do you know what I saw in you from the start? I saw greatness. I see a beautiful girl behind that—" She tried to brush Hattie's hair back with her fingers but stopped when they caught a knot. "Ugh! This chestnut mess you call hair!" They both laughed. "Now, scoot."

Hattie headed up the stairs. "Oh, and don't think I didn't see those eyes rolling," Livy said as she turned and entered her office, calling for her aide as she went.

"Cora? Put some coffee on, please. We need to be ready for the Middletons. They're on their way to meet Hattie." She shuffled some papers together and glanced out the window.

Cora stepped into the office, duster in hand. "Yes'm, Miss Marigold. It's already on." She had been employed by the orphanage even before Livy had arrived. She knew how things worked, and her face showed her reservation toward the day's visitors. "D'you think—"

"No, Cora. We are going to stay positive and hope for the best." She sighed, then interrupted her own train of thought. "And how many times do I have to tell you to call me Livy? You could be running this place yourself."

Cora shrugged and Livy put an arm around the woman. "We'll see what happens. You could do me a favor though. Would you make sure the children stay outside? I don't want any disturbances, and. . . I want to talk to these people before Hattie comes down."

The tone of her voice had changed, and Cora glanced up at her in concern. "Miss Livy, you gonna be all right?"

"Yes. I'm just nervous for her is all." Through the wide window, they both watched as a shiny black Packard eased its way onto the lane next to the house. "Okay, Cora, you know the drill."

Cora grabbed her hand, gently kissed it, and held it to her chest. "Th'only one in control here," she murmured, "is God. You need to trust Him. He'll make it right for our Hattie."

They stood for a moment longer, holding on to each other, until the Middletons were at the orphanage door.

~

The Middletons were an elegant couple, impeccably dressed and exuding an aura of superiority. Livy didn't usually warm up to that sort, but she'd set aside her personal opinions for the sake of the children.

"Mr. and Mrs. Middleton, hello. Please sit down." She welcomed them quietly, indicating seats near her desk.

"Miss Livy—" Cora popped her head in and stopped to admire the couple. There was an uncomfortable silence in the room until she realized she was staring. "Oh, I'm sorry. I have coffee if anyone would like it."

Livy seated herself at the desk. "Yes, would you like some coffee? Or Cora could get you some tea."

"We are fine, thank you," Mr. Middleton responded. He looked at his watch. "May we see the girl?"

This is already off to a lousy start. "Her name is Hattie," Livy replied pointedly. "I'd like to ask you a few questions before you visit with her, if you don't mind."

"Of course," he responded, and his wife glanced at him nervously. "We just don't have a lot of time. We would like to look at the girl. . . Hattie, of course. We must return to New York as soon as we are finished here."

"New York? I didn't see that on your application. I have a local address here in Charleston." Livy shuffled through her papers. *Something is not right.*

Mrs. Middleton spoke up. "Our main residence is in New York; that's where our business is. We travel back and forth, and Charleston is one of the *many* homes we have, Miss Marigold." She turned and smiled up at Cora. "I'll take a tea, please."

Cora nodded and left the room.

Livy pushed on. "Okay, let me get this straight. You are looking to take Hattie to New York, then? She will not be living here locally?"

"No, she will be in New York at our main residence," Mr. Middleton responded. "She is sixteen, yes?"

"Yes, she is. Just turned, in fact." Livy flipped through the adoption papers again. "It says here that you have a small local business—a textile mill? Is that correct?"

"Oh, we closed our textile mill here in Charleston months ago. We're operating out of New York exclusively now, and times are not as. . . well, not as good for us. We cannot afford to have multiple facilities and pay for labor. And Black folk are only allowed to sweep the floors and clean the machines. We need healthy White girls to operate the machinery—" He cleared his throat and shifted in his seat. "May we see her, please. How is her health?"

Mrs. Middleton looked pained.

Livy sat quietly, watching them closely. She could not dislodge the uneasy feeling in her chest. "She is healthy, strong, and capable." She knew where this was going now. "Cora!" She shouted the name, not leaving her desk or looking away from the couple.

Cora bustled in from the hallway, carrying Mrs. Middleton's tea. She set it carefully on the table then turned toward Livy. Her eyes widened when she saw her face. "Miss?" She asked carefully.

"Bring Hattie, please. The Middletons are waiting." She sat back in her chair, twisting a pencil in her fingers.

"I'm here, Miss Livy." Hattie spoke from the doorway. "Miss Cora already called me." She looked beautiful in her borrowed dress. Her brown hair fell smoothly to her shoulders.

Livy looked at her, smiling. "Come in, Hattie. I'd like you to meet the Middletons."

Hattie walked over and reached out her hand. "I'm pleased to meet you," she murmured.

Mr. Middleton smiled coldly and looked Hattie up and down as though he were looking at a prized cow at the county fair. Livy had had enough. She set her pencil on the desk and stood up.

"Thank you, Hattie. Now run along." Cora was standing at the door and ushered her out, looking back at the couple and at Livy. Livy motioned for her to leave too, then strode to the door and closed it firmly. She stood there for a moment with her arms crossed, then shook her head and spoke.

"I think this transaction is finished. It's time for you to go."

Mr. Middleton stood. "What are you saying, Miss Marigold?"

Mrs. Middleton reached up and grasped his sleeve.

"I'm saying, you need to leave. This is an adoption agency, not Market Street. My kids are not bought and sold like cattle. You need to leave now."

Mrs. Middleton stood up. "I'm sorry, Miss Marigold. You misunderstand our purpose. We can give her a good life—"

"A good life? Working in the factories? She is a sixteen-year-old child looking for a home. She is not a warm body to fill the seats of a cheap labor force!" Livy opened the door and motioned for them to leave.

Mr. Middleton became outraged. "Show some respect, woman! We are doing her a favor. Do you really think she is adoptable with that—that *scar* of hers? No one will want a child at sixteen for anything other than work. And we are willing to give her work *with pay*."

"Look," Mrs. Middleton spoke earnestly. "Times are not good for us. We need help in our factories. This would be the best thing for a girl like her. She will learn a trade."

"The *best thing*? All you want, madame, is cheap labor. You cannot do this to a child—adopt her and then send her off to work in your factory. She needs love and a family, not to be cast out onto an assembly line." Livy couldn't stand to look at them any longer. "Get out. *Get out!*"

Mr. Middleton took his wife's arm and shoved her toward the door. With his chin high in the air, he turned back for a final word. "Good luck, Miss Marigold. Eventually, you won't be able to *afford* care for all these children, and the state will *make* you do it. There's no sense in being proud about it—it's one less mouth for the county to feed. And this one! Looks to me, with that scar and being sixteen already—" He snorted. "You give these kids airs, make them think they're worth more than they are. You think you're helping them? Don't make me laugh." He stomped down the hallway and out the door, still talking.

Livy couldn't remember the last time she'd been so angry. Shaking, she closed the outer door behind him and returned to her office. She sat at her desk, arranging papers and fighting back tears.

One less mouth for the county to feed. The callous words resounded in her mind. She knew he was right. Eventually, the lack of funding would force her to do the inevitable.

No. I have faith, she thought. She wasn't entirely sure what that meant, but it sounded good. Times were bad, but surely good things would come. Someday. Right now, her responsibility was to the children, and as long as she breathed, she would not allow them to be sold like cattle.

She straightened the Middletons' paperwork and placed it carefully in a drawer. It was time to move on. She stood and strode to the door, planning to head to the kitchen. Instead, she found Hattie huddled at the end of the hallway, a hand on her scar and her hair covering her face. She had heard everything. Her tears gave it away.

"I told you, Miss Livy."

Livy grabbed her and held her close. "Now, you pay those monsters no mind. You were meant for bigger and better things." She held Hattie's face in her hands and looked earnestly into her eyes. "You listen to me, girl—bigger and better. I promise."

In the weeks that followed the Middletons' visit, Hattie immersed herself in books and kept busy helping Livy with the children. She was sixteen after all, and it was about time, she told herself, that people thought of her as an adult.

She and Livy hadn't talked about the Middletons after that day, but the disappointment lingered—not so much because she had wanted to be adopted, but because of the rejection that always came. Her own father hadn't wanted her—he hadn't even wanted her mother at the end. But as always, Hattie pushed those unbidden memories aside and focused on making herself valuable around the house.

"I might just be here forever," she muttered as she browsed through the books in Livy's office, looking for one to take her mind elsewhere. "But then again, maybe forever isn't such a bad thing." A hollering outside caught her attention, and she pulled the drapes aside to get a better look. She raised the window, a grin on her face. The children were running circles around Livy, playing some game.

"Hey, y'all better stop all that carrying on out there! I'm coming out with my books, and you better find somewhere else to play." The truth was, she didn't mind them being out there at all. They were family.

Taking what looked like a brand-new copy of *The Grapes of Wrath*, Hattie walked past the garden and headed to her place of refuge. She'd heard talk of this one. A few pages of John Steinbeck should be enough to get her mind off things. She stretched out under her favorite oak tree, looked up at the Spanish moss tangled in its branches, and gave a nice, long sigh. Opening the book, she took a minute to appreciate the smell of its fresh pages, then started to read. Not more than a minute later, it seemed, someone was calling her name.

"Hattie!" Livy called again. "I need you inside to help with the chores. Mr. Wallace will be by this afternoon. We need to get things cleaned up a bit. What are you reading, anyway? It's certainly had you enthralled."

Hattie glanced down at the book, surprised to find she'd read several chapters.

"You had a new book in your office. I thought it looked interesting." She showed the cover to Livy, whose eyebrows rose in response.

"Oh, that is a good one. It's not an easy story to read, though. Kind of gets a little close to some of us sometimes." She shrugged and reached out a hand to Hattie. "Anyway, right now I need you to help me straighten up and get dinner ready."

Hattie rolled her eyes and shook her head. "And you want to adopt me out of here," she teased. "Looks like to me, you need me around to keep things in order." She let Livy pull her to her feet, then stopped and looked at her, standing with her hands on her hips.

"Miss Livy, you know I love you, right?" She smoothed the dirt around with her toe. "I mean, I know I don't say it much but. . . I really do appreciate all that you do for me." The breeze lifted her hair and blew it gently against her face.

Livy dusted the dirt off Hattie's shirt. She fixed her collar, then rested her hands on Hattie's shoulders. "Baby, if ever I was born into anything in this life, I was born to love you and every one of these kids we're raising. And did you hear me? I said *we*. We are in this crazy thing together, you and I, and I won't let anyone hurt you, ever again."

She reached up and traced the scar on Hattie's face with a gentle finger. "Whatever happened to you, whatever ugliness gave you this, I am going to take it all away." She cleared her throat. "Now, let's go take care of those kids."

Chapter 2

*All things work together for good to them that love God,
to them who are the called according to his purpose.*
ROMANS 8:28

December 1860

Julia Summerton took a sip of her tea, placed her mother's fine china on the breakfast table, and picked up an issue of *The Liberator*. She smiled as she remembered her recent visit to Boston with her father. It had been a business trip for him, but Julia had used the time for adventure. She had even managed to secretly attend a meeting in a Quaker community that was active in its campaign against slavery. Finding people who were likeminded had been both refreshing and invigorating. Acquiring a few recent copies of *The Liberator* had been an unexpected coup. If Father had known where she'd been and what she'd been doing. . . she shook her head.

It had taken some effort, but she'd managed to smuggle the newspapers home and had kept them carefully hidden since. Concealed within this issue of the paper's pages, she also had two pamphlets, reprints of material written years ago by the Grimké sisters, well-known abolitionists who had once lived in Charleston.

She pulled out the documents and set them in front of her. Most of the Southerners she knew would consider the publications blasphemous; they were surely contraband. She glanced through Angelina Grimké's letter to the editor of *The Liberator*, originally published in 1835, then picked up the second pamphlet—equally dangerous, Sarah Grimké's *An Appeal to the Christian Women of the South*. She studied it for a moment, then carefully placed the pamphlets back inside the newspaper.

Julia admired the bravery of the women for speaking out against the degrading nature and sin of slavery, and their mutual desire for the emancipation of slaves. She felt an affinity with these women, a sense of kinship that could not be denied. She sided secretly with her friends up north, but in Charleston. . . she was alone.

She took a deep breath and placed the newspaper neatly on the table. She had been keeping herself informed on the national cries of potential rebellion in the Southern states over the last few months, and now there was rumor of secession. She didn't know what the future held for South Carolina, but she knew what she was hoping for. The pathway there, however, felt entirely obscured and impossible.

She didn't want to be a pesky pessimist, but it was clear that change was not coming to South Carolina anytime soon. Yet she couldn't help but hope that eventually a new South would rise from the ashes of its sin.

She stood from the Chippendale table and looked out the large window. From here, she could see the row of slave homes and life bustling on the plantation. She wondered what her father thought about when he looked out this window. He, sitting beside the table in sheltered richness, and the slaves, in constant movement, working no matter the condition of their environment, working always within the confines of shackled sin.

"What a contradiction," she said aloud. It was a Southern standard, set by Southern men in a world she didn't want to belong to. Frustrated, she moved to her father's cabinet and poured herself a drink, the kind Southern women weren't accustomed to.

Returning to the window, she looked up and out. . . and something beautiful caught her attention. Like wisps of hope, a light snow was falling from the sky. Highly unusual for South Carolina, but perfect for what she was planning for the evening. Christmas was less than a week away. Lost in the moment, she felt a sense of peace wash over her as she thought about the days ahead.

"Miz Julia." She turned from the window, startled but pleased with whom she saw. It was Ned, her father's field supervisor. "We ready, Miz Julia," he said with a grin on his face and his hat in his hands. "Got all the kids ready. We's headin' up to the praise house."

Ned couldn't contain his excitement as he paced back and forth, almost giddy. They looked forward to this every year, especially when William wasn't around. Christmas was a time for reading and learning, where the slaves gathered in the praise house, waiting for the words. The birth of Christ would lead the way. Freedom. *Freedom, indeed.* The story of Jesus gave them that. *Even if it is in secret.*

"Well, what are we waiting for? I'll get Mother's Bible, and we'll get started." Gathering her skirts, she moved toward the small table where the Bible waited. She glanced back toward the window, her smile growing.

"Ned, make sure there's plenty of wood for the fire in the praise house. Can you believe it's snowing? In South Carolina! It's a sign—I know we've got good things coming. Well, come on!"

She grabbed her wrap and rushed out the door, calling for Chloe. Chloe had been Julia's companion as a child, then as they got older, she'd become her personal maid. But their relationship went far beyond slave and lady of the house. Chloe was a friend and confidante.

She found Chloe in the music room, standing at the long windows, watching the snow fall. "There you are! Come on, let's go! Father will be back from Beaufort tomorrow, and we must get a move on. There is no telling what kind of mood he'll be in."

There were always risks when she involved herself with the slaves and their personal lives, but Julia took full advantage of her father's frequent absences. She was an oddity, she knew. She had no friends to speak of, nor did she need any. While her position as a Summerton could have afforded her a busy social life with the other wealthy landowners in Charleston, she seldom participated. She knew where she belonged, what she believed, and what she wanted to do with her time, and she did it—despite what society would dictate.

Truth be told, Ned and Chloe were more like family to her than her own flesh and blood. Her father's temperament had declined over the years since Julia's mother's untimely death, and that had affected her social activity as well. But as his field supervisor, Ned had always been close to her father; in fact, she would dare to say they shared a mutual respect, despite her father's outward attitude otherwise.

Ned was special to the Summerton family. He'd apprenticed at twelve, and Mr. Summerton himself had made sure he'd gained skills in carpentry, farming, blacksmithing, and basic bookkeeping. With that knowledge, Ned was a valuable asset for Mr. Summerton. He trusted him to direct the Negroes in their agricultural and other duties—and thus managed to avoid interaction with his other slaves.

William Summerton divided his time between Charleston and his deceased father's rice plantation on the Combahee River. Much of the crop from that plantation was brought up to Charleston, where slaves sold the produce at the market downtown. When Father was gone, Ned managed the slaves and the fields at Summerton Place. Her father's frequent travels were a blessing for Julia and the slaves, because during those times, she taught them how to read and write.

Secrecy was key. Once when she was a child, her father had caught her teaching a slave how to read by reading stories from the Bible. Instead of punishing Julia, her father punished the slave and made her watch. Julia didn't attempt to do it again for years, until Ned had begged her to teach him. He reasoned that it was worth the pain if caught, to have the knowledge and abilities needed to function in the world.

Sweet Ned. He was a believer. He believed that one day, God would set them free. He wasn't sure when or if it would happen in his lifetime, but he was sure it would. He made a point of remaining steadfast and informed. . . waiting, much like Habakkuk or Job, people from his favorite books of the Bible.

"If'n God's people can do it," Ned would say, "so can I. I will wait for my God. I will wait and listen for His voice, Miz Julia." He would ponder the verses, then put his hat on, stand up tall, and go back to tending the plantation. Ned's was a righteous path if ever there was one. Julia admired his strength, even when she questioned her own.

They walked down the trail, crossed a footbridge over a narrow part of the river, and headed to the church on the other side of her father's plantation. Along the way, children ran out from the slave cabins, reaching to touch Julia's skirts as she walked by. Chloe would have shooed them away on a normal day, but not today. Today everyone was invited.

The snow fell gently on the long line of oaks as, together, they entered the praise house.

Outside, the church bristled with the chill of the evening. A bonfire snapped and crackled in the yard. Inside, too, a fire burned brightly on the hearth, tended carefully by a field hand. Slaves of all ages sat in the pews, anticipation on their faces. The children sat in front, closest to the roaring fire as they hummed the songs of their African ancestry. Others recited the Lord's Prayer in Gullah dialect. Both joyful and rhythmic, they worshiped together in the praise house.

The Bible was a dangerous book to the Lowcountry African. Christianity was encouraged here, but reading was not—hence the secret lessons and avid memorization of verses. But secrecy gave the people a love of Scripture, a determination to learn, and hearts that yearned for Jesus. In the praise house, you could hear their shouts of joy, see their arms outstretched as if to touch Him from the very place they sat.

Julia felt most comfortable here, surrounded by her father's slaves as they worshiped and sang songs both Christian and African. Occasionally, she danced alongside Chloe in their joint celebration of salvation. Julia was often astonished by the closeness these people felt with the Father, the peace they experienced despite their bondage. How did they manage that? Maybe they were closer to the Lord than she was.

In time, the dancing and singing subsided, and the room settled into silence as the people gathered to listen to the reading of God's Word. Today, they would read about the birth of Christ. Ned read the first verses, then Chloe, then Julia. When the reading was finished, the children began reciting their memorized verses, and it was like music to Julia's ears—beautiful, solemn, and joyful, all at the same time.

She watched as they celebrated, marveling again at their confident and buoyant spirits in this world of human travesty. Christian virtue was strong in their moral character, and they were eager to learn. They were like sponges soaking up the Word, their ardor unlike anything she'd experienced in far grander churches in town.

Yet even in the joyful celebration of the praise house, Julia's apprehension stirred. Father would return tomorrow, and her time with them would end for now. It was late, and they all had responsibilities in the morning. With a sigh, she closed the book and stood. She looked out the window and noticed the snow had stopped falling.

Part of her was disappointed, and she couldn't help but think of the irony of it all. For those gathered in this building, hope was alive, even in their bondage. Yet her own hope diminished as the thought of her father's impending arrival permeated her soul with dread. How easy it was for her to lose the value of what she came here to teach. She was teaching about grace while forgetting her own. She felt like a hypocrite.

A strange sense of doom pressed upon her shoulders, but she shrugged it off and forced herself to smile. This was a joyous day, a celebration of their Lord, and for that she would be thankful. The children gathered around her, but her attention was caught by Ned and Chloe, whispering together in the back of the church.

She moved through the children toward her friends. "What on earth are you two whispering about?" They were up to something. "C'mon now, cat got your tongue? What's got you two smiling so big?"

"Miz Julia, we got something to ask you, if you don't mind." Ned walked up to Julia as Chloe clung to his side. "Me and Chloe. . . we want to—"

"We want t'jump the broom, Miz Julia! We want t'get married!" Ned and Chloe looked at each other, smiling from ear to ear.

"Married?" Julia had known for a while that her friends were secretly attracted to each other, but she hadn't realized it had progressed to this. She looked at them warily. "Really? You sure?"

The smile they exchanged told her all she needed to know. "Well, then. Looks like we have us a wedding to plan. When shall we do this?"

"*Now*, Miz Julia. We want to do it now." Ned paused, gripping his hat in his hands. "Seeing as how Mr. Summerton is coming back—Chloe and I was hoping to do it before tomorrow."

Julia knew what he meant. Father didn't take kindly to relations among his favored slaves. It was an unwritten rule, and it would apply especially strong to Chloe. Marriages were usually encouraged by slave owners because married men were less likely to be rebellious or try to escape, but her father was different around Chloe. Julia knew that was true, though she did not want to understand why. Not long after Julia's mother had died, he had become obsessed with Chloe, almost as if he desired her, but Julia had stubbornly shrugged off that thought, unwilling to think it of her father.

But this? It would change everything. "I am afraid Father would not approve," she said slowly.

"I know you's worried about your father, but she my life. You know how I feel about her. Please do this for us."

Chloe held his arm tightly, her eyes beseeching Julia's help.

"Well. . ." Julia hesitated, then took a deep breath. "All right. Let's do it now then. But you let me tell him, in my time. Do you hear me?"

"Yes, ma'am." They said it together, both grinning from ear to ear.

"What are we waiting for?" Julia shrugged, her own smile beaming. "Someone get me a broom!"

She married them beneath the frozen stars on that cold December night. The light of the moon shone down on the praise house, blessing the event. She read a few Scriptures to the couple, and then, as the lady of the house, pronounced them man and wife in the eyes of God. The celebration ensued late into the night as they danced and sang in the vibrant Gullah tradition.

The party ended abruptly when a field hand tending to the bonfire outside saw the carriage moving along the frosted, oak-lined road. Master Summerton was home.

Chapter 3

Rest in the LORD, and wait patiently for him:
fret not thyself because of him who prospereth in his way,
because of the man who bringeth wicked devices to pass.
PSALM 37:7

Julia was up early the next morning, uneasy about her father's sooner-than-expected return. She didn't have to look long to find him in his library, already at the books and orchestrating the daily affairs on the plantation.

"Father!" She swept past him and glanced out the window. "You're back, a full day early. How is grandfather's—"

"What was all the commotion outside the church last evening?"

"Commotion? Oh." She laughed nervously. "Some of the Negroes were roasting corn on the fire. Isn't it a gorgeous morning?" She glanced back to find her father unimpressed. "I'm sure they were just celebrating the upcoming holiday, Daddy. Have you forgotten, Christmas is only a few days away."

He looked at her as if not quite sure what to make of her explanation or if he should trust that she was telling the truth. "Looked to me like there was something more to that celebration than the birth of our Lord and Savior." He looked hard at her, then shifted his gaze to the desk, shuffling some papers.

Julia bit her lip. The hypocrisy of her father's beliefs played hard on her sensibilities. Christianity was alive and well, but so was bondage and the sin that came with it. *There is no Jesus in slavery*, she thought, but she pushed away her growing resentment toward him. Choosing her words carefully, she changed the subject.

"How was your visit to granddaddy's plantation? Are the fields ready for the winter?"

He ignored her question, his expression stern. "I see you are occupying your time with William Lloyd Garrison, rather than tending to your father's business." He threw the copy of *The Liberator* on the table in front of her.

How could she have forgotten? She snatched the paper from the table and turned away from him.

"There is no harm in reading the news and staying informed, Daddy. Even if you don't agree with what is said." She turned back and kissed him on the cheek, hoping to soften his demeanor. "Welcome back." She could feel the anger growing in him. Lying to him wasn't easy.

"Your love and affection for our Negroes has not gone unnoticed, young lady. And now, you are reading about the abolitionist sentiments in the North?" He took back the paper from her hands and strode to the fireplace. "I will have no daughter of mine reading such blaspheme. Today, I was informed that we have seceded! They are our enemies now. They work to take away our way of living, Julia. I won't have you sympathizing with the enemy. And you are far too friendly with the darkies."

Julia watched as her father crumpled the paper and tossed it on the fire. *He's almost painfully beautiful,* she thought, *but it seems I hardly know him anymore.* His high cheekbones, his square jaw, his jet-black hair, and those piercing green eyes—they had attracted many in his day, but in his rage, he appeared distorted to Julia, ugly in nature and form, no better than the fallen angel himself. But he was her father, and she loved him despite his darkened soul.

A quiet voice broke the moment. Ned, hat in hand, breathed light into the room. "Welcome back, Mr. Summerton, sir." He smiled, his head held low in deferential subjection. "May I stir the fire and get you something to eat? Mus' be hungry after such a long journey." He paused, still assessing the situation. "All is well on the plantation, sir. I made sure of it."

He hesitated, as if wanting to add something more. Julia stepped between him and her father.

"Ned," she interjected, "see to it that Father gets a nice breakfast. I will tend the fire." She knew he wanted to share the events of the previous night, but her father was in no mood for that news. She shooed him out the door with a murmured, "In good time, Ned. Not now."

She looked back at the paper, now curling in the flames. She shook her head. "Father, don't you have a plantation to run, rather than scold me for keeping up on matters that impact our daily affairs?"

"I'd say your relationships on this plantation have everything to do with my daily affairs." William strode to the window to watch Chloe walking toward the mansion with a basket in her hands. Without taking his eyes off her lithe form, he returned to his earlier question. "I'll ask you again. What exactly were you and the Negroes doing last night?"

"Oh, Father, please! I told you—we were singing and worshiping. It *is* nearly Christmas, and our slaves have always been welcome to celebrate at the church. I don't see why this bothers you so dearly." She knew why.

He shook his head, clearly perturbed. "Seemed like a bit more than a holiday. Field hands, women, children. It was late when we arrived. And you were there as well." He turned toward her, his eyes accusing. Of what, neither knew for sure.

Chloe entered the room, and William's demeanor changed completely. Discomfort tickled at the back of Julia's mind, but she shrugged it off. It had to be her imagination.

"Father, please pay it no mind. Let's not get distracted from our business matters."

He barely acknowledged her words, and the hair on her neck rose slightly.

Chloe gave William a nervous nod.

"Welcome home, Mr. Summerton, sir. Miz Julia, I have the medicines ready. We got enough sick around here with the cold weather this winter. It snowed some las' night and—"

"Father, we need to tend to our chores," Julia said. She kissed her father's cheek, then grabbed Chloe's arm. "Be careful not to get too worked up on these matters. I must tend to the needs of our slaves, and you must see to the needs of this plantation."

And with that, Julia and Chloe began their morning ritual of tending to those who were sick in the slave quarters, then passing out the daily provisions. With twenty-five field hands, as well as the house and garden servants and their many children to look after, the daily provisioning took a great deal of time and thought.

They passed Ned in the hallway outside the library door. Chloe gave Ned a knowing smile and let out a little giggle. Julia looked back at her father to see if he had noticed. The brooding look on his face had her urging Chloe out of the house as quickly as she could.

William sat down to his breakfast as Ned reviewed the itinerary for the day. He sat silently, not responding and not hearing a word.

Chapter 4

Delight thyself also in the LORD:
and he shall give thee the desires of thine heart.
PSALM 37:4

July 1939

Wallace Hayes, the estate and business manager at the old Summerton plantation, enjoyed bringing food and supplies for the children at Palmetto Manor. His kind and attentive manner endeared him to the children and Livy alike, but she had noticed that Hattie was especially enamored with him.

Wallace spoke of hope and eloquent things, and the girl found him a fascinating friend. In fact, the words he shared often seemed as much anticipated and appreciated as the items he delivered to benefit the children and the orphanage. Today was no different.

"Do you think Mr. Wallace will stay for a while?" Hattie paused in her chores to ask. The hopeful look on her face tugged at Livy's heart.

"We'll see, dear. He may have time to chat for a while. I'm just hoping he brings in enough food for us this week. If it weren't for him, I'm not sure where we'd be." She sighed. "Donations are rare these days, and let's face it, money is scarce. The state is not providing us with everything we need."

Livy wasn't sure how they stayed afloat, but somehow they always managed. So many orphanages had shut down recently due to lack of money and the inability to provide necessary food, supplies, and clothing to keep them operating—but funding for Palmetto Manor continued to come in. She didn't know where all of it came from, and she didn't ask questions when checks from anonymous donors arrived. It didn't really matter who gave the money, as long as it came in. They were the lucky ones, and Livy knew it.

One thing she did know for sure, though—they had a guardian angel, and his name was Wallace.

Finished with the chores, Livy went outside to gather the children. They were playing behind the orphanage when the familiar pickup truck arrived at the house. She grinned when Wallace gave a quick blast with his horn.

"Wallace is here! Wallace is here!" The children shouted, dropping what they were doing and running to welcome him. He stepped down from the truck and braced himself for the oncoming wave of adoring children.

"Glory be!" He laughed and stretched out his arms to gather them in. Finally, he turned their attention to the load he'd brought in. "Go see what's in the bed of my truck now," he said, "before you hurt this old goat's back!"

The kids fell off him and swarmed to his truck. They pulled out a few balls and board games, then food and other items.

Livy shook her head. "You sure do spoil them, Mr. Wallace. I'm not so sure they deserve it." She giggled as she watched the kids tear apart his truck.

"They're worth it, Miss Livy," Wallace said. "I'm just glad that God provides, is all."

"Me too, me too. I don't know what we'd do without you." She smiled at him, then turned to the kids. "Okay, come on, guys. Let's get this stuff inside," she directed.

Wallace watched as the children followed her like ducklings behind their mother. As the commotion settled down, he turned to look for the girl with the scar. She was probably in a quiet corner somewhere, lost in a book. Her books took her to places far from reality, an escape from the circumstances of her life. He understood the release books provided, and he had a heart for the introspective and sometimes withdrawn girl.

There's just something about her, he thought for the umpteenth time. She was perfect, and he knew she was the one. He opened the cab of his truck and pulled out a book that was worn and tattered around the edges.

He stood still, looking at it as if its very presence had ignited a precious memory. He opened the book, and the wind rustled through the pages. It made a beautiful sound. *Just like wings of angels taking flight to some unknown destination.* He smoothed a hand over the open page, then gently closed the book. *Today,* he thought, *that destination is Hattie's hands.*

He looked for Hattie under her tree, but she wasn't there. He strode through the back door and into the hallway. Livy was coming toward him, a distracted look on her face. She startled when he spoke.

"I brought something special for Hattie, Livy," he said. "I figure since she reads and all, she might like to have this. I can't find her though."

"Oh, she's in the kitchen, helping with dinner. Hey, Wallace, would you like to eat with us tonight? The kids would love to have you stay."

"Maybe I will. Maybe I will. I'll let you know." He smiled at her and headed to the kitchen to look for Hattie.

"Mr. Wallace!" A delighted Hattie ran to give him a hug. The book he was holding fell out of his hands and onto the floor. Embarrassed, she leaned down to pick it up. She dusted it off and held it out.

"No, it's for you, child."

The smile on Hattie's face as she flipped through the delicate pages made his day complete. "Oh, it's beautiful," she breathed. "It looks old. There's writing in it—is it yours?"

"Some of the writing is mine," he agreed. "But many of the notations are from my grandmother, some from my father, and others from another very special person I used to know. You remind me of her. Her name was Julia. She passed on when I was ten years old. But yessuh, I remember her kindness and love for my family. She passed her mother's Bible to my grandmother. They were the best of friends." He looked at the book as if it were worth everything in the world to him. In essence, it was. "Mama Chloe passed it down to my father. . . then he passed it to little ol' me. And today—" He took a deep breath. "Today, I'm passing it to you, Hattie. I marked a few things in it especially for you. Just read it. . . when you need to."

She looked at him quizzically. "When I need to?"

Wallace thought for a moment, then reached out to gently move the hair from her face. His fingers lingered on her scar. "You read this book, child, when times are hard and when times are good. Read it when you're sad and when you're thankful." He smiled as he spoke to her. He put his hands over hers as she held the book. "This is God's Word, dear one. When you don't understand, the answers are here."

He looked up to see Livy standing in the doorway watching them. He let go of Hattie's hands and turned to the older woman.

"Now for you, Miss Livy. Let's get the rest of those supplies in here. I don't see everything I brought. Send out some of the older boys to help me unload. I'm betting they left all the important stuff in the truck."

"You're such a godsend, Wallace," she said softly. "Make sure you tell your boss thank you."

***

Life quickly returned to normal after Wallace's visit. He'd left them with visions of hope, barrels of laughter, and more importantly, supplies. Though they never knew when he'd be by again, he was never far from their reach. He stopped by to say hello as often as he could on his way home from the market.

Livy continued to work tirelessly with the children, while Hattie read from Wallace's old Bible in her spare time. The children returned to their normal routines, and Livy and Cora dealt with the daily affairs of running the orphanage.

One day, early in August, Cora returned from town with a letter in her hands. "Miss Livy," she said. "I've got a message for you from the city office."

Livy looked up from her desk as Cora handed her a letter from the commissioners of the orphanage. She opened it, read it, and sighed.

"Another child's arriving, Cora." She shook her head, worry showing clearly on her face. "A boy, sixteen. And he's German."

Cora's face showed her surprise. "Sixteen? We're taking a *sixteen-*year-old boy?"

Livy shrugged. "Apparently, his parents left him at the downtown office and have returned to their country. It doesn't say whether he speaks English." Livy set the letter down on the desk and rubbed her forehead. She was puzzled by the situation herself.

"He is older than our usual intake, but they set the rules. We're barely making it as it is, but he will be welcomed here." She placed the letter in her desk drawer and stood up. "Cora, I'm heading to the downtown office. They are asking to see me personally when I pick him up. I'll need you to watch the children." She thought about the recent episode with the Middletons. She still hadn't heard anything from that. She figured it was about time. She gathered her things and headed out the door.

On the way out, she noticed Hattie sitting with the children in the yard. She and the boy were the same age. Maybe her presence would ease his transition. "Hattie, come with me. I'm heading into town to talk to one of the commissioners and to check on a boy we are bringing home." She paused dramatically. "He is your age."

Hattie's hand when to her cheek, and she ducked her head. "Are you sure? I don't want to scare him off."

The action broke Livy's heart. "Child," she protested, "you are the most beautiful girl I've ever known. No scar is going to change that." Hattie's scar may have grown invisible to her, she wasn't sure—but there was more to it than that. The girl really was beautiful—inside and out. She continued firmly. "One day, you will wake up, and you will not see that mark any longer. You will *know* that you are someone special. The only thing that matters, dear, is that you are loved. By all of us. Now let's go."

Hattie took a deep breath and sighed. Then she stood tall and followed Livy into town.

They walked down Calhoun, passed the Old Citadel on Marion Square, and turned onto Meeting Street. The city was bustling with activity as they pushed through the crowds of people. Many of them were still out of work and soliciting for jobs, others were there selling what they had mustered up from farming.

Hattie wondered if Wallace was on Market Street with his grass baskets and seasonal vegetables. She wished they could stop and find him, but Livy was on a mission, taking her to God knows where and for what. *Since when does she want me to meet boys, anyway?* She rolled her eyes heavenward as Livy tugged her on through the crowded streets. *And why is she in such a hurry?*

Finally, they stopped in front of an official looking building with large white columns at the entrance. A big granite sign read, "Department of Social Services." People waited outside the doors in long lines, but Livy didn't stop there. Taking Hattie's hand, she marched past the line, up the stairs, and into a waiting room filled with desperate looking adults and children running wild.

Hattie paused, a little overwhelmed by the atmosphere in the room, but Livy gave her an encouraging smile. "It's okay," she said. "We have an appointment." They walked through this room, too, and into a large office area. A woman who was looking at some files in a corner glanced up at them over her glasses, then stood and came to meet them. She didn't look happy.

Livy stiffened a bit, then turned to Hattie. "I'm going to have to speak with this lady for a few minutes before we can move on, dear. Why don't you take a seat by the window, and I'll be back as quickly as possible."

Hattie did as directed, wishing she'd have had time to grab a book. She still wasn't sure why Livy had insisted she come along.

⌒‿⌒

Livy turned from Hattie and waited for the onslaught of questioning. It was time to answer for her behavior toward the Middletons and her refusal to release Hattie. The wealthy had such influence over the state. There often seemed to be little concern about what was best for the children—instead, it was all about catering to the rich. *Well, it's time to pay the piper.*

"Ah, Miss Marigold. We've been waiting for you. We've much to discuss. Follow me, please." The woman turned and headed for a small, windowed room along the wall.

Livy was ready for her. "If you are talking about the Middletons—"

The gray-suited lady with freakishly large shoulders stopped in her tracks. "Of course we are talking about the Middletons. You've left us with a problem, Miss Marigold. The board of directors is asking why you didn't allow them to take that girl—" She scratched her chin. "Umm, what's her name?" She flipped through her papers. "Hattie Whitmore?" She let out a loud sigh, put her free hand on her hip, and glared at Livy over the glasses perched on her long nose.

Livy was about to blow a gasket. "Mrs. Danville." She stopped to regain her composure and to think before she spoke. "Mrs. Danville. It is my right as the director of Palmetto Manor to make decisions based on what's best for the children—"

"And you thought it best to not let her go to one of the most influential, well-established families in Charleston? Do you understand how few couples are out there right now with the means to support additional children? They can! And not only did you not let them adopt her—you offended them!"

Heads turned to look, and Livy tried not to wince. Mrs. Danville motioned her to a chair in the little office and closed the door.

"So what exactly do you possibly have to say for yourself, Miss Marigold?"

"With all due respect, Mrs. Danville, I know—" She stopped, looking for the right words to alleviate the situation. "Look, I did what I had to do for Hattie. Something in that situation was just not right. I couldn't let her go to them. But that's not why I'm here. I received a letter today about a boy who's being sent my way. Could we move past this and discuss his situation, please?"

Mrs. Danville stopped, took a deep breath, and fixed the glasses on her face. She gave Livy one last, hard stare, then shuffled through the files on her desk. "Yes. Ezra. He's been here since last week. He is sixteen years old. He migrated here last year from Germany with his parents. They were unable to find lucrative employment, I believe, so they left him here and headed back to Germany." She flipped through the papers in his folder, then sighed. "I don't know for sure, but I suspect the War has something to do with it. I'm sure you've heard about what is happening in Europe, Miss Marigold."

"Of course," Livy responded. But in honesty, she seldom listened to adult fare on the radio, only occasionally when the children were otherwise occupied. She tried to listen to FDR's fireside chats when she could, but she worked hard to protect the children from unpleasant things. That did mean, though, that she wasn't always abreast of the latest news. "I'm surprised we're taking him in at sixteen?"

Mrs. Danville waved a hand. "Mitigating circumstances. The boy is quite shy, speaks only a little English. He is currently in a foster home. He has a benefactor who wants him in your care, for some reason. We wanted to talk to you first before handing him over to you. He'll need to learn English, of course. You'll have to get him ready for school in the fall."

"Okay." Livy had a teaching certificate. Made sense. She thought about Hattie, waiting for her in the outer office. She would be a great help. "That's no problem. We'll teach him." No hesitation, no reservation. She thought of how frightened and alone the poor boy must be feeling. "What did you say his name was?"

"Ezra. Ezra Wolfe."

As Hattie waited for Livy in the busy office, moments long for-gotten from her own life prior to arriving at the orphanage washed over her. Memories of the desperate nature of her father and the sweetness of her mother. A wistful smile at her mother's memory lingered on her lips as she looked up to notice a boy her age entering the room. He was with a lady who carried herself stiffly, no warmth to her demeanor. His eyes were downcast, but she caught a glimpse of blue as he passed by.

He must be with a social worker, she thought. *There's obviously no connection between them.* A distant memory of her own social worker touched her heart. The boy sat down across from her, and she watched as he fidgeted and looked around the room. Another child tried to talk to him, but he didn't appear to want to engage in conversation.

Something about him intrigued her. She didn't know if it was his manner or the empty look in his eyes. He sat quietly until he looked up and caught Hattie's curious gaze. They sat for a moment, looking at each other without saying a word. The boy had the bluest eyes and, from what she could tell, the sweetest face she had ever seen. There was an air about him that felt familiar. *I wonder what your story is*, she thought.

The boy returned her awkward gaze with a look that suddenly made her feel uncomfortable. She felt hot and self-conscious and quickly covered the scar on her face. Why hadn't she remembered? He'd caught her off guard—and that was not easily accomplished. He started to say something to her in an accent she did not recognize, but they were interrupted by a social worker who motioned for him to follow her.

Hattie watched as he walked away and was startled when he stopped to look back at her. She wasn't sure, but she thought she saw him smile. The intensity in his eyes threw her off guard again, and she was left with no choice. She smiled back, and then he was gone.

Livy stood up as the boy walked in. She looked at him carefully before introducing herself. This one seemed different to her than most boys who'd been left behind by their parents. He was well-dressed, clean, and appeared to be healthy.

"It's nice to meet you. I am Livy Marigold. And you are?" As she reached out her hand, the boy looked up and smiled. She was stunned by the blue in his eyes, *Oh, my. . . you are a handsome thing.*

He shook hands politely. "I am Ezra Wolfe." Aside from an accent, his words were clear, and he was not the boy she had pictured.

Mrs. Danville interjected. "There is talk that his parents are involved with the wartime effort and have family overseas who need help." She paused, then continued. "There was some secrecy on the matter that they would not discuss with us. They left him with some money to tend to his immediate needs. I'm afraid there is no word on when—or if—they will return. There is some speculation that his ancestors used to own some estate on the Battery. I believe it was used as a hospital at one point before the War Between the States, but we don't know for sure."

Ezra stood silent, looking uncomfortable as Mrs. Danville went on.

"I suspect his parents didn't want to return to Germany with a child when the country is on the brink of war with Poland. I imagine they wanted a better future for him here where he would be safe." She stopped and sighed. "He speaks only broken English. I'm sure he'll need help with school and integrating into the system. I imagine some of the older children at your house will be able to help?"

Livy had been listening intently. This was all important information, of course. At this question, however, all she could think about was Hattie and how relieved she was that she had brought her along. How strange it must be for the poor boy to be left alone in a strange country with no family that they knew of. She wasn't sure how long his family had lived in Charleston, but it couldn't have been that long. Especially if he hadn't already been enrolled in a school. She smiled at him to ease the tension, but he appeared to have withdrawn into his own little world, gazing emotionlessly out the window.

"Of course," she responded to Mrs. Danville's question. *What a weight he must be carrying on his shoulders*, she thought. "We will take good care of you, Ezra." She touched his arm to draw his attention. *What a beautiful name.*

Instantly, his intense eyes were on her again. "Thank you, Miss. I am German, but I want to be American. I can understand what you are saying." He formed his words carefully. "Teach me how and I will learn. I will be no problem for you." He'd obviously understood more of their conversation than they'd thought. Livy put her hand on his shoulder.

"Ezra, how much English do you understand?"

Ezra shrugged. "People think I do not understand, but I do. I do not talk because I do not want them to hear my accent. They tease me. They call me Nazi. I am *not* a Nazi. I am—" He stopped. He looked down at the floor then back up at them. "I will learn to be American, yes?" He fixed his blue eyes on Livy.

Her heart broke for the young man, shy and withdrawn, but eyes wild with curiosity. She thought of Hattie again. *He reminds me a little of her.*

"Yes, Ezra. You will. Wait here. . . I want you to meet someone. She is your age, and I think you will like her. Her name is Hattie."

Hattie had settled herself in a corner where she could watch the people around her. She almost laughed when Livy burst back into the room, calling her name.

"Hattie! C'mon, I've got someone for you to meet!"

She followed Livy into the office, puzzled at her excitement.

"Ezra, I'd like for you to meet Hattie."

Hattie raised an eyebrow in Livy's direction. She looked a little too proud of herself. Then she noticed the boy standing at the window, watching the traffic in the street below. She gasped as he turned around. It was him—the boy with those amazing eyes. A strange sense of falling threatened her equilibrium as he enveloped her in a stunning smile.

"It is nice to meet you, Hattie." Despite his German accent, he was fully confident as he reached for her hand.

Hattie looked down as their hands joined in a perfectly decorous clasp. Yet she was struck by his touch. Suddenly, inexplicably, everything was more exciting and colorful. This was more than a handshake—she felt his presence and energy down to her very soul.

She swallowed hard, then managed a quiet, "Nice to meet you too." His blue eyes delved deep into hers, taking refuge in the timeless recesses of her being. Breathless, she wondered how someone she had just met could feel so familiar to her heart.

Chapter 5

Now faith is the substance of things hoped for,
the evidence of things not seen.
HEBREWS 11:1

E zra walked out of the building with Miss Marigold and Hattie, juggling his suitcase and another bag. Hattie had offered to carry one, but he could manage. They were on Meeting Street, heading home, according to the ladies. *Home?* Was there such a thing anymore? Ezra thought back to the last place he'd called home, to another time when things had been happier for his family, another place, an ocean away. He remembered green pastures, castles, love, and laughter. *That* was home. Then, things had changed. Suddenly, there were whispers and arguments and pointed looks from folks in town. A whole new culture of danger had encompassed his family.

Of course, he knew the actions of his country's leader. He knew his parents had brought him here for his safety. Some of his friends had already been pulled into the Hitler Youth movement, but his parents were determined he would not be. And his heritage had begun to cause friction between himself and those friends.

Finally, declaring that they wanted a better life for their son, free and safe from the confines of a growing, violent regime, Ezra's parents had packed up everything they could carry discreetly, and one deep, dark night, they had left all that they knew and headed west.

America, he thought. His family had tried to make a life in Charleston, but as news of his relatives in Germany trickled in, his parents became increasingly restless. Secrecy was imperative; he was told never to tell anyone who he really was. Their way of life, traditions, belief systems—and maybe even their existence—were in jeopardy.

Ezra had learned early that trust was not something he could freely give. The plan now was for him to integrate into American culture and learn their ways. He could still hear his father's voice, broken with tears and desperation. "This is the best place for you, son. You will be safe here. Everything we do, we do it for you." Tears, hugs, whispered words of courage and comfort, and they were gone—leaving him to follow these women through the streets of this bustling town.

Ezra was apprehensive about his new life. Would he make friends? Would they accept him? The girl now leading the way down Meeting Street seemed to like him well enough. *Hattie*, he thought. *I don't know what it is, but there's something special about you.*

As they neared Market Street, Hattie stopped. "Miss Livy, can we look for Mr. Wallace? He has to be here; he always comes to market on Wednesdays. May we please? I want Ezra to meet him."

Livy stopped and sighed. "I suppose that will be all right, but only for a minute. We need to get back home."

They passed the entrance to the market and meandered through the busy street full of vendors. There were people selling baskets, fruits, vegetables, baked goods, and whatever else they could to make money. They found a few folks who must have been familiar, because they stopped to enquire.

"Have you seen Wallace?" Hattie asked, looking around. "He's usually right here on Wednesdays, is he not?"

"He doin' some business down the street. You can wait here, miss. He shouldn't be long." The vendor's thick Gullah accent was difficult for Ezra to follow, but Hattie's actions made it clear. Disappointed, she shrugged, and they left the busy street.

They were almost to Calhoun Street when the women spotted the man they were looking for. He was speaking with a well-dressed older man outside the bank. Ezra watched as the man named Wallace spotted them. He handed his companion an envelope, then turned to greet the ladies. The other man, Ezra saw, quickly disappeared into the bank.

Hattie ran to him. Her excitement over meeting this Black gentleman was intriguing to Ezra. They spoke for a few moments about the day's events, until Wallace looked over at Ezra, who was standing quietly behind Hattie.

"Well, do we have a new friend, Miss Hattie?" He looked at Livy, then at the bags Ezra was carrying.

"Yes, we have a new boy, Mr. Wallace. His name is Ezra."

"Ezra," Wallace said it at the same time Hattie did. "What a nice name, young man." He held out his large hand, and Ezra automatically stretched out his own.

There was something familiar about this Wallace, but Ezra could not place him. *How does he know my name?* But there wasn't time to dwell on it, as Wallace quickly redirected them with talk of visiting the orphanage and taking the children to the farm.

"Oh, I can't wait." Hattie bubbled with excitement. "We'll take Ezra and show him the animals, and you'll tell us stories and read. Oh, Mr. Wallace, you must read to us like you do with me!"

Livy interrupted. "Hattie, you and Ezra run along ahead. I'm just going to talk with Wallace for a second."

"Okay, Miss Livy. C'mon, Ezra. We're almost home." She dazzled him with a smile that would have him following her to the moon if he could.

For a moment, Ezra looked back at Wallace, and the old man nodded his head as if to reassure him about something he did not know or understand. He tilted his head, puzzled, then turned to follow Hattie.

As soon as the kids were at a distance, Livy turned to Wallace. Perplexed, she asked, "You know each other?"

"I know his parents. Well, mostly, I know his family," he responded, watching the children walk down the street. He knew she would ask for more information. "I met them about a year ago when they first came to this country. . . . His father held a prominent job in Germany before things started to change for them. He was a physician, as were most of his family for generations. Yessuh—but don't you worry your pretty little head over it. Our Ezra is in a safe place now."

Livy looked at him, dumbfounded. Wallace always surprised her with his knowledge about the world. There was so much more to this wonderful man than met the eye.

Other questions filled her mind, but she shrugged them off. Wallace had already changed the subject. They discussed the farm and how the harvest was going. He asked how she was and how things were at the orphanage. They exchanged idle chit-chat, ignoring the elephant in the room. *Which is what?* Livy wasn't sure.

In good time, they made a few plans for his next visit and said their goodbyes. Wallace headed back to the marketplace and Livy back home. Questions crowded forward again, but she had an odd sense of peace about Ezra. Whatever Wallace knew, he would share it with her when it was time. She trusted him, so she left it at that.

Chapter 6

Fear thou not; for I am with thee:
be not dismayed; for I am thy God:
I will strengthen thee; yea,
I will help thee; yea, I will uphold thee
with the right hand of my righteousness.
ISAIAH 41:10

December 1860

Julia and Chloe walked out of the house, their arms laden with supplies to be dispensed on their rounds. The meticulously land-scaped gardens, once the pride and joy of Julia's mother, had suffered a bit with the frost from the night before. Julia paused to inspect the camellias, glorious just yesterday, now withered and drooping. They looked much like she felt after that scene in her father's library.

She wondered at times how her mother had managed to keep everything running so smoothly—the house and gardens always maintained to perfection, social activities always planned and well-executed, field hands and house servants always happy and healthy, and William always satisfied and complete. Under her mother's hand, everything had worked like a well-oiled machine.

Of course, Father had been different back then.

Julia missed her mother. She missed the man her father had been, and truthfully, she missed who *she* had been before her mother died. How different times were now. She often wished she could go back before everything changed. She'd been fourteen when Mother took ill, fifteen when she died. And by sixteen, instead of becoming the young lady of society her mother had envisioned, she'd taken on the role and responsibilities of the lady of the house.

Most of the time, Julia didn't mind the turn her life had taken. She enjoyed keeping the plantation running smoothly, and she still had friends in town, though she didn't see them often. But she would be forever grateful to her mother for recognizing and allowing the bond between her handmaid's daughter and her own. Chloe had long been Julia's best friend and confidante, despite their obvious differences in life and station.

Theirs was a tender attachment, one of love and loyalty, each equal to the other in Julia's mind, even as society dictated otherwise. *Well, no,* Julia thought. *Not equal.* Chloe was far more precious to her than just an "equal." Through Chloe, Julia had learned important life lessons, lessons on bondage and freedom. Through Chloe, Julia's love for her companion's people had grown, and she had learned they were her brothers and sisters—in her heart and in the eyes of God. Equals? *Hardly.*

Together the women made their rounds, distributing medicines to the sick and the provisions for the day. As they had when Mother was alive, spinners weaved cloth for blankets, skilled slaves made tools and pottery, and the field hands prepped the fields for winter. Other slaves were busy caring for the animals in the stable yard.

As they passed by one cabin, a child just recovering from a bout of a putrid sore throat, ran out to greet them.

"Miz Julia," he called, tugging on her skirt, "you gon' read to us like las' night? I didn't come 'cause I's sick."

Chloe gently turned him around and headed him back to the cabin. "Josiah, you run 'long now and go help your mother. Miz Julia's busy, and she can't be reading—"

"No," Julia interrupted. "I can swing by tonight and read you something special, Josiah. I believe we can work something out." She thought about the day ahead. "It may be late though," she warned.

If her father knew, he'd reprimand her for sure. But Julia had long since decided the risk was worth the censure.

Josiah's mother looked up from her spinning wheel as her child approached.

"Mama, Mama!" he cried. "Miz Julia's gon' read to me tonight!" A smile blazed across the woman's face, and she gave Julia a thankful nod. The slaves knew the cost of what Julia did for them and the chances both they and she were taking. But they also knew the cost of not learning the stories she taught. Religious principles were their staff of life, and they derived much strength from listening to Julia. The stories she told differed from what the slave handlers and men like her father had taught them. Master Summerton emphasized the ultimate need for obedience to the master. But Julia's desire was not to teach social control of master over slave, but to emphasize the biblical themes of redemption and hope even in suffering.

Finished with their daily rounds, Julia and Chloe headed back to the main house. Ned was busy coordinating the affairs of the day and directing the house servants. Chloe headed to the kitchen while Julia found her father in the garden, where he appeared to be reprimanding one of the gardeners.

Watching them made Julia nervous. Reading to the Negroes was one thing, but there was the other matter. *Had he found out?* She was certain her father would not take well to the nuptials of the night before.

Yes, he encouraged slave unions—that's how children were born and how his slave holdings increased. But Ned and Chloe were different. They held a higher status than the plantation slaves; they were preferred and given much more responsibility. Marriage—a family— would only hinder the hold he had over them.

But deep down, Julia was afraid. Somewhere in her soul, she knew there was something more to her father's no-marriage rule, particularly as it applied to Chloe.

She watched as he stomped out to the stable, where a groom handed him the reins to his favorite horse. The last she saw of her father that day was his rigid back as he rode swiftly off toward town.

The saloon was filled with sailors who'd just arrived by merchant ship, and women of the night slithered from person to person. The dank air smelled of rotting wood and salt. The sound of waves crashing along nearby docks mixed seamlessly with the more disreputable sounds within the bar, but William paid no mind to any of it.

He was well into his fourth mug of rum, and he had other things on his mind. A bawdy woman made her way to his table, but he shrugged her off and instead motioned to the barkeep for another drink. He was in no mood for her toils, but drinking—that was a whole other thing.

From his spot in the corner of the saloon, he spotted a young, dark-skinned girl making her way through the crowd of men. This one was different. She reminded him of someone, and he couldn't help but watch. She caught him looking and turned her gaze directly on him. Her smile grew and her dark eyes sized up the pathetic soul sitting in the chair. Like a hauntingly beautiful wolf to her prey, she circled him as if waiting for the right time to devour him. He knew what she was doing, and though anger filled his heart, he surrendered to her lure. Darkness overtook him as the temptress of night encouraged and nourished the growing ire within his heart.

A quiet, cold December storm hovered over Charleston as he left the saloon, riding home with drunken intent.

William arrived back at the plantation stable yard to find it empty. Not so unusual, considering the time of night, but he could see lights and hear noises in the distance. Another celebration? Maybe they needed more to keep them busy. He stabled his horse himself, then headed unsteadily toward the praise house. Between the oaks, he spotted the bonfires and heard the slaves as they sang joyfully and danced into the night. The rumor he'd heard earlier in the day resounded in the drunken fogginess of his mind. He stood in the shadows, watching, and his rage grew deep within him. It was time to claim what was his. Chloe belonged only to him.

He looked for her among the jubilant crowd—and then he saw her. Dressed in white lace, holding her hands to the heavens, dancing to the exuberant music. She moved around the fire to the steady beat of the drums.

She mesmerized him with the way she moved, entranced him with her innocent beauty. He imagined himself as her only audience, a spectator who would take her as he pleased. *Why not?* He mused. *She is mine. She is my right.*

Suddenly, there was Julia. She stepped out of the praise house and began interacting in a way that was far more familial than what was appropriate for mistress and slave. She looked to be a part of them, an equal with only her alabaster skin setting her apart.

He watched in disbelief as his daughter joined the slaves in the dance. Then Chloe caught his eye again, glowing against the backdrop of the night. The firelight danced on the damp of her skin, and William could not look away. . . until Julia stopped dancing. Until Ned took Chloe's hand and led her through the crowd. Until the others joined them with shouts of joy and mutual affection as they danced together under the moonless sky. Until he realized this was not just any celebration.

Chloe was beautiful, and the thought of her with anyone else was more than he could bear. Thoughts of her consumed him. Temptation haunted him. Past longings raised their head. *Please, Lord.* For a split second he remembered who he was. *Stop me.* Silence echoed through the empty chambers of his heart. He turned and stumbled toward the house.

His wife—God rest her soul—had insisted Julia have a companion, so when William acquired her seamstress mother to work in the house, Chloe had become Julia's constant, cheerful shadow. They were the same age, and he had allowed their close relationship at his wife's insistence. He had come to appreciate the child's happy disposition and useful existence. And then his wife had passed, and he began to realize that Chloe was becoming a lovely young lady. He chastised himself at first, but her constant proximity, coupled with his increasing loneliness, had only fueled his desire. He had tried to take her once before—an unplanned moment of opportunity—but Julia had walked in just before he moved.

She'd nearly caught him then, but she wouldn't this time. By rights, the girl was his.

He stood at the library window, nursing a drink. Dark obsession drew him down, far from what he knew was right. The maker of lies whispered deep in his soul, and closely, he listened. He was a fool.

Chloe seemed preoccupied as the women walked back toward the house. Concerned, Julia wrapped an arm around her friend. "I have a gift for you," she said. "A wedding gift—something Mother gave me, but I want you to have it."

Chloe shook her head. "You done so much already, Miz Julia. Just you lettin' us jump the broom is enough."

Even in the dark, she could see the worried look on her friend's face.

"Chloe." Julia stopped on the top step. "You seem bothered about something. What is it? You can tell me." The wind picked up, and they moved quickly to the door.

"I don't know if I should say," Chloe said. She stopped to look back the way they'd come. Julia opened the door and they stepped inside. Chloe took a ragged breath. "It's—I'm worried about Massah Summerton. 'Bout how he'll be when he finds out about Ned and me. I have a bad feeling that jus' don't escape me, all day. It's like your father is watching. . . like he's out there, jus' watchin' and waitin'. He ain't never been the same since your mama died. Sometimes, I think—"

"No." Julia interrupted. "Pay no mind to my father. You let me worry about him. I'll tell him my way. You just forget all those thoughts. So many things in this world to worry about—let's not worry about Father. Besides, we both saw him leave this morning. Who knows when he'll be back." She gave her friend a quick hug and led her to the music room. "Now, you wait for me here. I'll be right back."

Julia hurried to her room and shuffled through her jewelry box, looking for her mother's locket. Finding it, she held it for a moment, caressing the engraved surface—a beautiful silhouette of an oak tree encased within a cameo. She opened it and admired the tiny script inside, a complete copy of the Lord's Prayer. With one last, gentle touch, she placed it in a velvet pouch, then carried it from the room.

She ran down the staircase and past her father's library. The door was open. She stopped. A candle flickered on the mantlepiece, and a drink was on the table. *Is he home?* He usually stayed out all night when he left the way he had this morning. Fear overtook her as she heard faint, muffled sounds coming from the music room.

Chloe's fingers froze on the keys of the pianoforte as William stepped into the room. Her back was to the door, but she would recognize the sound of those shoes sliding across the wooden floor anywhere. Then she felt his breath on the back of her neck and his hands on her arms. He pulled her from the bench and pushed her to the floor. "No," she begged. "Please don't do this."

But William took her, violently and quickly. When it was finished, he looked up to see Julia standing in the doorway. It didn't matter. He didn't care.

Julia stood on the threshold, unable to move. Her mother's locket slipped through her fingers, out of its velvet pouch, and crashed to the wooden floor. She watched as the abomination that was her father pulled himself together and strode victoriously out of the room. She could scarcely catch her breath as she reached down to pick up the locket. She cradled it in her hand as she went to Chloe who lay on the music room floor. The dress that had clung lovingly to her body as she'd moved around the bonfire was now torn and hanging from her small shoulders.

Julia gathered her friend in her arms and took her to her suite. With loving care, she bathed her and put her to bed in the tiny room beside her own. Ned would have to wait.

Chapter 7

Be strong and of a good courage;
be not afraid, neither be thou dismayed:
for the LORD thy God is with thee
whithersoever thou goest.
JOSHUA 1:9

Julia lit the lamp on her desk and tried to process the depth of her father's depravity. She paced back and forth across her room, unwanted images flashing repeatedly through her mind. How could she not have known? Why couldn't she have stopped him? She'd been too late, she knew, but—*why didn't she stop him?*

In her distraction and distress, she put her hand in her pocket and encountered the locket. She hadn't given it to Chloe. There had been other things to attend to.

She stood motionless now, gazing at the oak tree carved into the cameo. A tree that had been symbolic to her and her mother, a representation of a secure place where they could gain strength from a just God who would right the wrongs in the world. She clenched the locket in her fist and held it against her heart. She opened it and let her finger trace the engraved letters inside. With tears streaming down her face, she fell to her knees beside her bed and recited the words she knew were there. "Our Father which art in heaven, hallowed be Thy name. Thy kingdom come, Thy will. . ." her voice broke. "*Thy* will be done." She was silent for a long time. Then she swiped at the tears and straightened her shoulders fiercely.

"I must be strong," she muttered.

"Give me the strength, dear Lord, to carry through and hold the hands of the pained and grief stricken," she prayed. "Let me find a way to carry out Your will as I tread down this unknown path. Oh, dear God. Lord. . . why my father? *Why?!*"

She held the locket and prayed for Ned and Chloe, even as she struggled to find meaning in the devastation she had just witnessed, the betrayal by her own flesh and blood. She knelt there for a long while, her eyes closed, her heart broken. Finally, she took a deep breath and stood up from the floor. She moved to the window and looked out.

In the distance, the sun was just peeking up across the fields. The storm clouds had lifted, and the morning sky looked clear. A silhouette caught her eye, it was Ned. He was beginning his day.

A slight shuffling sound from the hallway caught her attention. She hurried to the door but saw no one. A house slave, perhaps, stoking the fires for the day. She turned, unsure of what to do next. Exhaustion beckoned, but then a thought occurred. Chloe!

She opened the door to the girl's quarters, thinking maybe she had awakened. Her heart crashed to the floor as she realized her friend was no longer there. But she mustn't go to Ned. Julia had to think this through. Ned couldn't know; he just couldn't!

She shoved her feet into her shoes and grabbed a cape from her chair. With silent urgency, she raced down the hallway. Her father's door was open, and a shudder ran through her body. She stopped. Surely, he hadn't taken—but no. She could see him, silhouetted against the wall, huddled in the corner by his fire. A faint whisper came from his direction. She wasn't sure what it was—perhaps mumbled despair? Or was it grief and shame? It mattered not. Cold was the air that passed by his door.

On silent feet, she ran down the stairs and out the door, headed to Ned's cabin.

"Chloe?" She lightly tapped on the door.

She wasn't there. Where else would she have gone? Julia thought for a moment, then turned toward the praise house.

Chloe was there, huddled in a blanket on the floor. Julia reached for her and held her in her arms. "My precious friend. . . I am so sorry." She put her hand to Chloe's face and looked into her tearless eyes. "I need for you to listen to me. We must go back to the house. I'm sure Ned is wondering where you are." She tried to help her off the floor, but Chloe would not budge.

"I want to stay here for a while, Miz Julia," she said. "I don' want to leave this place ever, not ever. I jus' want to remember this place. My weddin' night, how it was before—before he. . ." She began to cry.

"You can't stay here, Chloe," Julia said. "You need to go to Ned. I'm sure he thinks I required your services in the night." She stopped, her eyes wide. "And. . . and that's good. He must never know what happened, Chloe." She reached for her face again. "Do you hear me? Ned must never know!"

Chloe shook her head, opened her mouth to protest. "But—!"

"No. I don't know what he'd do; what either of them would do. But it wouldn't end well for anyone, and especially not for Ned. Or you. At least for now, we need to keep this quiet."

Julia's heart broke at her friend's expression.

"It's for the best, my friend. I promise." She wiped the tears from Chloe's face, then reached into her pocket. She pulled out her mother's locket. "Here. I want you to have this. I want you to hold on to it. It will give you strength, just like it has for me."

Chloe looked surprised. "That's your mama's locket. Your father will think I stole it."

She was right, Julia knew. Her own tears threatened. "Yes, but—I am giving it to you. I need for you to have it, Chloe. Do you remember when we were kids and I got sick and you made me a sweetgrass doll, so I'd feel better? Do you remember what you said to me? You told me that you wanted it to give me strength; that you'd wished upon it and prayed that I would feel better just by touching it and feeling the love that you put into it." A tiny smile lifted Chloe's lips. Julia squeezed her hand. "You were such a wise girl, Chloe. I've learned so much from you."

"I remember," Chloe said, "but that doll didn't cost no one nothing. I made it from grass. This here's a piece of fine jew'lry that your mama meant for only you to have."

Julia shook her head. "That grass doll meant the world to me. You made that with your heart, and it was so precious to me. We are forever connected, my sweet friend. As God is my witness, I will always protect you. You have given me hope when all around me there was none. You have loved unconditionally. And you know what—I always got better."

"I r'member, Miz Julia. I r'member your mama especially, how she took care of me an' took me in when my own mama died. I miss her spirit. I feel like I know her soul, like I seen it. Your mama was all good."

"Mother would have wanted you to have this," Julia said as she put the locket in Chloe's hand and closed her fingers around it. "Take it. I want it to help you like it helped me. Just like you told me whenever I got sick. It's the most precious thing I have. It's yours now. The Lord's Prayer is on the inside of it. I've prayed over it so many times—" She stopped and swiped at the tears on her cheeks.

"Even last night. . . I prayed for you, that through the love of God you will be healed and restored. And though this awful sin has been committed against you, we will pray for God to heal this home and for you to be blessed with His favor. That is my fervent prayer for you."

A ray of morning sun tumbled through the window.

Chloe ran her fingers across the locket and opened it. "It's beautiful," she said. Her eyes ran down the familiar lines etched inside, and she whispered the words. "Forgive us"—her breath hitched—"as we forgive those who trespass against us.. . . Forgive him?. . . I will forgive him. We *both* will, Miz Julia. For *all* our sakes."

Outside, a bitter wind beat against the door, but inside, where love abode, a cleansing, pure, refreshing breeze surrounded them. Evil would not have the final say.

Chapter 8

*Commit thy works unto the LORD,
and thy thoughts shall be established.*
PROVERBS 16:3

August 1939

Livy found Ezra to be a quick study. He mastered her English lessons easily, so she decided to give Hattie the responsibility of helping him integrate into everyday life. This had given Hattie a new sense of purpose, and Ezra—well, he made her feel alive.

She was getting ready to run an errand in town for Livy on Thursday when suddenly Ezra appeared before her, a saucy grin on his face.

"*Guten Morgen,*" he said. He waggled his eyebrows at her, and Hattie's heart zinged.

Oh, my, that boy! she thought. *And what is wrong with me?!*

"Yikes! Ezra. . . you spooked me!" She put her hands on her hips, pretending outrage. It didn't last long, as a giggle erupted right after. "*Good morning* to you too."

She was delighted to recognize the phrase he'd used in German. Ezra was teaching her almost as much about language as she was teaching him.

"Say," she continued. "I was looking for you. Livy asked me to walk to town and pick up a few things. Would you like to tag along?"

"Tag along?"

"Oh! Ummm. . . would you like to go with me? She said it would be okay."

"I would like it very much." Ezra scratched his chin. "I will have to remember 'tag along.' And 'spook.' It means frighten, yes? I am glad you are teaching me how to speak better English."

"Well. . ." Hattie giggled. "I don't know if that's *better* English, but it's how we kids talk. Anyway, I think you're doing great."

"*Danke*. I know English better than some people think, but the way I say the words, they think I don't. Sometimes they think I am a *dummkopf*."

Hattie's eyes widened. "Dummkopf? D'you mean *dumb*? You're not dumb, Ezra. I think you might be the smartest person I know."

He shrugged. "Not you, Hattie. Everyone has been very good to me here, thank you. But when my family was still here, we have. . . funny looks." He sighed. "I miss them. They went home to Germany to find my Tante Greta and Onkel Klaus. I think it is not good. I hope they will come back, but sometimes I am afraid. . ."

"Oh, they'll be back." She said it, but she wasn't sure she believed it. Most kids who ended up here never got to go back home. But he didn't need to know that. "Don't worry—we will make your stay pleasant!" She picked up the little change purse with money Livy had given her for her errands. She needed to go. "I'm ready. Are you coming?"

He grabbed a cap from a table in the hall and followed her out the door. They were quiet for a few moments, then he asked, "Why are you here, Hattie? Are your parents coming back for you?"

The question made her stumble the tiniest bit. She looked up at the sky before answering. "No. My momma died, and my daddy left me here. He said he couldn't afford to keep me, but I know that was a lie. He told me a story about going to fight in a war, but there wasn't one. . . at least there wasn't then. I don't think he will ever come back." She stopped, her eyes the tiniest bit hard. Then she shrugged. "But that's just as well. I like it here. I get to help Livy with the other kids. Besides, I've given up wishing—"

"Where did you get that, that *wunde?*" He saw the look on her face. "No, it is not the right word. The—" He reached out and touched her face.

Hattie's heart fell to the ground. With him, she had almost forgotten she had a scar. How dare he ask her that! She slapped his hand away. "I'm not sure how you do things in Germany, Mr. Wolfe, but here in Charleston, we mind our own business. You don't need to come with me today." And she stalked off.

Ezra tripped over his feet, catching up to her. "Hattie! No, don't go. I just want to know. Did someone hurt you?"

She stopped. Turned his way. Overhead, birds called loudly to each other and the leaves rustled in the breeze moving through the palmettos.

"I am sorry," he said. "I am."

Hattie stared at him, at the regret on his face. Maybe he wasn't as forward as he seemed. Maybe he hadn't meant to pry. She swallowed hard, and a tiny piece of her wall crumbled. Maybe he would be safe to—*no!*

This was not something she would talk about. She hadn't told Livy, and she wouldn't tell him. If he had to know, he'd get the same story everyone else did. The one her father had made her tell.

"It was an accident. I was playing with my mama's garden snippers." *And that's all I'm saying.* "So, hey, I was thinking that the next time Wallace comes by, we should ask to go to his farm. It's so peaceful there, not at all like it is in the city." Embarrassment grew, but she plowed on. "He has animals and grows his own vegetables and lives near a river and we can go swimming—" She knew she was rambling. She took a breath. "I mean, maybe sometime, anyway." *Don't ask me anything else.*

"I would like that very much," he said, not taking his eyes off her.

"Okay." She didn't like feeling vulnerable. Enough was enough. Composure was the key. She was in control. She was not going to cry. *Stop looking at me like that.* "Well, don't just stand there. Let's get to the market."

They spent the rest of the morning walking around the neighborhood, both studiously ignoring the conversation that didn't happen. They purchased the things Livy had requested and returned to the house. Then Ezra suggested they read to the children under the oak tree in the backyard. Hattie agreed, but quickly became uncomfortable because he stared at her so intently while she read.

Finally, she slammed the book shut and handed it to him. "Here. You read. It's your turn."

"Me? I cannot—"

"Yes, you can. It's a children's book. Read!" His face turned red, but he took the book and began to read.

He didn't need her help with English.

But she might need help with him. She couldn't stop herself from watching him—his lips, his face. His hands as he turned a page.

They took turns that afternoon—reading and staring at each other. It wasn't long before the kids caught on, and the giggling began.

⁓

As the days passed, the news from Europe became increasingly alarming. Ezra spent hours hovering over the radio, listening for the announcement of victory, for the eradication of the Nazi war machine. He'd not heard from his parents since they'd left.

Hattie and Livy tried to reassure him that they were probably safe and waiting it out, hidden from Hitler's marauding armies. He didn't argue, but he wasn't comforted as he learned daily about new atrocities that were happening in his homeland. It was too much for a sixteen-year-old to carry on his shoulders, but carry it he did.

Even so, the orphanage was a lifetime away from the sorrow that was war, and he was still enough of a child that life there could distract him. As the weeks passed, the bond between him and Hattie grew, and they were better for it.

Chapter 9

*I know the thoughts that I think toward you,
saith the LORD, thoughts of peace, and not of evil,
to give you an expected end.
Then shall ye call upon me, and ye shall go and
pray unto me, and I will hearken unto you.*
JEREMIAH 29:11–12

Wallace spent the morning at the river, watching the ebb and flow of the water as he prayed and asked for guidance. The trials of time had gotten him to this point, and direction was what he needed. Finally, he got to his feet and made his way back to the barns. "'Time and tide wait for no man,'" he muttered. "Lord, I'm gonna do what You're telling me to do. It's time."

He was beginning to feel the effects of arthritis in his hips and knees, an affliction passed down by his father, and he groaned a bit as he loaded the pickup truck with all that he could spare. Clarence, a trusted friend and field hand who lived on the property, helped him.

"Wallace, you don't need to be carryin' a heavy load like that," Clarence admonished. "I'll do it. Ain't no need to rush; them kids ain't goin' nowhere." He took a container of food from Wallace's arms and tossed it in the truck. "You ain't gettin' any younger neither. Y'might need to think about hirin' some more help."

"Nah, I've got enough help," Wallace scoffed. "Besides, I've got you, Clarence. Don't need much else besides what God has provided." He put a hand on Clarence's shoulder. "I got you and your kids and the others."

He stopped for a minute and looked down the long line of ancient oaks to the row of old slave homes. "I got them too," he said. "They're with me always. Alone? I'm never alone." He pulled a piece of an old brick from his pocket and rubbed it thoughtfully.

"No suh. We are not alone. But we do need to start thinkin' about what to do with them homes. We need to start rebuildin' or makin' more fields. Maybe start growin' tobacco again. Think about makin' more money to help them kids."

"We don't need to worry about money." Wallace smiled, slapped Clarence on the back, and hoisted himself into the truck. "Now, I'm planning to bring a few of the kids back with me today. I asked Mary to get some vegetables and some fresh chicken ready for this afternoon. . . mmm, and some sugared pecans. Yessuh, we're gonna have a good day today! We should enjoy this excellent October weather, don't you think?"

Clarence watched as his friend got himself settled behind the wheel. "Yep. Warm enough to get in the river, for sure! Maybe I'll get in too." He laughed, then thought for a moment. His face was serious when he asked, "Wallace, you gon' tell her?"

Wallace engaged the ignition and pushed the starter button on his truck. It chugged to life, but he sat still. Finally, he looked out onto the plantation and to the ruins of the old house. He scratched his head, then slapped his hand on the side of the door. "When the time is right,

Clarence. When the time is right, I'll tell her all she needs to know. You get the place ready. We gonna have some visitors today!"

Wallace arrived at the orphanage, determined and with purpose. He pulled into the long driveway beside the house, honking the horn and carrying on.

Livy was the first to greet him as she ran outside. "Wallace, what is all this noise?" Children tumbled out of the house behind her and surrounded the truck. "And look at this, now," she scolded. "I didn't know you were bringing a full parade with you!"

Wallace's grin rivaled the bright morning sun as he pulled on the brake and turned off the motor. Before he could get out, the children had wrapped themselves around him, giving him warm hugs.

"I've got some food for you in the back of the truck," he told the children, reaching for his cane. "Why don't you all grab something and take it in the house for Miss Livy? Go on, now." He shooed them away, and they did as he asked. He wiped his forehead and took a breath that felt a little too heavy. Livy noticed the struggle.

"Wallace, let's get you out of this heat." She put her arm in his and helped him walk toward the house. "Come in. Let me get you something to drink."

He settled on a chair in the kitchen where he could look out on the backyard. Ezra was there, sprawled under the oak tree. Hattie sat more primly by his side. Wallace watched them for a moment. "I see Ezra has found a friend."

Livy handed him a glass of lemonade. "Yes, he has. He seems to be fitting right in. Hattie has been a wonder, helping him find his stride. So. . . you look like you've got something up your sleeve. What are your plans today?"

Wallace looked at her and grinned. "You can always tell, can't you, Livy? I'm aimin' to take those two to the farm today. In fact, I'd like to do it on a regular basis, if it's okay with you."

She laughed. He'd asked, but he already knew what she'd say. She wasn't prepared for the next question though.

"I'd like for you to come as well, my dear. I have the day planned— we will picnic by the river. Clarence and his wife are makin' us a nice meal. Yessuh, his wife can cook." He rubbed his belly; his smile stretched from ear to ear.

Livy could not resist him. Somehow he always showed up at just the right time. "Wallace, you can't know how nice that sounds today. I've been working with the books all week; the Baylor twins have been nothing but fractious. . ." She sighed. "I can't leave the rest of the children though."

"Yes'm you can. I already spoke to Cora. She's ready to stand in your stead."

Livy hesitated a moment longer. "Oh, I shouldn't. I do love spending time at that old plantation house, though. Even though it's in a shambles, something about that place just sets me right." She poured herself a glass of lemonade. "I'll talk to Cora, make sure. . . I truly would love to go. What are you planning to do with it, Wallace? The house, I mean. Have you thought about that? You should rebuild it, make it into something real nice."

Wallace laughed. "Lots of places on that plantation need tendin' to." For a moment, they watched Ezra and Hattie, immersed in conversation under the oak tree. The teens were oblivious to everything around them. "But everything has its due time, my precious lady."

He reached across the table and took Livy's hand in his. "I have learned to wait on my Lord to lead me; my heart waits to hear His call." He turned his gaze back toward the teenagers, then closed his eyes. "In fact, I hear Him now. I hear Him sing His song. I see Him dance on the fields. He walks along the ruins and swims in the river. . ." A distant memory touched him, and a tear ran down his weathered, gentle face. "He is everywhere. In the sorrow, in the pain. . . and in the blessing." He looked at her. "Sometimes, we just have to wait for it, the blessing. Do you understand?"

"I think I do." Livy found comfort in Wallace's steadfast beliefs—that all was in good order and working according to plan. She couldn't say her own faith was as strong, but she felt secure that Wallace knew something she didn't, and she was quite fine to rest on that. For now, she would take one day at a time, resolving herself to another's belief that all was well.

She brushed aside her curiosity on Wallace's mystery and stood up. "I'll get Hattie and Ezra moving," she said. "And I'll need to speak with Cora before we leave." He nodded, and she hurried out.

They didn't have all day, she thought. A picnic on the Ashley River was just what they needed.

***

Hattie was more than excited to join Wallace on a visit to the plantation. Any reason to leave the monotony of the orphanage was a welcomed treat, but today was special. Ezra would be joining them! She was finding herself affected more and more by the time she spent with him.

Ezra's presence gave her a new sense of exploration—one she could share and not need to contain within her dream world of fabled stories. He was real, not a fictional character she'd written about or imagined in her dreams. She loved how he made her feel—most of the time anyways. He did occasionally withdraw to places in his heart where she could not follow.

It was an understanding between them that needed no words or explanation—she gave him space, and he allowed her to hide away her truest, most personal feelings. They were both guilty of holding back, though they could not have said why themselves.

She gathered her things, remembered to pack something to swim in, and reminded Ezra to do the same. She followed him around the house, telling him about the river, the tree swing, the animals—everything she could think of about the farm that might interest him. Breathless, she tried to curb her excitement, but anticipation had her out of control. Livy was quick to save the day by shutting her down with a tiny motion of her hand on her lips to "zip it."

She chuckled as she said, "Child, please! What has gotten into you? Leave the poor boy be; he will see it for himself!"

Ezra winked at Hattie and poked her side as they got into the truck.

"Can you tell me one more time about the river? What else should I see there?"

Hattie rolled her eyes and spent the rest of the ride looking at everything on the way to Wallace's farm—everything but the bothersome boy beside her.

They crossed the Ashley River bridge, and Wallace pulled the truck over so they could watch the boats going by. He pointed out various monuments and spoke clearly of their history. Hattie and Ezra both were happy to listen. Hattie basked in the stories he told, listening with her eyes closed and enjoying the cool kiss of the ocean breeze on her face. *Why don't we do this more often?* she wondered. She was completely content.

It was midday when the familiar line of ancient oaks appeared that led the way to the plantation. The occupants of Wallace's truck were silent as they wound their way down the dirt road that led to his home. Eyes were wide as they surveyed the stately trees and the humble slave cabins that stood untouched in the distance.

"Can we show Ezra the cabins, Mr. Wallace?" Hattie asked.

"I'll take you to the cabins after lunch, child. Yessuh, that's a story I don't think you will ever forget. But for now, we're gonna find a place and eat. Clarence and Mary have some good, down-home cookin' waiting for us, I'm sure."

He pulled the truck to a stop in front of a house, and Wallace laid on the horn again. Clarence came out of the house, shaking his head.

"It's 'bout time, Wallace. Food's ready, and I bet them kids are ready to get in the river."

"You know what I always say, Clarence," Wallace chuckled. "'Time and tide wait for no man.' Let's feed these people."

Livy looked amused as she came around the truck. "Well, if he's nothing else, he sure is predictable. Right, Clarence?" The two exchanged a quick hug.

"You get purtier ever' day, Miss Livy. What's your secret?" Clarence asked.

"Oh, goodness! And you must get more blind every day, Clarence," she teased. "Speaking of pretty, I sure hope your family is joining us!"

"Yes, ma'am." Clarence nodded toward the house as his wife and kids came through the doorway, smiling. "My kids ain't missin' nothin' happening here today. They been waitin' all day for you!"

"Well, I expect that they will be sitting with me too, you hear me?"

The excited group gathered baskets and blankets, food and drink. Then Wallace led the way to the river, singing a spiritual hymn to light the way to the place where everything had begun and where fate had dealt him the blow that had changed it all.

Though the sting of it still clung to him, he would be obedient to follow the ebb and tide of all that brought him to this day. It was time to make things right.

Chapter 10

Be strong and of a good courage,
fear not, nor be afraid of them:
for the LORD thy God,
he it is that doth go with thee;
he will not fail thee, nor forsake thee.
DEUTERONOMY 31:6

April 1861

Life on the plantation changed significantly as winter dragged into spring. Unable to face his own personal demons, William distracted himself with the demons of the day—war was on the horizon, and he immersed himself in the Confederate effort. Most days, guilt drove him from his home and into town, where he poured himself into his work, leaving most of the daily plantation affairs for Julia and Ned to manage. When that wasn't enough to keep his mind occupied, he disappeared for lengthy visits to his father's plantation on the Combahee River.

Julia, on the other hand, spent her time piecing together the affairs of the day and of the heart. Hers was not a purpose of war, but a purpose for God. She prayed daily for her state and a lost country. While the thought of war repulsed her, she knew deep inside there was a purpose in it; a purpose measured with an outcome known only to God. Regardless of what this war might mean to the average person, to her it meant the possibility of future freedom for those she loved.

Yet even as she pondered the hardships of war, the personal hardship of her father's actions haunted her. *What of the truth, my Lord? What has my father become?* She tried with every part of her to forget the images of him, rising off the floor, towering over Chloe, and then looking at her with those hard, empty eyes. She shuddered to think of his fall to such a dark place, and she mourned the man he had been when her mother was alive. Yet she was confident that, even in her father's darkened state, her Savior loved him, as He did all sinners.

Determinedly, Julia chose to push forward in God's grace and to share the love of who He is. She continued her regular lessons for the slaves in the praise house. She increased her activities on their behalf, though most of it, she did still in secret. Even if it meant risking everything, even if the trials of the world around her became greater than what she could imagine, she would be steadfast and true. This was the gift of her faith.

She remembered one morning though, not long after Christmas, that had cost her heart much. Ned had stood in the doorway as Julia sat at her father's desk. His hat was twisted in his hands.

"Miz Julia," he'd said. "I need talk to you 'bout something."

Expecting some problem with the crops or the livestock, she'd smiled at him. "Of course," she'd replied. "By all means, have a seat. Tell me." But Ned stayed standing.

"I's wonderin' about Chloe. . . has she done talked to you 'bout anything?" He stopped and looked at the floor. "She ain't the same.

She just empty inside, like she in another place. She ain't with me. I don't know what I done." His dark eyes had looked up imploringly, and Julia's heart had stopped.

"No, Ned. She hasn't spoken of anything to me. I'm sure you're fine. I—I know she loves you." She'd shuffled some papers on the desk, looking for a new subject. "How are your preparations for spring planting going?" She'd stood up and walked across the room to the window.

She was sitting in the very same place this noon, ostensibly going over the month's expenditures, but instead, the memories filled her mind. As if she had conjured him, suddenly Ned was in the doorway, standing much as he had done that January day.

"Ned! You startled me. Is there a problem?"

"No, ma'am; no problems. Crop is good and all the field work in place." He hesitated, and Julia waited. He shuffled his feet. Despite his assuring words, worry was written all over him.

"Then what can I help you with, Ned?" she prompted.

"Uh. . . yes. They is something else, Miz Julia."

"What? Ned, go ahead—you can tell me."

"It's Chloe. I's worried 'bout her. She done taken to the fever and been sick since las' night. I was wondering if we could—"

"Enough said," Julia interrupted him. "I will have—no, wait." She stopped. "I will go see her myself, Ned. Then if we need to, I'll have you draw up the horse and carriage, and we will take her into town."

"Town?" His eyes widened. Julia tended to the sick on the plantation, and when she couldn't help, a colored nurse or local physician came in. They were competent and devoted in tending to the sick. Going into town was unusual, and Ned knew it. But Julia's concern was different than his.

"I just want to be sure she doesn't have an infection is all," she assured him. "I want her tended to with the best of care and. . .

and with discretion." She hoped he would understand and not be alarmed. She set her papers aside and followed Ned to the cabin he shared with his wife.

Despite the warmth of the spring day, Chloe lay by the fire, wrapped in a woolen blanket. An older slave was tending to her.

"She not well, Miz Julia. She warm and been throwin' up all morning."

Julia touched Chloe's face, concerned by the heat emanating from her body. Chloe's eyes were dull and listless. Julia stood and turned to Ned.

"Get the carriage ready," she ordered. "I have friends downtown on the corner of South and East Battery, a physician and his wife. We'll take her there."

Ned had their transportation ready in record time. Together, they bundled Chloe into the carriage and set off.

They arrived in Charleston early that evening. They traveled down King Street until they reached South Battery. The air was significantly cooler here than back home. Chloe shivered uncontrollably, and Ned gathered her close. Julia urged the coachman to move quickly.

They arrived at the corner of East Battery and looked out onto Charleston Harbor. A bevy of supply ships were positioned around Fort Sumter. It was Julia's turn to shiver.

They turned the corner and pulled up to a large mansion where a house slave met them at an iron gate.

"I need to see Dr. Levine," Julia said.

"You better hurry," the man replied. "Somethin' is happenin' at the fort. You come 'round back." He hopped up next to the coachman and directed them through the back gate, through the gardens, and on toward the back end of the piazza.

There, they disembarked, and Julia stopped to stare, stunned at what she saw at the front of the home. The Levine's wrap-around piazza commanded a fine view of Charleston Harbor and the activity happening there. But what caught Julia's attention was the crowd of onlookers gathered on the piazza, all observing the harbor. Wives, mothers, daughters. Husbands, fathers, sons. Where the men were, excitement filled the air. They spoke of strengthening batteries and resupplying the fort. Among the women, worry and prayers. A bevy of debutantes vied for the attention of the younger men, but their efforts were not against each other but against the action in the harbor.

It was certainly not the quiet discretion that Julia had hoped for, but it was better than answering to her father, should he come home this evening. He would quite likely be curious about Chloe's condition, and that she would not share.

Few people paid them any mind as the slave led them to a small room at the back of the mansion. "My name is Solomon," he said. "Make y'self comfortable. Dr. Levine and the missus, they busy right now, but I'll let them know you here. Miz Summerton, if you'll come with me?"

Julia hesitated, then turned to Ned. "I'll be back momentarily," she assured him.

Solomon stepped aside so she could exit first. She swung her skirt free of the narrow doorway, glancing back in time to see the fear and worry on her friends' faces as Solomon followed. He closed the door firmly, then led her out to a larger, more gracious room.

"Please wait here," he said. "The doctor will want to speak with you first."

Chapter 11

I will praise thee;
for I am fearfully and wonderfully made:
marvellous are thy works;
and that my soul knoweth right well.
Psalm 139:14

Julia wandered the room, admiring the beautiful paintings on the walls. Then she gazed into the gardens and out to the piazza where the onlookers still gathered. She stayed inside, for fear of being recognized. She wasn't here to socialize or to speculate over the gathering threat in the harbor. She was here for a friend, not to participate in the morbid curiosity that filled the crowd this day.

The late afternoon sun's warm, golden rays filtered through the trees outside, and Julia realized how late it must be getting. Maybe the doctor had gone to see Chloe and Ned without her. She turned to find her way back to the clinic but stopped as a single ray of sunlight burst through a nearby window and lit a painting on the wall. Julia caught her breath in admiration. The landscape was magnificent, and she couldn't help but wonder what it would be like to live in such a peaceful looking place. She stepped closer to examine it.

"It is beautiful, isn't it?"

She jumped a little and turned in surprise. Alexander Levine stood next to her, looking up at the painting.

"I am sorry," he apologized. "I didn't mean to startle you. My parents commissioned this painting before they fled Bavaria. It is of my childhood home. We left when I was ten. We were Ashkenazi emigrants. Curious, isn't it, that we fled European slavery, German oppression, and Hessian taxes to come to America, to liberty—yet here we are, surrounded by slavery again." He paused, immersed in the irony. "Thousands fled in order to avoid serving a tyrannical government with brutal, anti-Semitic armies. Now, where are the Africans to go?" He shook his head and gave Julia a rueful smile. "But let us address your matter. How are you, my friend?"

Julia was speechless. She didn't know the Levines well, but she'd always felt a certain kinship toward them. She'd had no idea that they were Jewish immigrants. No wonder they seemed to mutually understand the plight of a people in bondage. Her thoughts returned to Chloe.

"Oh. I am well, but my companion has fallen ill and is in need of medical attention. I've had my field supervisor bring us here. Can I trust that we can keep our visit. . . quiet? My father is busy with all this talk of war, and I don't want—"

"I know your father well," Dr. Levine interrupted. "My brother is an accountant in town, and he deals with him frequently on a business level. Ah yes, Mr. William Summerton. And why, may I ask, the need for secrecy?" He turned and led her to the hallway. Solomon joined them.

Julia scurried after the men, hurrying more to find an answer than to follow. "I—I believe there's an underlying issue. A delicate matter—"

The doctor paused outside the room where she'd left Ned and Chloe, a quizzical look on his face. Then he turned and opened the door. Chloe lay on the cot, a blanket stretched across her body. Ned had been seated next to her, holding her hand, but he jumped to his feet as they walked in.

"Oh, I see." It was not standard to take one's slaves to a physician's home, but if the Summerton's mistress required secrecy, he would not question it. But with the looks of this, he'd need his wife as well. He turned to his house slave. "Solomon, bring Anna to me."

Solomon left the room and soon returned with the lady of the house. Alexander introduced his wife, then asked Solomon to take Julia and Ned to another room while they attended to Chloe.

The evening slipped by, and eventually, the noise from outside faded as the crowd dispersed. After what seemed like hours to a nervous Ned and an exhausted Julia, Anna stepped out of the room and gently closed the door. She was smiling. She was a lovely woman, small and delicate in stature, always pleasant and soft-spoken. She had a beautiful presence about her and a gentle nature that Julia found particularly comforting this evening.

Ned immediately stood to greet her. "How is she?" Julia stood next to him, silent and watchful.

Anna waved them both back to their seats. "No, no, please. Sit down. Please relax. I know you must be tired from your trip and the long wait this evening. Alexander and I insist on you staying here overnight. We have rooms where you can stay. Traveling tonight would not be wise, as the hour is late and much is happening on the harbor, as you know." Her sweet, almost melodic voice was mesmerizing.

"How is Chloe?" Julia asked.

"Oh! Chloe, such a beautiful name." Anna sighed as she washed her hands in the basin outside the exam room door. She looked at Ned as she patted her hands dry. "I gather she is your wife?"

Ned jumped to his feet again. He towered over her small frame.

"No. . . sit down, please. I insist." Anna laughed and continued. "She has a minor infection that we believe will resolve itself with some rest, but"—she looked at Ned almost giddily—"she is also pregnant. We suspect probably about three and a half months along."

A grin grew across Ned's face until it was nearly as wide as he was tall. "A baby?" he cried. "Well, thank the Lord, Chloe be all right."

Julia stood in silence. Anna's words confirmed what she and Chloe had discussed, but the timing made the news more horrifying than beautiful. *Three and a half months.* She had worried; she had suspected. . . but now it was confirmed.

That night they stayed at the mansion on East Battery, but they awakened before the sunrise to the sound of a large gun firing and then another and another. The war had begun.

Chapter 12

*Be content
with such things as ye have:
for he hath said, I will never leave thee,
nor forsake thee.*
HEBREWS 13:5

The battle continued for the next thirty-four hours. Many Charlestonians spent the day in celebration, sure the battle was theirs to win. When the white flag rose over Fort Sumter, they considered it proof that the war was also theirs to be won. But others were not so confident.

The Levines insisted that Julia and her company stay at the mansion another full day before risking the journey back to the plantation. That would give them time to monitor Chloe's response to medication for the infection, as well as to allow them to find safe passage. Anna tended to Chloe as Ned and Julia prepared for the trip back home.

It was well into the second day when Alexander stepped onto the piazza where Julia was pacing. Anna was close behind him. "I had Solomon run into town to make sure that the roads are safe for travel," the doctor announced. "He says you should be safe to make it home, as long as you travel quickly. We're readying your carriage now. If you make haste, you should be home by nightfall."

"Thank you so kindly, Dr. Levine. We are grateful for your hospitality. And Anna. You have been so wonderful, taking care of Chloe." Julia's voice showed a relief of her tension. "I'm not sure what we would have done without your care. You've spent countless hours with us. It is much appreciated."

The doctor smiled. "Yes, my wife is a godsend to me. She loves her work. She finds joy in devoting her time tending to the needs of others—and not just the sick but to everyone around her."

Anna hushed him gently. "I could do no less," she assured Julia. "We're all God's children."

"Do you have children, Anna? Dr. Levine?" They weren't the words Julia had expected to say, but they came out anyway. Surely, she'd overstepped her bounds. Anna looked away, her eyes distant, but Dr. Levine smiled and asked Solomon to bring them some tea.

"We have had disappointments over the years," he said.

Solomon returned with their tea, and in the gardens below, they spotted Ned and Chloe, walking arm in arm around the courtyard.

"We've been trying to have children, but—" He paused, his eyes sad. "It would appear that children are not in God's plan for us." They sat quietly for a moment, then the doctor smiled and looked at Julia. "Ours is a life of servitude, it seems, for others; not for ourselves."

"I'm sorry," Julia said. "I didn't mean to—"

"It's all right," Anna assured her. "We have a good life, one that we love, just the two of us. We have prayed for a different life, yes— one filled with children. But in place of children, God has put people, lots of them, each one needing us in some way."

Dr. Levine reached out to touch his wife's arm. "Anna is a blessing to everyone she meets. That is her gift." He stopped to look at Solomon, then watched Ned and Chloe in the garden again. He chose his words carefully. "You see, Miss Summerton, we have a bigger purpose, one that involves freedom. One that involves a greater good."

Julia understood precisely what he meant. His was a true purpose for God. She could identify with that.

They sat on the piazza for a while longer in companionable silence, recognizing they walked a mutual path. Finally, Julia stood and placed her hands, one on the doctor's shoulder and one on his wife's.

"We are only pawns, my friends. We are held in the hands of One we may not always understand, but we can press forward in our faith, knowing that ours is a walk for God, not for ourselves. Now I must go. Thank you, again."

With the carriage ready, Julia gathered Ned and Chloe, and they left the mansion on East Battery to begin the journey home.

William had been angry when he'd learned Julia was in town on the twelfth of April. She'd had no business being there. Did she not know the extent of the threat that had been looming? But she'd made it back safely, she and her companion and his foreman. Why on earth she'd taken them along, he hadn't gotten a straight answer for yet, but that didn't surprise him. They hadn't spoken beyond the barest civility since that fateful night in December.

Now, midway through May, he sat motionless in the gardens that overlooked the Ashley River. A light breeze wafted in from the waterway, providing a much-needed respite from the already oppressive air. His face looked as if carved of stone; his eyes were wide but vacant as he focused instead internally, where his thoughts lingered on the laughter and joviality of his past. A past he was barely able to remember. All was lost to him, it seemed, either by the travesty of war or through his own stifling personal sin. *It's too late for me*, he thought. *I cannot take it back.*

He looked once more through the papers he held in his hands, his decision almost certain. *I have nothing to lose but my life, and what's left of that isn't much.* After all, he reasoned, his soul was already lost. He put his pen to the paper, then paused.

No, there was another matter he needed to attend first. Enlisting with the Confederacy would have to wait until he was sure of his predicament.

Julia had not been comfortable in his presence since she had found him with Chloe in the music room. That night, the temptress had cajoled him, and even now, he heard her laughter as he contemplated losing himself to the darkness of war. His days were filled with restlessness and anxiety. He'd spent most of this year in town, away from the plantation and away from the consequences of his sin. Even now, after losing his daughter in his shameful quest for control, he still desired the slave. Somehow, he loved her, but he hated her too. He would not act on his thoughts again, but there were days when his vile desires and the constant whisperings of deceit threatened to drive him mad. Still, responsibility rode him hard.

With a frustrated groan, he gathered the papers in his hands and stood. Perhaps he could catch Julia in a moment of reason before he left. With that decided, he strode toward the house. As he reached the slave quarters, however, he stopped.

Chloe sat on the raised porch outside her cabin, weaving a sweetgrass basket, a craft she had learned from her mother in childhood. She was working on a large piece, diligently and artfully weaving the threads of grass in gracious form. She looked almost as if she were dancing, her delicate fingers working rhythmically through the weave; the basket, her imaginary partner in a ballet of artistic expression.

She stood and lifted the basket, turning it around and around to examine it. As she did, her clothes fell gently in place around her body, leaving one shoulder bare to the blazing sun. Her skin was radiant against the heat of the day, and once again, he was captivated.

He watched a gentle smile cross her face as she inspected the finished piece. She set it down and walked around it. She hummed as she did, then danced around the basket in a tender, graceful motion. She was pleased with her work, he could tell. He loved her like this, in her innocence—the way he'd known her before he'd allowed his depraved nature to steal away what he'd loved most about her.

Is it possible that she has forgotten? He wished he could take it back.

She turned again, in a lithe, elegant motion. . . and then he saw the full contour of her body. What he saw stunned him. Her belly had grown, and what he had wondered before, he now knew for certain.

She put her hand on her belly, looked up, and caught his gaze. Her smile disappeared and her beautiful features froze in fear. His eyes were intense as he looked upon her, at the life that was growing inside her. Her gracefulness left her as she looked desperately for a wrap to cover herself. Finding none, she turned from his unwelcomed gaze, but not before her eyes pled with him to leave.

Ned appeared from the stables, leaping the stairs from the ground to her side. He kissed her cheek and leaned over to admire the basket she had created. The sweetgrass crib.

A bitter wind of regret swept through William's soul as he turned and made his way to the house. He would stay awhile longer. The South could wait to claim his soul.

Chapter 13

*Whatsoever things were written aforetime
were written for our learning,
that we through patience and comfort
of the scriptures might have hope.*
ROMANS 15:4

August 1861

Moonlight illuminated the small cabin. Whispers of a new dawn, just on the horizon, promised a renewal of faith that would begin and end with trusting a good and just God. The wind rustled gently through the ancient oaks as, nearby, the women lifted songs of praise in hopes of a healthy delivery. But none of that mattered to Ned. He looked up at the stars and closed his eyes. Everything in his life had led him here. Even with the treachery of the times, the promise and blessing of this event filled him with a sense of affirmation that all was well on its way to fruition.

Inside the cabin, a midwife cared for Chloe and readied the room for the birth. Finally, she called, "Someone go get the missus—dis baby 'bout ready t'be born!"

Ned ran to the main house to rouse Julia. She had given strict orders to let her know as soon as any sign of the impending birth occurred, regardless of the time. He hurried to her room and rapped quietly on the door.

"It time, Miz Julia," he whispered when she answered. He stopped to catch a breath. "Should I let Massah Summerton know?"

"He doesn't need to know anything right now, Ned. I'll tell him later, once the baby is born. I shall be out directly, as soon as I am presentable." She closed the door, and Ned waited quietly in the hallway. Finally, still fumbling with a shoe, she opened the door.

"Well, what are you waiting for?" she exclaimed. "Come on!"

They hurried down the stairs and out the door. As they ran down the path, they heard Chloe scream. The sound cut Ned to the core.

"Miz Julia! She gon' be all right?"

"Of course she is," Julia assured him.

Ned stopped short of the door. "I know she in good hands but. . ." His voice shook; his fear was obvious.

"Ned, she is having a baby. She will be fine. You'll be a father in no time. Focus on that." Then she entered the cabin. Ned peered in through the doorway. The midwife was at Chloe's side, trying to make her comfortable and preparing her for the birth. When Chloe spotted Ned in the doorway, she turned imploring eyes on Julia.

"Miz Julia," she whispered, "make him go. Please, I don't want him here!" Both were fearful of what was to come. Julia nodded, her eyes full of compassion.

She returned to the doorway, strategically blocking Ned's view of his wife. "Ned," she said, placing a hand on his shoulder. "Why don't you wait outside. It won't be long now."

It didn't take much urging for Ned to follow her instruction. He found a tree outside the cabin to lean upon, and from there he gazed up at the praise house on the hill, just visible in the growing dawn.

Amid the backdrop of Chloe's cries, he tried to focus on all the good in his life. He thought of his wife, of their joyful wedding that cold December night, and of the celebration that had followed. He thought of Chloe and how radiant she had been as she danced around the fire. But even as content as he was with the life God had given him, he wondered how happy his wife was and if he could ever be the man she deserved.

Many times since, Chloe had been distant toward him, and he had worried about her. But tonight, he would focus on the blessing this birth would bring and not on any shadowy apprehensions that might lurk in the recesses of his mind. He took a deep breath and closed his eyes for a moment. He opened them again when a newborn's cries filled the night air.

Ned returned to the doorway and watched as Julia stood and, with relief on her face, looked down at the child in her arms. She cleaned the precious baby boy, then wrapped him in a blanket, and handed him to Chloe. Both women burst into tears.

Chloe held the infant in her arms and called for Ned to join her. In seconds, he was at her side. Ned looked at the baby's sweet face and reached to touch him. He was beautiful. He was everything—a culmination of faith and servitude—bundled up in a blanket.

Chloe's eyes grew wide, and she put a hand to her belly. The midwife moved closer, then turned to Ned. "You—out," she ordered.

Julia looked puzzled but took the baby from Chloe and handed him to Ned. "Here—take him outside. We'll clean Chloe up a bit, and you can come back in."

The slaves outside admired the child, then gathered around the bonfire and sang old Gullah songs of praise and joy.

Ned was standing with his son by the warmth of the fire when William suddenly appeared. He said not a word as he pulled the blanket back and examined the child. Then, with no emotion, he touched the baby's face and walked away.

In all his years, Ned could not tell of William bothering to attend another slave-child's birth. He watched his master leave, then shrugged. He pulled his baby close again and tucked the blanket back around the tiny form. But as William disappeared into the plantation house, Ned heard another sound.

"Juuuliaaaa!" Chloe's frantic voice sent a shudder through his body. Another scream and then silence. A baby's cry, but not from the one he was holding. And Chloe, wailing. He turned and ran back inside.

Chloe lay on the bed, sobbing. In the corner, Julia washed another baby clean. *Twins!* Ned stepped forward to see—this one was a girl.

A girl with lighter skin and familiar features. A girl with green eyes that tore at his soul.

The smile on his face, the delight in his heart—both were extinguished in the single moment it took to look at the child and know.

The babies were not his. The similarities were undeniable, and as he realized the travesty that had transpired between his master and his beloved wife, he staggered to his knees. He looked down at the beautiful boychild in his arms. He shifted the baby to one arm and motioned for Julia to give him the other. Hesitantly, she did, her eyes brimming with compassion and shame.

Oh, God, his heart cried. *Why?* He looked into their faces, one light and one dark, but both with the deepest evergreen eyes. He watched them as they reached for one another, sweetly connected and complete. They were breathtaking, and despite their bloodline, Ned found himself overcome by the urge to protect them.

With a shaky sob of his own, he cradled the babies close. "The Lord gives," he murmured, his eyes now on Chloe. "The Lord gives, and we is blessed. We gon' raise these babies to serve Him."

As the women worked to get Chloe clean and comfortable, Ned cradled the children in his arms, huddled in the corner of the room. In the depths of his heart, he knew the gut-wrenching reality of what his path would be. These babies were not his, but neither were they William's. They were God's.

"Ain't no need to worry, little'ns," he comforted. "We gon' love you ever' bit the same. Sin might'a done made you, but God can grow good from sin. You gon' be good babies, and me an' Chloe, we gon' be a good mama and daddy for you." The babies cooed in his arms as the light from the fire danced on their cheeks.

Tears fell down his face as Ned looked up toward the heavens. "I will do well by them, Lord," he declared. "No matter how they come to me, I will love them as my own."

Chapter 14

Julia stepped away from the bed and went to Ned, who was kneeling with the twins in his arms. His eyes were closed; he was praying over the babies.

"Ned?"

He looked up at Julia, his eyes filled with tears. "They his, Miz Julia. . they your daddy's. You know what this means."

Julia knelt and put her arm around him. She leaned her head against his shoulder. "I do know, Ned. And I'm so sorry." As she spoke, a beam of early morning sunlight through the window caught the cross she wore around her neck.

Ned squinted against the reflection. He thought for a moment, then swallowed hard. In a voice he barely recognized, he said, "I see theiface of Him who ransomed me. It drowns out the whisper of sin with the fear of God." He looked down lovingly at the babies and shook his head. "God din't make no mistake, no suh. He done created them in His image, after Himself, male and female."

As the words from Scripture made themselves known, Ned's demeanor changed. He stood, and he became more resolved as he spoke. "God allowed this, Miz Julia. He allowed it to happen for good. It gon' be hard, but we gon' see this through. Your father gon' know, the boy now, he look like me, but her—she look like you and your daddy. He come to see the baby after he born. I understand now, he looked at his face, and he thought he was mine."

Ned looked at the twins and smiled sadly. Then he looked at Julia and spoke deliberately. "She. . . this girl baby. . . she still have a chance."

Julia, too, looked at the twins and knew that Ned was right. The girl was lighter skinned and had her father's eyes. He would know, but she would still be half of Chloe, and that would mean she'd still be seen a Negro. She still would live a life in chains.

But not if Julia could help it.

"We'll figure this out, Ned. We'll make it right. For now, let's get these babies back to their mama. They need some food and mama's kisses."

They turned back to the bed, where Chloe was attempting to stand. She struggled against the nurse who was insisting that she sit back down.

"Ned!" She searched her husband's face for any sign of retribution or hate.

"Chloe, it be all right," he assured her. "They be beautiful, my love. They be from God."

He gave her the girl, then cradled the boy himself. His son. His daughter cooed against her mother's skin. Chloe held her closely and kissed her tiny head. They were quiet together for several moments. Finally, Ned broke the silence.

"We gon' name her Hope," he said to Chloe as she stroked the child's dark hair. "An' this one"—he smiled as he looked at the baby in his arms—"we gon' name this one Moses. He gonna lead us one day, just like Moses in the Bible. He gon' lead us out of our chains and to a place that God done prepared for His people." He looked at his son and smiled. "Yessuh. This'n's Moses Hayes."

Julia's heart constricted as she watched her friends relinquish their pain and accept what had transpired. With quiet steps, she left the cabin, determined to give them time alone.

Such faith they had! She admired them in a way that even she did not understand. With all the treachery now in the open, they still reached for the Rock deep within, the strength they clung to in times of tumult. She wished her own faith were as strong.

Even now, as she questioned her beliefs, her father's slaves stood strong, evidencing more faith and honor than any of her words had ever taught. How was it possible that a life lived in bondage could teach one who lived in privilege and affluence about a deep and unwavering love for the Savior, a love that brings real freedom and hope beyond measure?

I am the one in chains, she thought.

Julia sat outside by the dwindling fire and took a deep breath. She looked up at the sky and closed her eyes. The early morning air had shifted, and a cool breeze filtered around her. The wind rustled in the trees above as the warmth of the fire hit her cheeks. *Help me, Lord,* her heart cried. She sat still, listening for His voice—a whisper of direction or a path defined. She wasn't sure what the future held, but she knew she needed wisdom from above.

She listened to the sway of the Spanish moss draped across the branches of the oaks. The smell of the dying fire and the bright sounds of morning filled the air. A twig snapped nearby, and she opened her eyes to find Ned standing beside her.

"Miz Julia, we need to speak to you."

"Of course," she said. She walked into the cabin where Moses now lay sleeping in a sweetgrass basket. Hope suckled peacefully at her mother's breast.

Chloe had been crying, but her eyes held a steadfast intent. She looked directly at Julia. They had come to an excruciating decision. "You got to give her another life, Julia. Ain't no one can ever know. You got to find her a home where she be free." She stopped to look at her daughter's face. The child's emerald-green eyes peered up at her trustingly. "She gots a chance. I want that for her. I don't want her life to be here. She can *be* somebody out there."

A sob threatened as Chloe drew the baby close. "Do this for me, please." She kissed her daughter's cheek, then held her out to her childhood friend.

They waited until evening, then Ned and Julia rode into Charleston, headed to the only place Julia knew to find help. Ned handled the carriage as Hope lay nestled in Julia's arms, the little girl's future foremost in their minds.

As they neared East Battery, Julia looked down at Hope, memorizing her face. She was an elegant child, remarkably like her father but with a touch of Chloe's graceful features. One would not know from her innocent face the dire circumstance that had brought her into the world. Her beauty contradicted what Julia and Ned left unspoken as they traveled together.

It broke Julia's heart to know that under his faithful soul, Ned had been ripped to pieces over knowing the truth about the twins.

But no matter what connection to the child they shared, a life of slavery would be her future if they didn't act quickly. Hope's would be a life hidden from her true identity and hidden from her natural father.

Charleston was unusually somber as they made their way to their destination. Gone were the spectators and that unnatural interest in the war that had crowded the streets months earlier. A few Confederate guards allowed them to pass on their journey downtown, asking only for their identity. The Confederacy was at a momentary standstill, and the sounds of Julia's horse and carriage on the cobblestone road was all that broke the quiet. That and the faint cries of a baby girl on her way to a new life.

They reached their destination late into the night, and Ned was quick to settle the horses while Julia stood at the iron gate of the Levine mansion with the child. Together they sounded the bell. Solomon arrived at the gate in his nightclothes, and Julia watched as a lamp suddenly brightened the windows of the mansion. "Miz Summerton?" Solomon asked as he opened the gate. Ned was quick to respond, as Julia still held Hope.

"We have a matter of great importance to discuss with Master Levine." Ned made his voice sound certain, authoritative. Then Hope whimpered, and Ned turned, taking her from Julia's arms. He turned back to Solomon, his eyes pleading. "We ain't got much time, we got to get back to the plantation before—"

"We have something of dire importance to Dr. Levine," Julia interrupted. "It is imperative that we see him now." She looked up to see Alexander on the second-floor balcony.

"Let them in, Solomon," Alexander said as he tied his robe. "I'll be down momentarily. Make yourselves at home in the grand foyer." He disappeared inside.

Julia allowed the opulence of the mansion to distract her as they waited for Dr. Levine. The place was far more ornate than she remembered, much more so than just the beautiful paintings she'd admired. In the flickering lamplight, she studied ancient artifacts perched on marble pedestals, glorious vases ensconced on heavily carved tables, and tiny trinkets reflected in wall-sized mirrors. The place took her breath away. She closed her eyes and briefly allowed herself to be swept up in the historical significance of all that was in the room; allowed herself to forget, if for just that moment, the grim nature of their mission.

She wanted to look again upon the resplendent painting that had hung in the grand hall, where Alexander had proudly shared with her the landscape of his beloved childhood home.

Jewish, she thought. She wasn't sure why, but she felt a sort of kinship toward the couple, an inexplicable bond. Theirs was a life of history and religion, of a deep-seated need to be connected with their traditions and the past, especially in times of turmoil and questioning. The Levine home epitomized who they were and what they would always be, even in the midst of war and significant uncertainty. Julia felt both comfort and envy in that thought.

She watched Ned as he held the infant child, still swaddled in her mother's linens. She couldn't fathom how he had managed to stay pure in the face of evil and circumstances beyond his control. In his face, she could see the inner torment that buffeted him. She felt his deep sadness; his sense of grief that went unmeasured and overflowing, yet hidden behind the Rock of his salvation.

They had named her Hope, the one he held in his arms. Hope was what he held in his heart, so it was no wonder he loved her so. There were no coincidences here, nor would there be in her future. Hope's destiny would be delivered, surrendered to another path at God's direction. It was a path they would be true to follow.

No, there are no coincidences, she thought. *Not today, not tonight. Certainly not tomorrow.* She smiled to herself and looked up to find Anna on the staircase.

Anna descended the stairs, her eyes fixed on Hope. Ned looked at Julia, unsure of the next step. No words were said, but Anna stopped next to him and held out her arms. He hesitated, pulled the child close for one more moment, and then handed Hope to Anna.

Grief overtook him. He took off his hat and crushed it in his hands. Tears streamed down his face. Julia, her own tears flowing, embraced him.

Alexander appeared and walked quietly over to his wife. He looked at Julia, puzzled at first, but suddenly he knew. His late-night guests were leaving without the baby. The child was theirs.

"We are merely servants of the Most High, Dr. Levine," Julia said as she and Ned turned to leave. "Pawns in the bigger picture. Her name is Hope. Give her what we cannot. . . a life without chains."

Chapter 15

Yea, though I walk through the valley
of the shadow of death, I will fear no evil:
for thou art with me;
thy rod and thy staff, they comfort me.
PSALM 23:4

Chloe was too frightened to sleep. If William found out—oh, if he *knew*! Her heart stuttered and her lips moved in silent prayer. Across the room, baby Moses whimpered in the basket she had made for him. She rolled to the side of the bed, then pushed herself to a sitting position. She was so tired! The baby fussed louder. She must keep him quiet. They must not draw William's attention any more this night.

"Do he know, Lord? Did he see? Do he know she gone?" At her whisper, her son quieted. She lifted him from the basket and caressed his cheek. "Oh, my baby. If'n I could, you'd be with yo' sister, livin' another life. I'm so sorry, Moses. Ned, he ain't yo' blood, but he yo' daddy in the just eyes of God. He gon' raise you as his own."

She swaddled him closely. With a gentle hand, she wiped his tears. She could see her beautiful daughter in his sweet face.

He opened his eyes and looked up at her. Her heart stopped. She shifted closer to the lamp, examining her son in the glow of its flame. She was sure she'd seen William for just a second. . . in his face. . . maybe his green eyes? How had she not noticed that before, the resemblance to his father? Was it her imagination? Surely the flickering light was playing tricks on her. With effort, she made her way back to the bed, shrugging off the sense of William all around her.

"He can't never know," she whispered into the night.

It was almost dawn when she heard the carriage approaching. Her heart raced as she willed the wheels to turn soundlessly. She focused her mind on Moses, refusing to dwell on the image of Julia and Ned, returning without Hope. "It's for the best," she muttered fiercely. "Both my babies, they in God's hands."

Ned arrived at the cabin, weakened from the emotional journey. He stopped in the doorway, transfixed by the silhouette of mother and child that danced on the wall beside the fireplace. "She safe now, Chloe. I promise you that. They good people."

He crossed the room and took them both in his arms. On the wall, the silhouette grew to three—a firelit waltz of fate, of sorrow, and of blessing; each leading the other in a pirouette of uncertainty.

He helped Chloe get comfortable in their bed, the baby beside her. She was asleep in moments. With a sigh, he stretched out on the edge of the mattress, facing his son who lay awake and quiet. His tiny eyes were open and fixed trustingly on Ned. "We gon' be all right, little one," he whispered. He hummed an old Gullah hymn, one he remembered from his own childhood. With a gentle finger, he touched the baby's face, soothing the child to sleep. The events of the day slipped away, and Ned too, fell deeply asleep.

Outside the cabin, the approaching morning breeze cooled the damp in the air, and the darkness of the night faded. The sun began its journey to light the fields of the plantation, and one by one, the birds commenced their morning concert of praise. For a moment, it was peaceful at Summerton Place. . . but a storm was still on the horizon.

William stood at the window, watching. He watched as the sun came up, and muttered a curse. He watched as his slaves left their cabins and took to their work. Men, women, children. All his property. His responsibility. His. Every one of them. Chattel with which he could do as he pleased. And they dared to defy him.

The one he'd been waiting for appeared, making his way toward the manor house. As if it were any normal day. William slammed his empty glass to the tabletop, his whole being shaking with fury. He schooled his expression and turned as Ned stepped through the doorway.

The man pulled off his hat and tipped his head downward as he spoke. "Massah Summerton, the fields is tended. Everything be smooth and in order."

Not as smooth as you think, Ned, my boy. He cleared his throat. "I hear congratulations are in order." He turned to pour himself another brandy and was surprised to find the bottle empty. Which was good because somehow it landed on its side and twirled around the table. *A bit clumsy this morning, aren't we, Willy?*

"Thank you, suh. God is good." Ned's eyes widened, and William turned to see what he was looking at. Several bottles littered the tabletop. All empty. William belched.

"Has you ate breakfast yet this mornin', suh?"

Ignoring him, William went back to the window. He pushed the heavy drape aside just in time to see Chloe leave the cabin she shared with his overseer. Stupid woman. She left the comfort of her room in this house, to live in a slave cabin. His laugh was deep and bitter. More of a snort, really.

"Well, look at that."

"Suh?"

Ned joined him at the window and they stood together, watching the new mother as she gathered water and turned back to her cabin. William's hand settled on Ned's shoulder, his grasp tight.

"Ah, that Chloe. . . She is quite the beauty, isn't she? You know, I raised her after her mother died. I brought her here, inside this house." He turned and locked eyes with his slave. "I clothed her, fed her, looked after her.. . . I made her a part of this family. *My* family. She is *mine*." His teeth bared in a snarl and spit flew as he continued. "So tell me, old *friend*. Tell me why you—why she—" He shoved violently at Ned, intending to throw him against the wall, but the action only upset his own stability. He grabbed for the man's shirt and missed. He went down, still shouting, fighting as Ned tried to catch him. "You took my property. My woman. That child—"

His head hit the floor with a sickening thud.

Finished with her morning chores, Julia was heading out to check on Chloe and the baby Moses when she heard the commotion coming from her father's library. A sudden silence, then Ned's voice in a frantic scream. "Miz Julia!"

She turned and ran, arriving in time to find Ned on the floor, her father's head cradled in his arms.

"Father!" She raced to his side. "Ned, what happened?"

"He was drinking, Miz Julia. He angry. I think he know."

Julia looked around the room, taking in her father's collection of emptied bottles, both on the table and next to his chair by the fireplace. She shook her head. "He might, indeed," she muttered. *But what is it he knows?* "Help me get him to the settee."

Hours passed before William awoke. Julia sat nearby, waiting. She'd seen him drunk on occasion, but never had he lost consciousness. Never had she known him to consume so much alcohol at once either. Ned's account of the incident had her heart in her throat as she waited to see what her father would remember when he awoke.

When he finally stirred, it was to shield his face from the afternoon sun slanting through the windows. Groggily, he sat up and looked around the room. His bloodshot eyes settled on Julia, and the first words out of his mouth were a growl. "Where is that ingrate?"

"Daddy—you're awake! My, you had such a fall. I've been worried I might have to fetch a physician from the city to—"

"I said, where's Ned? And what role did you play in taking a piece of my property to the city without me knowing?" He struggled to his feet, his voice rising to a roar. "Every child born on this plantation is my property, for me to choose to do with as I please. They are my slaves, young and old. And you—my own daughter—have smuggled a slave out of my home. But I will deal with you later." He staggered to the large window, a hand to his head. "You'll take me to the brat once I've dealt with its father."

Fear overtook Julia. She grabbed his hand, but he pulled away. "Daddy. . . no. Wait!" He pushed past her and stormed out of the mansion. She ran to the back of the house. *Ned, where are you?* She didn't dare call his name, but she had to warn him. She ran frantically through the halls to the back of the house, where she found him in a utility shed, cleaning the bandages they'd used to staunch the flow of blood from her father's head.

Ned looked up from the sink as she entered the structure.

"Run," Julia cried. "You must run, my friend!"

Chapter 16

For God so loved the world,
that he gave his only begotten Son,
that whosoever believeth in him
should not perish,
but have everlasting life.
JOHN 3:16

October 1939

The sun hung low over the Ashley River, sliding in and out of the furrowed clouds. Thunder rumbled in the distance and the trees swayed as a damp breeze cooled the air. Tummies full from their picnic, Ezra, Hattie, and Clarence's children splashed and played joyfully in the river. All were oblivious to the darkening skies and the flock of snowy egrets crossing above them. Wallace and Livy, perched on the riverbank, kept a watchful eye on the children and the encroaching storm.

Hattie shrieked in delight as Ezra grabbed her hands and swung her around in the water. Watching them, Livy sighed wistfully. Wallace grinned in response.

Almost embarrassed, Livy picked up a pecan cookie and took a tiny nibble. "That right there is young love, Wallace. It's the beginning of everything, isn't it?" She laughed softly. "Don't it just beat all?"

Wallace tipped his head and looked thoughtful. "The beginning of everything? Well, no. That, Miss Livy, was a love pure as the white driven snow, endless as far as the eye can see," he said. "Yessuh, that's a love we can't hardly imagine."

"Wallace, there you go again, talking in riddles." But she knew what he meant. She chuckled and turned her gaze back to the teenagers. *Pure as the white driven snow.* "He barely notices her scar, you know?" She looked at him. "Have you noticed? He pays it no mind, like it's not even there. That's true love." *As far as the eye can see.* "Doesn't it beat all? I saw it in them from the start. The minute she looked at him, and he, her. He's really brought out the sparkle in her. She is not the same girl."

"Love does that," Wallace agreed. "It brings out the best in us. She is surrounded by people who love her, but she still has to find her own way. For those who care, the mark on her face only makes her more beautiful—Ezra looks past it and sees who she is. I believe that together, in time, they will both find all that they are themselves and all they were meant to be together."

"Well, I sure hope so. Hattie has been through a lot with her daddy leaving her. She doesn't talk about him much, but I know there's something she hasn't told me. She's hiding something."

Wallace shrugged. "We all have our stories. Just need the time to get 'em out. Her story is wrapped up in that scar of hers. That boy doesn't see it because he feels her pain and accepts her for who she is. He loves her for what she gives him—something he can trust. Something real. The good *and* the bad." He sighed. "Our Ezra has his own challenges. He comes from a long line of heartache. Generations of it, in fact."

Livy leaned forward. "Wallace, you've not told me how you know him. I know so little. What can you tell me?"

"Oh, I don't know him personally, but I'm familiar with his family. A few generations ago, they lived in Charleston. My father told me when I was a boy about how they left right after the War between the States began. And they had someone very special with them that day, yessuh, they did." Wallace smiled and winked at Livy. He looked at her for a moment, then continued.

"Ezra is Jewish, you know, and from a very old family whose roots grow deep in Charleston soil. There's so much history around here, Livy. Lots of untold stories, waiting to come out of the dark." He chuckled. "Yessuh, and the Lord has filled me full of 'em—good ones and bad. But I do His work, and when the time comes right, I'll tell 'em."

"Well, I'd like to hear them when that day comes, Wallace," she said.

"Oh, you will, Livy, m'girl. You will."

Hattie couldn't be happier. She was fully aware that her hopes and dreams were quickly becoming tangled up with this boy who had stolen her heart.

A distant rumble of thunder caught her attention, but it didn't worry her. She loved thunderstorms. What did worry her was the level at which Ezra was roughhousing Clarence's children. Not that they seemed to mind. They were giving as good as they got. But still—

"Ezra," she protested. "I'm simply all nerves watching you with these kids. Could you try to be gentler with them?"

"It's okay, Miss Hattie," the oldest one cried. "He ain't hurtin' us. In fact, *we're* gettin' *him* good!" And somehow, they did, knocking Ezra off his feet and under the water.

When he popped back up above the surface, Hattie was practically in tears from laughing.

"Ach!" He sputtered. "You think that's funny, ya? Maybe it's your turn!" He spread his arms and started wading her way. With a yelp, she turned to flee. The children cheered him on as she ran. Suddenly, her foot got caught on a root in the riverbed, and she lost her balance. Before she knew it, she was underwater. . . but she wasn't afraid. Eyes open, she allowed herself to go limp, to stay beneath the surface. She heard Ezra shout her name when he realized she might be in trouble. Then he dove in to find her, and she grabbed his hand to pull him under too.

They wrestled each other under the water until finally, breathless and gasping for air, they both popped up. Hattie was laughing, but she sobered quickly as she caught sight of Ezra's face. He was embarrassed.

"Why did you do that?" he shouted. "Are you crazy?"

"Oh, shoot, Ezra, it was just a gasser!"

"A what?"

"It was a joke." She crossed her arms. "Did I scare you? Were you afraid? Nah, you just hate to lose, isn't that right, y' big baby?"

Ezra turned around slowly, his expression still grim, but Hattie recognized the twinkle in his eye just in time.

"Oh, no!" She shrieked and turned to run as Ezra took a quick dive in her direction. She didn't make it—he caught her and pulled her under, daring to tickle her in the process. When they broke the surface again, something had changed between them.

A loud clap of thunder startled everyone, and lightning flickered in the distance. Livy jumped to her feet and called for everyone to get out of the water. Hattie looked shyly at Ezra and he took her hand. Together, they hustled the children to shore, then stood for a moment in silence. Finally, he reached down and grabbed two towels from the bushes that lined the bank. He handed one to Hattie, then turned to head to higher ground. Hattie caught his hand.

"Wait," she said. "Do you know what the best part of the storm is?" He turned back to look at her. "It's that moment after you hear the thunder and right before the rain starts."

They looked up at the sky, and it began to rain. The bushes hid them from everyone else. Hattie stepped closer as Ezra raised his free hand. Gently, he touched her scar. She closed her eyes and did not resist him. Then Ezra leaned in and kissed her cheek. A deluge of rain washed over them, and the cool Charleston breeze embraced them, as if to bless them where they stood, right there on the banks of the Ashley River.

Grabbing up baskets and blankets and leftovers from their picnic, the group headed to the stables as fast as they could. There was no staying dry in this downpour. They raced across the fields, past the tumbledown cabins and the remains of the plantation home, straight into the refuge of the barn. Panting and dripping and laughing, they stopped just inside the doorway to find that Clarence and his wife had set out a long table with snacks and drinks to refresh them. Quickly, Livy and Hattie added the leftover food from their picnic to the table.

Wallace stood nearby, a big grin on his face. "Well, I'll be jiggered. I didn't even realize I was hungry again till I walked in. Thank you, Mary, Clarence. This is gonna hit the spot. Let's give God thanks for this bounty."

He held out his hands to Hattie and Livy, standing on either side of him. The others quickly joined in, forming a circle around the table. Together, they bowed their heads. "Holy Father," Wallace began, "thank You for this food and for this very special day. Thank You for the refreshing rain, Lord. It cleanses us and makes us pure. Let us receive Your word as we sit here today surrounded by family and our most treasured friends, humbled and accepting of Your never-ending love. In the name of Jesus, amen." He looked up, a grin on his face. "Let's dig in, folks!"

They filled their plates, then found places to perch around the barn. Wallace sat alone on a feed barrel, watching them all as they ate. Hattie and Ezra had chosen an empty stall. Livy and one of the children were perched on a hay bale. The other children lay sprawled across the center aisle of the floor. Clarence and Mary leaned against a high watering trough. It all reminded him of another story, an ancient one, when a gift was given to all people. He thought about the gifts he planned to give to each of them. They didn't know it yet, but they were each part of the puzzle set in motion so long ago.

He stood up from his barrel and made his way to the barn door. He wasn't feeling well; his time was running out.

Thunder rolled across the trees and echoed through the fields. He peered out through the rain, thinking of Bessany. He could picture her running across the fields and over the bridge. She'd been everything to him—his whole world wrapped up in that beautiful white lace dress Ida had made for her. Her short life had led him here, to this barn, to this family—the family he would lead until he drew his last breath.

"Wallace?" Livy called. "You okay?"

"Yup. Jus' seeing if the storm was passin' by or if I'd be fixin' to make you all sleep with the mules tonight." Clarence's kids protested, and he laughed aloud.

Outside, the storm had arrived in full force, but within the weathered walls of the barn, a powerful peace reigned—the same peace that dwelt within Wallace; the same peace that someday would change the world. His heart swelled with pride as he looked over his chosen family. They had no idea the impact they would have on generations to come. He had a plan for each one. Even better, *God* had a plan for each one.

He watched Livy as she sparkled and laughed and made sure each of the children had what they needed, both Clarence's and the older two. Her heart for children who were not her own amazed him. He knew who she was and where she came from. Her story was the darkest, the one that touched him in the deepest places. He had looked for her for so long. Her hair, jet black; her eyes, the greenest emerald. He would have to wait to tell her as Hattie and Ezra needed her now. Right now, she was their hope. He smiled at the irony of it.

"Lord, You are so good. So very, very good." He said quietly as he watched his family interact with each other.

The rain stopped just as they finished eating. The sun emerged from the clouds, turning the lingering raindrops into colorful, sparkling prisms in the grass and on the trees. While Livy and Hattie helped Mary clean up, Wallace asked Ezra to take a walk with him. It was time, he decided, to get to know the boy better. The two headed out down the river path, dodging puddles along the way. Strolling along the marshy edge of the river, Ezra stopped abruptly to watch some egrets feeding. The pensive expression on his face touched Wallace's heart.

"That's not something you see in Germany, is it, Ezra?" Wallace broke the silence.

"No. It is not. It is different here—everything about this place is different. But it is beautiful, Mr. Wallace. Thank you for bringing me here."

At the sound of their voices, the birds lifted off and flew away, leaving behind only their tiny footprints in the sand.

"Oh, we've chased them away," Ezra lamented.

"Don't worry," Wallace assured him. "They'll be back. They know the marshes offer them life, that food and water are plentiful here. It's ingrained in them—they don't think about it, they just know where to be. Home for the birds is a place wherever food is plentiful and the rivers flow with life."

Ezra was quiet for a moment, then gave a long sigh. "I don't know where home is anymore, Mr. Wallace. Or if I will ever see my family again."

"This place is far from your world, isn't it, son?" Wallace put his arm around Ezra. "But you know what I think? I think that the river flows in you—it flows in all of us. Our home is where the river is, where abundant life is, where we survive, and we eat the food that the Lord gives us. You *are* home, my sweet child. You are *home*. God has made a place for you here, with us."

He wanted to say more but instead, he shut his eyes and listened to the sound of the marshes. Ezra did the same. *Home.*

Chapter 17

Being confident of this very thing,
that he which hath begun a good work in you
will perform it until the day of Jesus Christ.
PHILIPPIANS 1:6

"Hey, stop daydreaming, Ezra!" Hattie said, snapping her fingers in his face. "What'd you and Wallace talk about on your walk? Did you talk about girls or did you talk about—"

Ezra grabbed her hands. "We talked about you and your chutzpah, is that what you want to hear? We talked about what a character you are!" He laughed.

Hattie huffed and rolled her eyes.

"You two need to stop your flirting and just get on with it and admit your feelings," Livy said, exasperated by them. "There is a lot to be said about being honest."

Hattie gave Livy a look and motioned for her to zip her lips.

Wallace got up from the table. "I think it's time for all of us to take a walk around the place. We can work off some of that good cooking." He looked outside. "How about a history lesson? I'd like to take you folks to the cabins before it gets too dark."

"History?" One of Clarence's children balked. "Nooooo. Let's go back to the river!"

"No suh. We are going to show our guests what makes this place so special."

"Come on, now," Livy said. "You didn't think we were just here for fun, did you? Let's go!"

"But we live here!" the child protested.

"Well, I don't," Hattie said. "You can show me what I need to know." It didn't take long before the whole group was up and out the door, following Wallace on a journey of discovery.

Wallace led them on a trek to the slave cabins that lay alongside the oak-lined path. The large trees provided a thick covering, with only speckles of early evening light shining through the Spanish moss.

The kids ran ahead, chasing each other and picking up twigs and stones to skip along the path. They passed the ruins of the plantation house. Livy and Hattie paused to take it in, eyes wide.

"It must have been beautiful once," Livy said.

"'Twas," Wallace agreed, "but there's beauty in the ashes, too." They kept walking till they reached a row of brick cabins. Wallace stopped outside the first one, then motioned for Livy and the others to go inside.

"Be careful where you step," he warned. "These are the original slave cabins. We have twelve of them still standing. They've withstood fires, earthquakes, hurricanes, and time. Yessuh, they stood here strong since the day they were built by the hands of the slaves themselves." He touched the cool wall of the cabin. He closed his eyes. "They're showing their age now, but sometimes I come here to listen to their voices. I can hear them. I hear them sing, and I hear their cries in the night. Sometimes their voices wake me up at night."

The children were silent as he spoke. Hattie's eyes were wide.

"Wallace, what is it that you hear? Who sings?" Livy asked.

He didn't answer at first, just remained in silent reverie. They waited for him to speak, while outside, the wind picked up and circled the trees. It whispered through the walls of the aged abode. When he finally responded, it was with a peaceful look in his eyes.

"I hear the voices of the faithful, the cries of their solemn hymns. I hear the sounds of the African drums as my people held to their beliefs in the midst of their great struggle." He smiled at them. "You see, they believed that the Lord would provide, and they never wavered. Hope—it's what they held on to. They had nothing, yet they had. . . everything." He stepped deeper into the cabin, and they followed him. "The family that lived in this very house endured much pain, even beyond the confines of the chains, yet they survived and held on to the hope that God would deliver them to freedom.

"This was my grandparents' home. I keep them with me all the time." Wallace pulled a small chunk of brick from his pocket and looked at it lovingly. "Yessuh, they are always with me." He looked around the cabin, then at his audience. They were transfixed on him. "And you'll see—one of these fine days, I will make it right for them. I have plans for this place."

The children were silent, their eyes full of questions. Hattie and Ezra stood together, hand in hand. Livy's hand was at her lips, her gaze swept the small room with interest. For a long time, no one moved, then Ezra stooped to a pile of refuse near the door.

Only it wasn't refuse, it was crumbled brick. He sifted through the pieces, then picked up a small chunk. He examined it quietly, then slipped it into his pocket.

Wallace smiled at him. "You are a leader, my son. Many will follow you. Your people know the pain and suffering that I am speaking of. Your parents love you very much. They did not abandon you; they

left you here so that you could live and make a future of your own."
He stepped over and put his hand on Ezra's shoulder. "We don't
know where they are today or what has happened, but we do know
they have done what they had to do to save the rest of your family
and get them to safety," he said. "The river we talked about—the
river of life—flows through them, just as it flows in you. Do not fear.
The river always comes 'round again, whether here or in the heavens."

Ezra's eyes were wide and shone with unshed tears. Wallace
squeezed his tight shoulders. "You come from old tradition and a
great love for God, my child. Be proud of who you are. Be vigilant to
where God is taking you." He reached down to gather several small
pieces of brick, then handed them to Ezra. "Be sure each person gets
a piece," he murmured.

Then he turned to look at Livy. "And you, my dear. You are our
hope, descended from sacrifice, but done so in the name of love."

"Whatever do you mean, Wallace—that I am 'our hope'?"

"One day, Miss Livy, you will build a place for orphans. A bigger
place, much larger than the one you are in now. You are precious to
the children you have. My hope is that you will provide not only for
the few, but for the many who will come to your door looking for
help. And I think you will do it right here on this plantation."

Livy's mouth dropped open. "Here? And how, Wallace? How am
I supposed to do that? You need money to build a place like that, and
last I checked, I don't have any."

"The Lord will make a way." His voice was firm and confident.
"In fact, the time will come when each of you will take your places
here by the river and by the great trees that line this beautiful place.
And you will bear much fruit by following the truth and providing
for the people around you." His face softened as he spoke. "Yessuh,
in God's time."

Chapter 18

Take unto you the whole armor of God,
that ye may be able to withstand in the evil day,
and having done all, to stand.
Stand therefore, having your loins girt about with truth,
and having on the breastplate of righteousness;
and your feet shod with the
preparation of the gospel of peace.
EPHESIANS 6:13–15

August 1861

Ned stood at the sink with William's bandages in his hands. He looked up as Julia entered the room, pleading with him to run. He had spent the last few hours in prayer, and now a quiet calm filled his spirit. It shone on his face as he turned to speak.

"No, Miz Julia. I will not run from my fam'ly. I been talkin' to God, and I gon' seek His kingdom by His pow'r and glory. I got things to do. I got me a wife an' a baby. I's change gonna to gon' stand this trial and protect what God done give me. I ain't runnin' out."

He placed William's bandages across the sink to dry. Then he pulled the plug and watched the dirty water circle out through the drain. "My life ain't worth nothin', Miz Julia, less'n I walk my path and do the work God gives me."

"But you're not worth anything either if you're whipped and dead, Ned! I've never seen him like he is today. He will kill you. Please!"

Ned turned to face her. "Where would I go, Miz Julia? When he find me, it'd be worse." The simple truth stopped her protest. He walked past her but stopped short of the doorway. "Do he know they his?"

"No. All he knows is that we smuggled one out." She put a hand on his arm.

Ned struggled to maintain his composure. "That be good. Don't tell him no diff'rent. An' you be strong, no matter what he do to me." He covered her hand with his own. "You take care o' Moses an' keep the promise we done made for Chloe. Hope's got her a new life. We gon' live through her. Me and Chloe, we be okay." He forced a smile and was gone.

Julia collapsed onto a nearby bench. "Why, Lord, why? Why must they endure such hatred, such unabated hardship? Where are You? How can anyone remain faithful in the face of this evil?" She looked up as if to shake her fist in the very face of God. "How is this loving? What have they done wrong?" A sob overtook her. She sat in the washroom, clenching her fists and pounding at the wall.

"Lord. Take me. Not Ned. Not him. He's honorable. He's a good man and faithful. Take me, Lord. I. . . am. . . nothing."

She raised her head and looked at the bandages Ned had left hanging on the basin. Suddenly, she knew. She stood up, wiped the tears from her face, took the rags from the sink, and headed out to the fields to find her father.

But first, she stopped and opened the armoire that held her father's guns.

Ned found Chloe sweeping the front yard, Moses bound to her body in a makeshift sack. He stood and watched her as she worked, until she looked up and caught sight of him.

"There you is," she said, her eyes worried. She pointed toward the stables. "Massah Summerton was jus' over yonder lookin' for you. He din't look happy."

"Chloe," he said, trying to stay calm.

"What is it, Ned? Do he know?"

He took her arm and urged her into the cabin. "Yeah, he lookin' for me, Chloe. I don't know how much he know, but he know enough." He looked outside the window. "Now you listen to me. I ain't got much time." He drew her and the baby close in his arms.

"You scarin' me." Moses began to cry, and Ned gently kissed his head. Then he tipped up Chloe's chin with a finger.

"Look at me." He looked straight into his wife's eyes. "I don't know what he gon' do. I ain't never see'd him like this. But Chloe, you gon' stay strong. For both our babies."

"But they his—"

"He don't know that. He only know we took Hope off and lef' her somewhere. He be yellin' 'bout me taking his property. That's what he mad at. We can't tell him diff'rent."

"But if'n we tell him, maybe—"

He caught her clenched fists in his hands. "No. He'd look for her and bring her back. You want her to live this life? She gon' grow up with her new family." Emotion choked his words. He swallowed hard and began again. "She gon' have purpose in her steps. She gon' be free. God done give her that—she look like the massah for a reason. The Lord, He gots a purpose in her livin' another life, a good life, diff'rent from what we got. She won't be a slave—that's all what matters."

Chloe stopped fighting him, and Ned reached out to touch Moses's face. "And Moses. Chloe, he gon' lead. He gon' learn and grow strong and teach his own children about the ways of the Lord, 'cause you gon' teach him, you an' Miz Julia. God gon' take care o' you. All o' you." He kissed her, then rushed out of their cabin to the praise house.

He had to have a word with God. If this was his last day on earth, he would spend it praying to the only peace he understood.

He opened the door and dropped to his knees at the altar. He held his hands above his head, his fists clenched. This place defined him. All the horrors in the world were understood here, clarity given even if the outcome was unwanted. He resisted the anger growing in his heart, the questions rising, and above all else, the fear of the unknown that raged against all the good planted within him. He fell on his face before his God. Bits of Scripture, long ago committed to memory, now fell from his lips.

"O Lord, are You not from everlasting? My God, my Holy One, I will not die! You have appointed them to execute judgment. You have ordained them to punish. Your eyes, they be too pure to look on evil; to tolerate wrong. But why, God? Why do You tolerate the treacherous?" He lifted his head and, with tears streaming down his face, caught a glimpse of the cross hanging above the fireplace. A cross, glowing in the golden light of sunset. He drew a breath and braced himself. God had met him here. He was not alone. And he was ready.

William threw open the door. "Take him," he roared.

Ned shook his head. "No need," he said. Then standing tall, he stepped outside.

At his composure, William's fury exploded. He turned to the field hands he'd brought with him, whip already cracking. With wide, apologetic eyes and shaking limbs, they pulled the shirt from Ned's body, bound his hands above his head, and tied him to the tree outside his beloved church.

The world stopped for a brief moment as Ned waited for the first blast of the whip. He would endure what God allowed, if only to keep Chloe's children safe. He looked up past his bound hands and out beyond the ends of the oak tree to the crystal blue sky. His body quaked. In the distance, he heard a faint hymn, the sound of a culture taken away from him. The calm rhythm of a drum called to him from his home beyond the clouds. From his Father.

His master's voice was faint and powerless over him as he felt the first fiery sting of the whip.

William beat him until the whip caught the rope that bound his hands and ripped it from the tree. Ned came crashing to the ground. William walked over to him, his breath hot and vile as he breathed into Ned's face.

"*Where is my property?*" he growled. "If you want to live, you'll answer me, boy. *Now!*" But Ned didn't reply, and William pulled back his foot for a vicious kick. "Well," he roared. Ned simply looked at him in silence. And William beat him into unconsciousness.

When he came to, he opened his eyes and reached for a handful of sand. He let it sift through his fingers, gathered more, and looked up. William, leaning against a nearby tree stump, watched in shock as his faithful slave, now broken and bleeding, lurched to his feet.

Ned stood tall and defiant, looking up at the sky. He stretched out his arms to his sides, ropes still hanging from his wrists. He clenched his jaw, whispered a prayer, and stood waiting.

William, whip in hand, stepped forward, his intent clear. Locking eyes with his once trusted slave, he raised his arm to swing. And then they heard it. A cry from across the fields, a voice known to both.

Chloe, Moses cradled close in her arms, was running toward them. "No, Massah, no. They yours! The babies are yours. Ned ain't done no wrong!" Another slave tried to restrain her, but she shook him off. Behind her, Julia ran too, her father's shotgun in her grasp.

"Chloe, no," Ned cried. William looked from one to another—

Chloe, Ned, Julia. Julia, who now had his own shotgun trained on his chest.

Julia looked him in the eye. "Daddy, if you touch him again, I will kill you."

He looked back at Chloe, holding a baby. *A baby!* Then where had Ned gone last night? Wait. Had she said *babies?* Were there two? Twins? William let the whip fall from his hand. He brushed past Julia as if she weren't there. He stopped beside Chloe. He looked down at the baby, bundled in his mother's arms. Her fingers shook as she pulled back the blanket that covered the child's face.

Eyes deep as the finest evergreen peered up at him from a tiny brown face. William stood motionless, unable to speak. It was his own face. He recognized it now. William looked at Chloe and then at Ned. His gaze lingered on Ned, and something deep inside released itself and the hold it had on his tortured heart.

"Tend to him." He could barely get the words out. "Julia, I want to see you in the library." He stalked away.

Chapter 19

Be still and know that I am God.
PSALM 46:10

William stopped at the top of the hill and looked back. Julia and Chloe were at Ned's side, trying to repair what he had sought to destroy. The events of the day confused him, as if he had watched them unfold outside of his body. What had he done? He had become a monster, unrecognizable even to himself.

"Massah Summerton." Thomas, Ned's second in command, had followed him. William interrupted before the slave could finish.

"I want him tended to. Make sure his wounds are cleaned. Send for a doctor from town if you need to. Tell Julia to come to me immediately. I will be leaving in the morning."

"Tomorrow, suh?" Thomas was confused. "But you was inspecting the fields tomo—"

"Plans have changed. Until Ned is well, you will work directly with Julia to keep things in order. Now go. I have things to do."

William stood in the doorway of his mansion before walking in. His breathing became heavy and his heart raced. *What have I done? I need to fix this.* His head hurt tremendously, both from the alcohol he had consumed—as evidenced by the collection of empty bottles still strewn around the library—and from the knot on his forehead. He wasn't entirely sure where that had come from either. In his distress and confusion, he began talking aloud to himself.

It was dark when Julia finally showed up. By that time, William had made some decisions. He was seated at his desk, a single lamp lit nearby, a stack of papers in front of him. He looked up when she entered the room.

"Is Ned okay?" Even with the lack of light in the room, he could see her expression.

"Why do you care?"

He was silent for a moment, then sighed. "You are rightfully angry with me. There is much I regret from today, but I need some answers."

"The answers are, Chloe bore *your* children, conceived through *your* sin. Ned, *her husband*, was providing for and protecting her. You beat him half to death. Your foreman who has never been anything but faithful to you!"

"I know that now. But where did he go last night? And if there were two children, why did I see only one? Last night and today?"

"There were two children, yes. He did not go alone. I was with him. He was acting under my authority." Her voice was cold, her speech careful and precise. "The second child was a girl. We took her to a doctor in town. She did not make the trip back home."

William was silent as he absorbed the message in her words. He shuffled the papers on his desk, then looked up. "I should have asked.. . . I've had time to think, Julia. I won't have another day like today. Chloe—" He stopped, swallowed hard. "She is my downfall, but I will not bother her again."

He stood and walked to the window. He looked out into the darkness, then turned. "I am leaving. My things are ready now. I have drawn up papers for you and for Ned and Chloe. The plantation is yours, to share with them. They are free."

Julia's breath caught, and she collapsed in a chair beside the desk.

He crossed the room and picked up the sheaf of papers. "I have no excuse for my actions, daughter. I will answer for them to God. But this is what I can do." He handed her the papers, looking down into her stricken face. "I love you. I'm going to Beaufort. I won't be back."

Julia sat in stunned silence, trying to make sense of the papers in her hand. The sound of her father's carriage leaving made no impression on her consciousness. One by one, she examined each page— her father had named her owner of the estate and left instructions for its management in conjunction with Ned. And he had drawn up documents emancipating Ned, Chloe, and the baby. Wonder filled her heart and tears threatened to fall. She stood and made her way to the main hall.

"Father?" She called. "Daddy?" The silence around her finally registered. And then she realized what he'd said. He was gone? He was gone.

She stayed at his desk far into the night.

The next morning, Julia walked into Ned's cabin, her father's papers in hand. A tired Chloe was at Ned's side, tending to his lashes. Moses lay whimpering in his basket.

Setting the papers on the table, she took the salve out of Chloe's hands. "I can do this," she said. "Why don't you take some time for you and Moses." Chloe opened her mouth to protest, but Julia turned her gently around and gave her a tiny push toward her son. "I can't give the baby what he needs. Only you can. I can help Ned." As if on cue, Moses began to wail.

Julia turned briskly to the bed where Ned lay silently, eyes half-mast as he watched the women. "Now, let's look at you." A pile of soiled bandages lay on the floor, but a bowl of fresh warm water and clean rags waited on the table next to the bed. She set the salve down next to them. Chloe must have just been getting started with a bandage change. She swallowed hard as she examined the wounds her father's whip had left. Several deep lacerations still oozed, and his ebony skin looked rough and inflamed.

She poured some whiskey from a nearby bottle into a tin cup on the table. "I'm going to clean these up a bit," she said, handing him the drink. "You're going to need this."

"He gon' be okay, right, Miz Julia?" Chloe looked anxious as she gathered her son from his basket.

"He will be fine; it's just going to take some time for these to heal. Has the doctor been here yet?"

Chloe shook her head. "No ma'am. Thomas s'posed to be sendin' someone to fetch him."

"I'll make sure he gets here. We need to keep these wounds clean or they'll get infected. I'll check the storeroom for more salve, too." She looked at Chloe, now sitting cross-legged on the floor, nursing her child. "Chloe, when you're finished feeding him, I want you to give Moses to me, then go get some food for yourself from the kitchen. Then you are to go to the house and get some rest. You can use my room."

"No, Miz Julia! I need—"

"Chloe, you just had a baby. You need to take care of yourself so you can care for him. If you get sick too, then what will we do? Now do as I say."

"But your daddy—" Chloe's eyes were wide and frightened.

"Oh, I didn't tell you. He's gone. You don't have to worry about him. He left for granddaddy's plantation in Beaufort. There's talk that the Union army is heading that way. My guess is they'll go to Port Royal, but all of Beaufort County and the Sea Islands are in their path."

"You sure he ain't comin' back?"

"I'm sure. He didn't say much to me directly, but he left a long letter with lots of instructions and some other papers we'll need to attend to. In fact, he didn't say so, but I think he's going to join the army." She stopped, her face somber. "He's too old, but that doesn't seem to matter these days. Anyway—your job for the day is to care for yourself and your beautiful son. Now, go."

She cleaned and bandaged Ned's back as Chloe finished feeding Moses and changed his diaper. Still protesting then, the new mother placed her baby in his basket and left the cabin. Turning to Ned, Julia said, "You just rest. I'll clean this up and be right back. We have some things to talk about." She gathered the dirty bandages and rags and placed them in a pile on the stoop. Then she picked up the wash basin and carried it out to empty it. Finally, she washed her hands at the pump and headed back to her injured friend.

She wasn't surprised to find him asleep. Picking up the baby basket and the papers from her father, she tiptoed back to the doorway. "I'll just sit out on the porch for a while," she murmured. "I need to talk to Ned when he awakes. I'm not sure what to think of this. Daddy left equal charge of the plantation to me and Ned. I'm no more superior in managing the affairs of this plantation than he is now. Such a strange thing." She set the basket in the shade, then sat down nearby. Moses continued to sleep, and she gently caressed his perfect baby face. With a sigh then, she sat back and shuffled through the papers one more time, smiling as she did. "God does work in mysterious ways, doesn't He?"

She sat quietly for a while, observing the smooth working of the plantation around her. Slaves came and went, doing their regular duties. A few looked surprised to see her sitting outside Ned's cabin, but she waved and smiled, and they went on about their work. She'd brought a basket of sewing with her in the morning, and as Ned and the baby continued to sleep, she pulled out a piece that needed mending.

An hour at least passed before Moses stirred again. Julia jumped up and lifted him from the basket. As she did, the bushes next to the cabin rustled and moved like something was there. She looked but didn't see anything. A shiver ran down her spine. Still holding the baby, she gathered her sewing and turned to go inside. She checked on Ned, thinking maybe she'd heard him, but he was still sleeping. His skin was warm to the touch. Too warm.

The room darkened as a body filled the doorway. She turned in relief, expecting to see the doctor, but a deep voice stopped her in her tracks.

"Julia."

She jumped, her arms tightening around the baby, who whimpered in response.

"Father? I thought you had left. What are you doing here?" She positioned herself between him and Ned's bed.

"I had to come back." William's shoulders were bowed, his demeanor unlike anything Julia had seen before. "I had to see my son." He stepped into the cabin and reached for the child. She hesitated, then held him out. Her heart stuttered as her father took her brother gently from her arms.

Moses stopped crying as William pulled the blanket away from his face and looked into his eyes. The baby cooed, and the edges of his lips curved upward. He reached out his little hand and touched

William's face. William held him a minute longer, smiling back at the newborn boy. Then he turned and placed him back in his crib. He moved to Ned's bedside and stood there, motionless. His voice was hushed when he spoke.

"Is it possible, Julia, to right the wrongs in this world? Is it possible that the vilest of us who live among the blessed can be redeemed from the shackles that keep us tied to the darkness?" He reached down to touch Ned's shoulder. The man didn't move. "This is someone that I've loved. I've known him since he was a child. But I took his wife. She wasn't mine."

His voice broke. Tears glittered in his eyes as he looked over at Julia. "Is it possible, daughter, that God can grow good from the sorrow in the world? The pain. . . my sin?"

"Daddy, I don't know. I—"

"No," he interrupted. "You know, in the face of that child, I can see it. I know God can turn anything to good. Doesn't the Bible say that too?"

"Yes, Daddy. God works all things together for good for those who love Him."

"Yes." He was quiet for a moment. He moved to stand next to Julia. He reached out and put an arm around her. "I will tell you here and now, Julia. You are my witness. I will make it up to all of you— you, Ned, Chloe. . . this child—every last one of you. And maybe someday, I will have earned a place at"—he pointed to Ned—"at his table."

He looked once more at the baby in the basket, at Ned, still motionless in the bed. He squeezed Julia's shoulder one last time.

"Forgive me," he said. And he walked out of the cabin.

Chapter 20

My grace is sufficient for thee,
for my strength is made perfect in weakness.
2 Corinthians 12:9

October 1939

Dusk had settled around them, but Ezra and Hattie took the long way back to Wallace's house. Fireflies danced across the fields as Ezra took Hattie's hand. A haze formed over the ripples in the river beside them, and the grasses along the shallows swayed with the flow of the current.

They came to a tree whose large, exposed root system reached out over the water. Cautiously, Hattie walked out onto it and sat down a few feet from the trunk. Her toes swung several inches above the water. The twisted mass didn't protest when Ezra tested it, so he joined her. Hattie smiled.

"It's so quiet after a thunderstorm," she said. "It's like all the wild in the air blew all the mess right across the horizon. I think that's why I like storms so much. God just comes right in and sweeps all the gunk away. He—"

"How did you get that scar?" Ezra interrupted. "What happened to you?"

Hattie's mouth fell open. "I don't want to talk about that, Ezra."

"But I care about you, and I want to know." He reached for her hand, but she pulled away. She swung her feet out over the water, wishing she could kick it and maybe soak her friend. But she couldn't reach.

"I'd rather just forget about it," she whispered.

The root swayed with Hattie's movement, and Ezra scooted back to where he could lean against the trunk of the tree. Silence hung between them. He pulled a pocketknife from his trousers and began to carve something into the tree.

After several minutes, Hattie broke the silence. "Why do you want to know so bad? Why can't we just sit here and enjoy ourselves without having to talk about serious stuff?" She lowered herself from the tree and splashed down into the water. "Maybe we should get back. I'm sure it's time to head home anyway." She stepped back onto shore, shook the twigs and grass from her skirt, and started for the trail.

Ezra jumped up and caught her arm. "I'm not ready."

"What?"

He looked deep into her eyes, his gaze hard and intense. At first, he almost looked angry, but then the tension in his gaze softened, and he touched her face.

"I need to know, Hattie. I want to know everything about you, the good *and* the bad." His hand cupped her cheek. "I have things I don't want to talk about just like you do. But I think sometimes it's good to talk about the things that make us uncomfortable. It's hard to just know things and think about them in your head and not be able to share it with anyone else."

She didn't speak, but wrapped her hand around his.

"Okay," he said. "I'll go first. I'm Jewish. You know that. I don't know where my parents are, but I know they went back to Germany to help our relatives. And now, I don't know if any of them are even alive anymore. I hear about those camps every day on the radio. And I wait and listen and I know nothing. And sometimes I just want someone to talk to about it." He took a step back. Tears trembled on her lashes as he continued.

"We're the same, Hattie. We both carry this. . . I don't know. . . the same sadness. Please, let me in. I have nobody." Ezra's voice deepened as he spoke. "I need you to open up to me, because I need to know that I'm not alone. I think, together, we can help each other get through this, this torment. I want to understand you and to know your pain because easing yours will help me with mine."

She pulled away and shook her head. "I can't. I'm not ready. It's too painful, Ezra."

If she told him, there would be no going back. There'd be no pretty picture of her past—imagined as it was. There'd be no denying who she was if she allowed him to see everything. Ripping her heart apart in public was not something she was ready to do. Not even for him.

She stumbled and caught her balance against the tree where they'd been sitting. Her fingers felt the roughness of the carving Ezra had made, but she didn't look. Instead, she dropped to the base of the tree, drew up her knees, and rested her head on her arms.

"You go back," she said. "I'm going to stay here awhile."

"Hattie! I'm not leaving you—"

"Ezra. I've been here alone many times. I don't need you to protect me. Just follow the path and go. Please." The coldness in her voice surprised her, and she could see it had shocked him. But right now, she didn't care. She turned her head away and sat motionless and silent.

After a long while, Ezra muttered a sullen "Fine." Another moment of silence, and he stomped away.

Tears rolled down Hattie's cheeks, but she didn't watch him go.

It was getting close to dark, and the kids hadn't returned to the house. Wallace wasn't worried, but he did know the treachery of the river, so he headed back out to check on them. He was surprised to find Ezra storming down the trail alone.

"Where is Hattie?" he asked sternly.

"By the river." Ezra muttered.

"You left her alone?"

"Just giving her what she wants. At least that part I understood."

"Young man! What is going on?"

"I don't even know," Ezra growled. "Ask her!" Then he stomped off.

Wallace watched him go, his eyebrows so high they'd joined his hairline. Then he turned, his eyes scanning the riverbank, looking for the girl. He did not allow any of the children to be alone at the river, and Hattie was no exception.

He found her sitting along the river's edge, her back against a tree and her head in her arms. The evening air droned in a cacophony of buzzing and chirping. Over her head in the bark of the tree, Wallace spotted freshly carved letters, and suddenly thought he understood. It wasn't difficult to read the young couple who refused to see the great love between them. They were a perfect match, caught in a tangle of imperfect circumstance.

Wallace grimaced as he settled down beside her. His old bones weren't too delighted about plopping down on the ground these days. Yet he didn't say a word. Instead, he looked up at the sky and out at the beauty that surrounded them. The harmony of the nocturnal hum continued unbroken around them for several minutes longer. And then the dam broke.

With a sob, Hattie raised her head. "Why, Mr. Wallace? Why does everything have to be so hard? Why can't we leave the things that hurt alone? Why can't life be kind for once? Why can't we just be friends? Why does he have to know?"

Her voice broke in a wail on the last word, and Wallace drew her close. "Oh, child," he crooned. "You just don't know how perfect you are. Life is hard, yes ma'am, but life is always hard. Easy things ain't worth having."

"Mr. Wallace!" she cried.

He squeezed her shoulder, a sad smile on his face. "Those are hard words, aren't they? But I want you to know something. Everything here, all the pain, all the suffering—it's all a part of a bigger plan. God's plan."

He pulled a handkerchief from his pocket and wiped the tears streaming down her face. Then he looked out over the water. His voice was rough when next he spoke.

"This place where we sit—" He cleared his throat and swallowed hard. "In this very spot, Hattie, I lost someone dear to me. God took her from me, and I endured the most terrible pain you could ever imagine." The power of Bessany's memory threatened to split his heart in two. "I think losing someone you love is about the worst possible pain anyone should ever have to endure. Especially your child."

Hattie looked at him, confused. "Mr. Wallace? I didn't know," she said. "I didn't know you had children."

"Only one. Her name was Bessany. And she was a child like no other." A wistful smile turned his lips upward.

"What happened to her?" Hattie asked.

"I lost her in this very river. She came down here to fish after church. I was busy working on the farm and—" The memory drew so close he could practically touch it, her voice calling out to him just as those of his ancestors did in the dead of night. He shook his head. "My Bessany. She's with my people now. And she's with the good Lord. Knowing that is what helps me walk this walk."

A gentle breeze blew a strand of Hattie's hair across her face. Wallace tucked it back behind her ear.

"I don't understand why God lets our paths turn down roads that lead to pain and suffering. But I do know that I can trust Him no matter what. I know I can count on God to lead me. If you rest on that, my sweet Hattie, you too will find your way." He drew her close for another hug, and she rested against him.

"Your heart is troubled," he continued. "Your past has left you with many struggles, many questions. I see hurt and sometimes anger in your eyes. But you mustn't let them rule your heart. From my own experience, I know you must forgive and allow those memories that you hold deep in your heart to heal. It isn't easy, but letting go of that past—learning to forgive—that's what moves you into the plan God has for you. Let your times of difficulty build you into who God intends you to be."

He stopped a moment, then bumped her shoulder with his. "Now, I know you and Ezra just had a little tiff. I don't know what it was about, but I got a feelin' that what's eating you ain't really him." She sniffed. "Whatever it was, though, you need to forgive him now. Don't let it dig its little roots down in there, in that place where you hide the hurts and terrors of your past. Those are the memories that will hold you back from your destiny. Don't let this in there. It'll grow and get tangled up with all the other things that worry you. It'll choke the good right out of your heart."

"He wouldn't leave me alone," she wailed. "Why does he have to know about my face? I thought it didn't bother him. He isn't like most people when he looks at me. He doesn't look at *it*, he looks at *me*! But today. . . he, he. . .Why does he have to know?"

So that's what happened. Wallace's eyes brightened as understanding dawned. He looked back at the bold declaration carved in the tree above them. Did she know?

"He loves you, child. He wants to protect you, to keep you safe. Part of that is knowing what happened in your past."

"But why? Why does he have to know? Why does anyone have to know?"

"Well, telling someone what happened might make you feel better. Sometimes what we keep inside gets too big for us to handle. Sometimes it gets so big it handles us instead."

She looked at him, wide-eyed. Then she nodded. "I can see that. Sometimes it's all I can think about. I can be having a really good day, and suddenly—wham! There it is. And I can't breathe."

They sat silently in the gathering gloom for several minutes longer. Then Hattie shook her head and drew a deep breath. "You wanna know?" She burst out. "I'll tell you. My daddy was gonna hurt my mama, Mr. Wallace. I had to protect her from him. He drank a lot, and when he did, he always got mad at Mama and at me. Most of the time it was just yellin' or sometimes he smacked us around. But the last time, he was really mad. Then Mama fell and, all of a sudden, he had a knife. I–I didn't think about it, I just jumped between them and. . . and he cut me instead of her."

A sob interrupted her words. Wallace's kind eyes watched her quietly, his hand stroked her back. The heel of her shoe dug a trench in the soft side of the riverbank. After a minute, she raised her chin and continued.

"Mama got sick after that, and he didn't yell so much, but. . . I think every time he looked at me, this scar reminded him of what he did. He is *not* a good man, Mr. Wallace. And then, Mama died and. . ." She shrugged. "He left me at the orphanage like I was a piece of trash. And now? I'm a nobody. No family, no people to share memories with, just hurt. There's nothing good to remember, so I'd rather just forget where I come from."

"You are *not* a nobody, Hattie. First of all, you belong to the heavenly Father. And you've got me and Miss Livy and now Ezra. We're your family, child. We choose you, and sometimes that's better than the family we're born to."

Hattie sniffed and wiped her face again with Wallace's handkerchief. "I know, but—"

"No buts. It's hard to forgive such a tragedy, child. But you have to let it go. One day, you'll look back and you will understand. Your pain and the suffering you endured—that's what makes you able to help others. You might not know it yet, but you are a gift to the people around you. But until you give it to God, until you trust Him, you will be stuck in hurt and anger and bitterness. And that's not what He intends for you."

"But He took Mama away, Mr. Wallace. If He loves me, why would He do that? Why didn't He stop Daddy from hurting us?"

"God didn't cause your daddy to turn down that road; he made that decision for himself. But the Lord was certainly in you that day," Wallace said. "He was in you when you stopped your daddy from hurting your mama. He was in you when your daddy marked your face. He was the courage that moved you forward. Your scar is beautiful, child, and it's there for a reason."

He tipped her chin and waited till she turned to look in his direction. "It's there so you will always remember that God was in you that day that your father cut you and not your mama. You saved her life that day, didn't you?" He looked at her intently. "Good is so much bigger than evil, Hattie. With God's help and through our resolve and goodness, evil will not win. People like you and me, Miss Livy, Ezra—we've experienced more suffering than most people do, because God knows we can handle it. When we give it to Jesus, He carries it with us, and He turns it into purpose, into good."

Hattie shook her head. "That doesn't make sense. Why does it have to hurt so bad? How can suffering be good? And why does loving someone hurt the most?"

"You know what, child? I don't know the answers. But I do know the One who made the heavens and the earth, and I know that He watched His one and only Son suffer on the cross—for us. For you and me. . . for your mama and even your daddy, if he would accept it. Imagine the pain God felt. But He did it because He loves us, and through that terrible pain, He gave us life." Wallace looked out over the river. "He gave us forgiveness of sins. He sacrificed His one and only Son. And Jesus—just like you put yourself in front of your mama, He put Himself in front of the sin that would send us to hell. The good that is in Him is *in you*. It is in all of us who believe in Him. You do believe in Him, right, Hattie?"

"I do, Mr. Wallace. I don't always understand, but I believe."

Chapter 21

Call unto me, and I will answer thee,
and show thee great and mighty things,
which thou knowest not.
Jeremiah 33:3

B y the time Wallace and Hattie made it back to the house, Clarence had gathered his children and sent them home to bed. Livy and Ezra were sitting together on the front steps of Wallace's home. Ezra turned his head away as Hattie approached. Wallace raised a brow but the only word he spoke was to his Father in heaven.

Livy was still concerned about their overnight plans. "Are you sure we're not imposing, Wallace? It's early enough yet in the evening to go back."

"Now, you just relax, Miss Livy. You know our Cora is quite capable of caring for the children in your absence. I wouldn't have arranged this otherwise. I'm happy for the company tonight," he declared. "I say we get a fire going, yessuh, just like the old days. We'll roast some corn, sing some songs, and tell some stories."

"Oh, I love it when you tell stories," Hattie squealed.

Wallace looked past Hattie to Ezra, whose nose was still in the air. "Stop sulking, boy," he said, "and help this old man get some firewood." Ezra ducked his head and followed Wallace to the woodpile.

Clarence brought the corn, and Livy and Hattie helped him prep it. Before long, a blaze was snapping and crackling, and the smell of roasting corn filled the air. Wallace took a seat on a strategically placed log near the firepit, and the others gathered round. They conversed quietly as they munched on their sweet corn snack. Wallace sat watching and listening, his eyes glowing in the light from the fire. After a while, he closed his eyes, and the corners of his mouth moved upward into a smile. He loved these people, every one.

He began to hum, and then, with his eyes still closed, he sang to them. It was an old Gullah hymn, a spiritual song of praise and worship. They grew silent as he sang, anticipation on their faces. Only Ezra had not experienced a night like this before. A tear made its way down Wallace's face. Not a sad tear, but one connected to the beat of the song. Like it belonged there, somewhere tucked within the emotion and a piece of the story he longed to tell.

With a sigh, he began to speak. "God makes no mistakes, my precious friends," he said. "Each one of us here right now, we're all a part of His family. And we are called to a greater purpose, whether we find it in the old stones of a slave cabin or in the music room of a once-beautiful plantation house."

He paused and looked at Ezra. "Man causes terrible things to happen, but God uses those things to bring good in the end. We must drown out the whispers and questions and replace them with courage and faithfulness and trust. He put you here, Ezra, to prepare you for your future. And you, Hattie, you must come to see the value in who you are now, even as you struggle in your doubts and sorrow."

Livy shifted restlessly. She'd heard these things before but still did not quite understand. "That sounds easy, Wallace," she said. "But it's a lot harder to do than it is to say."

Wallace nodded patiently. "It is, dear one. But if you give your heart to God, He will give you the understanding you need. When you put your trust in Him, the puzzle pieces will start coming together, and you will understand the purpose in all the hurt you have gone through. How *does* God show Himself in the destruction of a people, in the midst of bondage, in immense pain and struggle?" He stood and looked out toward the old slave cabins. "I see the face of the One who ransomed me. I will be still in His presence and wait patiently for Him to act."

He looked at Hattie. "Anger plants its seed in us and grows vines that do neither prosper nor bear fruit. Instead, it ruins our relationship with Him. I don't know about you, but I don't want to be chained no more. Christ—He is hope personified. Through Him, our chains are broken. Through Him, we claim all that He's promised—eternal life by His side, beside the trees, beside the river that flows through us all."

He stopped speaking and sat back down among his friends. They were silent for a great while, then Clarence broke the still in the air with more songs; some from the old days as well as newer ones they were familiar with. They sang along, and the mood lightened.

They ran out of songs to sing, and that's when the stories began. In his sweet old sing-song style, Wallace told them of the past, of the slaves and the history of Summerton Place. He spoke fondly of the people who had lived in the cabins and the family who'd resided in the mansion. His heart was rooted in the soil, in the ancient oaks that lined the road, in the solemn hymns that sounded on the evening breeze. He knew the secrets buried in the ruins too.

"Mr. Wallace," Ezra asked, "why do you leave the old house like that?"

"Ah, the old house. You are not the only one to ask that. People've been pesterin' me for years and my father before me." He laughed. "Even Clarence, here, has been after me to do something with the ruins of that. . . glorious place."

An odd note in his voice caught Livy's attention. "Glorious, Wallace? I hardly think it's glorious. It's in shambles."

"Aye. But I've been waitin' for a long time to fix it up. Knew it was only a matter of time before I'd see what needed to go there. It might not be glorious today, but it will be. I see a right glorious place, built upon this foundation." His voice was firm and proud. "There has been sorrow here, more than you can know. I am here today, a product of that sorrow. It's why you are here as well, Livy. We are connected to it—you and I."

She looked startled, but he continued. "You remind me of someone, a wise woman who lived here when I was very young. You look like her; you have her eyes. Yessuh, I see the family resemblance when I look at you."

"Family? I—" Livy's voice came to a quick halt as Wallace swayed. Both she and Clarence leaped to their feet to steady their friend. It took a minute, but soon Wallace waved them both away.

"I'm fine," he said. "No need to fuss. I ain't done here." He sat down next to Livy and patted her arm. "Now, as I was sayin'—"

"Yeah, as you were saying," Livy repeated. "Wallace, what do you mean? How am I connected to this place? I don't understand."

"Oh, that's a story I've been saving for you," Wallace said. "The time is almost here."

"But I've never known my family," Livy protested. "I grew up in an orphanage, just like these kids. Only with nuns, and all they could tell me was that my mother was older and she died giving birth to me."

"Yes, she grew up in a loving family, but when she learned who she was, she left everything she knew and loved—including those who raised her—to come to Charleston to find her twin."

"*Twin?* I don't understand, Wallace. And how do you know all this?"

Wallace moved to pat her arm but lost his balance on the log. His body shifted and he started to fall. Clarence jumped to catch him and keep him from the fire.

"Wallace, we need to get you to bed." He spoke firmly and began maneuvering the old man toward his home. Wallace didn't argue.

"I am tired tonight," he agreed. "But tomorrow, Miss Livy. . . Tomorrow, I will have all the answers for you. Tonight, my bed is callin' my name. You young'uns enjoy the fire and make yourselves at home in the guesthouse."

Chapter 22

For I am persuaded that neither death, nor life,
nor angels, nor principalities, nor powers,
nor things present, nor things to come,
nor height, nor depth, nor any other creature,
shall be able to separate us from the love of God,
which is in Christ Jesus our Lord.
ROMANS 8:38–39

The day had taken its toll on Wallace, and Clarence was quick to help him to bed.

"Wallace, d'you think she's ready? You 'bout told her everything. Of course, she needs to know. The sooner the better."

"We're almost there, Clarence, yessuh." Wallace reached down to remove his socks. "She's not expecting what's coming, but she'll be right fine." He stood up and made his way to the bedroom window. Clarence followed him, worry etched clearly on his face.

"No, it's Hattie I'm concerned about," Wallace continued. "I have to convince her. I have to tell her the story. She won't think she can do it, but she's the one with the gifts. And Ezra, he'll help her. Love will do that, bring out the best in us. They don't quite know it yet, but Ezra will bring that girl to all she was meant to be." He chuckled as he peered out the window toward the fire. "They aren't seein' eye to eye right now, but time pays no mind to fate's hold. It jus' refines and makes you better."

"Well, they seemed more like they were mad at each other tonight than in love." Clarence took Wallace's jacket from him and hung it on a rack. "I don't know, Wallace, but you do have the gift of foresight, so I'll trust you to know what you're doin'." He poured a glass of water and set it on the nightstand. "We don't have a lot of time left, my friend. We're both getting old, and we need to make it right. Why aren't they speakin' anyways?"

Wallace smiled. "Ah, pride infiltrates young hearts. But I'm not worried about them. Love will pull them through." He made his way back to the bed and climbed between the covers. Clarence stood beside him as he closed his eyes. "I will pray and ask the good Lord to place a blanket of truth over them, one that will stand the test of time."

"You do that, Wallace. And you get some sleep tonight, okay?"

"Mmm, there's legacy here, my friend. There's a future rich in possibility, but it's not ours no more, Clarence. It's time to give it over. You know, it's the wounded places that connect us. God gives us each time, and we determine the road we take. I coulda let Bessany's death destroy me. . . and after her, her mother. Ida's heart was not able to recover from it, much as I tried to help her see."

He stretched and yawned. "I'm feelin' mighty philosophical tonight, aren't I, old friend? But we find our most treasured gifts in the darkness of sorrow and pain. That's what I need them to know. It's what I'll tell them tomorrow."

"What do you think will happen to this worn-out old place, Wallace?"

Already half asleep, Wallace whispered, "Somethin' wonderful, Clarence. Yessuh. . . somethin' wonderful." He smiled, and visions filled his mind.

Tomorrow, he would tell them of their significance to the plantation. He'd been waiting for this day. Much like Habakkuk, one of his favorite biblical prophets, he had stationed himself on the ramparts and waited. He thought of the past, of the story he would convince Hattie to write. It was one of shackled sin, of unbelievable torment, yet unwavering belief that good would stand the test of time. And much like his ancestors, his own faith had been tested—in fact, the age-old question of "why" still lingered, especially in the night.

As he drifted off to sleep, he listened to the voices of the past. They comforted him in the night and encouraged him to press forward so they could be heard. All for a fallen world needing hope. And he waited for her to come to him, as she did every night just as he reached the edge of consciousness. He pictured her in her white dress, dancing around the hallowed fields. He listened closely until, in the wind outside his window, he heard her.

"Daddy. . ."

With a start, Wallace was awake. He sat up at the edge of his bed. *Just one night, Lord, can I just sleep through one night?* He lit the lamp beside his bed and made his way to the window. He had been dreaming of Bessany, and waking up from being with her was always unsettling.

Through the window, Wallace spotted Livy still sitting near the dying embers of the bonfire. *Ah, I see, Lord. There are things You want me to do.* He dressed himself warmly, then grabbed a blanket from the chair. With a whispered prayer for guidance, he headed outside.

"You look cold, Miss Livy." He draped the blanket around her shoulders. "Can I get you anything?"

She jumped. "Wallace! You startled me. But yes, I am a bit chilly. When that sun goes down, you'd think we were living somewhere way up north, not here in the Lowcountry." With an appreciative hum of pleasure, she pulled the blanket closer around herself. "This wrap is perfect. Thank you!" She patted the seat next to her. "Come, sit with me."

"Well, to be honest, I need to walk right now. These old muscles get cramped up sometimes, and I just need to move." He reached for her hand. "Would you walk with me? It's just you and me, awake in the world. I'd love to spend some quiet time with you."

"Gracious, what a surprise you are. Are you sure you're up to it?"

"Oh, I'm sure. The good Lord woke me from a lovely dream, just so's I could talk with you. It's such a beautiful night."

"It really is," Livy gushed. "I just couldn't go inside. The moon is so bright, it almost lights the way."

Together, they wandered the path worn wide through history, listening to the night sounds, admiring the stars, and despite Wallace's mention of a talk, enjoying a companionable silence.

Finally, Livy spoke up. "Are you feeling well, Wallace? I'm a little worried about you. I'm afraid you are holding something back from me. I mean, you've always been a little mysterious but—you were so unsteady this evening."

"Oh, I'm just getting old. Arthritis is getting the best of me, that's all. We had a big day today. I was tired. No need to worry."

Livy's feet slowed as they approached the ruins of the plantation house. In the moonlight, Wallace could see her furrowed brow.

"What is it, child?"

She laughed. "I'm no child, Wallace, though sometimes when I'm with you I feel like one. Especially when the young ones are around." Above them, clouds shifted and a shaft of moonlight spotlighted the broken wall of the plantation. Livy's eyes were captured by the sight.

"You must tell me, why *do* you keep it this way? It seems such a shame to leave the property in such disrepair." She shook her head.

"It makes me sad. You know, I have always felt a strange connection to this place. I don't know why."

Thank You for that opening, Lord. Wallace took Livy's hand. "I'd like to talk about that. There are, indeed, things you need to know. It's no coincidence that you feel at home here, Livy. Come, I want to show you something." He led her to a wide section of broken wall, low enough to sit on. Gingerly, he found a seat, and Livy joined him.

"I like to sit here," he said. "Right here in this very spot and look out toward the cabins. This room behind us used to be the music room. Yessuh, this is where the pianoforte was. . . my father used to tell me how well Miss Julia played. He could listen for hours, he said. It was Miss Chloe's favorite room, too, for a while. She was Mr. Summerton's foreman's wife. His name was Ned."

Livy shifted, her eyes wide. "You mean—"

"Yes, they were Mr. Summerton's slaves. They died when I was just a little boy, but I feel like I lived right b'side them, as much as I know about them. My father taught me everything about the history of this place, and now I get to share it with you. And eventually the whole world."

He paused and looked at Livy's skin, glowing in the light from the moon. He pictured her high cheekbones and green eyes. *Aye, she's a Summerton. All the way.* "That cabin over there?" He pointed across the way. "That cabin was Miss Chloe and Ned's. They lived here their whole lives, even after the Civil War ended and they were no longer slaves. They maintained the property with their son. His name was Moses."

He looked at Livy. "And Moses was my father."

"Your father? I've always wondered about your family, Wallace." A breeze picked up and chilled the air. She shivered, partly from cold and partly from an excitement she didn't quite understand.

"Yes'm. He had a hand in achieving some wonderful things for the Gullah population here in the Lowcountry. He went to school up north, to Howard University in Washington DC. Then he came back and became a teacher here in Charleston. He also had a hand in opening the first and only orphanage for our kind in the Old City in 1891." He chuckled quietly. "He made his mark on this town, for sure. Wonder how many of us he saved by what he accomplished. Helped orphans learn trades, produced items to sell in the market. . . yessuh. And music! Some of the kids learned music. Of course, Miss Julia helped run that department. Guess they named him right— Moses led his people to freedom."

"That's amazing, Wallace. I didn't know!"

"Yep, that was my father." He stopped and adjusted the blanket around Livy's shoulders. Then with a gentle hand, he lifted her chin. "And he was your uncle."

For a moment, the words didn't register. Then Livy's eyes flew open wide. "My— What?!"

He nodded solemnly, but his eyes twinkled in the moonlight. "Yes. And that means, I'm your—"

"You're my cousin? How do you know? I've never known family. I—" Her breath caught in her throat. Tears gathered on her lashes as she stood, then stepped away. "But I've known you for years. How. . . why?. . ."

Wallace looked up at the stars, then back to Livy.

"The Lord works in mysterious ways, child. When we discovered who you were, we were not free to disclose that information. But we kept watch over you. I made sure you were safe and cared for, though you have done well for yourself on your own. And then, well, the time was not right. I'm sorry, I—"

"So, I'm a Hayes?"

"Not exactly. You're a Summerton."

Chapter 23

For my thoughts are not your thoughts,
neither are your ways my ways, saith the LORD.
For as the heavens are higher than the earth,
so are my ways higher than your ways,
and my thoughts than your thoughts.
ISAIAH 55:8–9

"Is Livy still outside?" Ezra stood in the front room doorway. It was late—far later than Livy ever allowed them to stay up at home, but she was nowhere to be found.

Hattie shrugged. "She wanted to stay under the stars. I haven't seen her."

"Are you cold?" Hattie nodded stiffly. "Me too. Think Wallace would mind if we lit a fire?"

"I'm sure it would be fine." She watched as Ezra lit a small fire on the hearth. They hadn't spoken for the last hour. She knew she wasn't being kind, but she couldn't seem to help herself.

"May I sit next to you?" His voice was tight. She nodded, and he perched on the far end of the settee. She looked into the growing fire while he fidgeted.

"Why have you shut yourself off from me?"

Hattie jumped at the harshness of his voice. She started to respond, but he barged on.

"One minute, we're swimming in the river, laughing, and the next—you're all closed up. All I want is to get to know you." He stopped, waiting for an answer, but Hattie stayed quiet.

Frustrated, he crossed his arms over his chest and sat back with a growl. "I don't understand girls at all."

Consternation grew inside her. She couldn't answer him. She didn't know. The strange connection between them both enthralled and terrified her. She didn't understand it, but she was afraid to let him in. The circumstances of life had built a wall around her heart—one that had protected her well for many years. When she was with Ezra, her wall felt threatened. Did he really care? *Would* he care if he knew? Did she want him to? Silence stretched.

"Why won't you talk to me? What did I do?"

She shook her head, hard. "I'm just not comfortable talking about my past, Ezra. It's the past and I'm not proud of it and I can't change it. And I don't want you to know. Why can't you let it go?"

"Life isn't perfect, Hattie. I've already told you about my family."

"Your family, yeah." The mocking tone of her voice surprised even her. "People who leave you somewhere safe and go save other people. My father left me because *he didn't want me*. We are *not* the same."

"We don't have to be the same. And I think your father was a fool." He moved closer to her as he spoke. "I don't know what happened, but I know I want to get to know you. I can help you if you let me. But I can't if you avoid me all the time."

"I don't need help. I'm fine. There's nothing to fix—it's just who

I am." Catching a glimpse of his crestfallen face, she sighed. "I'm not avoiding you, Ezra. But sometimes. . . sometimes you scare me. When I'm with you, I forget who I am and I forget about this ugly scar. No one else has ever done that for me, just you. And I don't know what to do with it. What if I tell you and you don't like me anymore? What will I do then?"

"But you do the same for me, Hattie. You make me think things, feel things, I never have before." He touched her hand. "Talk to me. Let me in."

Her heart raced. It was hard to catch a breath. She hated this out-of-control feeling of being swept up in him. She jumped to her feet.

"Let's go for a walk. Let's go find Livy!"

"Okay, okay. But we're going to finish this conversation."

"Not tonight," Hattie tossed over her shoulder as she hurried out the door.

They found Livy and Wallace at the old mansion, deep in conversation. Wallace saw them approaching and murmured something to Livy. Her posture straightened abruptly. Hattie was sure she saw her wiping tears from her face, but when she turned to them, her usual smile was firmly in place.

"Is no one sleeping this night?" she asked.

"We were wondering where you were," Ezra answered. "It does seem to be a night for wandering though."

"Livy and I were talking about the history of this place," Wallace said. "But it would be good if we all headed inside." He held a hand to Livy. "Shall we?"

But Livy was no longer paying attention. She was looking out over the darkened fields. "So, what happened to Ned?" she asked abruptly. "If he was freed, why did he stay here after the war?"

Wallace dropped his hand, looked at the teenagers, then started them all walking back toward the guesthouse. "Well, everything just got a little bit crazy around here. Life changed in big ways, for the

Summertons and our people. Most freed slaves faced poverty and discrimination, but the slaves from Summerton Place stayed for a long time. Miss Julia was in charge, and she was kind. In 1867, the first free secondary school for Blacks opened. My father went to school, and so did my granddaddy, Ned. Mr. Summerton and Miss Julia had already taught Ned the basics, but at school, he learned new trades as well as a higher level of education. Mr. Summerton built and paid for that school himself." There was an odd mixture of pride and. . . something else. . . in his voice that caught Hattie's attention.

"Was Mr. Summerton nice to his slaves, Wallace?" she asked.

Wallace scratched his chin. "That's a story for another night, and one that I will tell you, especially, Hattie. When the time is right. But I will say that so much has happened here on this land. . . great sorrow has happened here. And yet, in the middle of it—blessin'. Yessuh, blessin' right along with the sorrow."

"You talk about that a lot, Mr. Wallace," Hattie said. "Blessing and sorrow together. I don't get it."

Wallace was silent until they were back at the firepit. Only coals were left, glimmering in the dark. He picked up a stick and poked at them thoughtfully before answering. Finally, he said, "It's kinda like this fire, Miss Hattie. We can look at it and think it's all done—the flames are all gone. But there's still fire smoldering underneath. It's not dead. Well, it was like that here too. The most amazin' thing happened right before the end of the War. Just when everything seemed ruined, let's just say, God was working overtime."

The confusion on Hattie's face must have tickled Wallace because he laughed. "I'm not makin' this any clearer, am I?" She shook her head.

"Okay," he said. "Let me ask you something. Do you think that when all else is failin'—at the point that you think all is lost—would you still hold on to the hope that God can deliver you to your place? That everything in this life is meant to draw you to Him? Even with all the sufferin' that man causes, do you think that, in the midst of it all, our sweet Lord is workin' overtime to make all paths righteous?"

She hesitated. The question was strange, but something in it tugged at her heartstrings. "Uh. . . I think so." She took a breath. "No, I know so. Yes."

Wallace nodded in approval. "Well, that's what He did. He took all the pain and sufferin' that happened on this plantation, and He turned it all to blessin'. All the hurts and evil—God was still able to touch hearts and change lives."

Hattie was transfixed. "Do. . . do you mean. . . forgiveness? Like, they let it all go and forgave?"

A smile grew on Wallace's face, so wide she could see it in the moonlight. "Oh, my sweet Hattie. I see now why God has chosen you. Why He brought you to us."

"Chose me? What do you mean?"

Wallace pointed back the way they'd come. "You know that row of slave cabins? You see the broken-up plantation home over there? There is a beautiful story here, my child. And God means for *you* to write it."

He turned to the others. "In fact, you all have a place here. All three of you. There are no coincidences in life. All of our paths were meant to cross. And God has His holy hands in all of it."

They looked at him, dumbfounded, and he couldn't help but laugh in delight. "And what's more," he continued, "I intend to give this to you. All of it—every acre, every brick, every stone—everythin' is yours.

"And I can tell you this: there is freedom in what I have planned for this place. In what *the Lord* has planned for it. Every tear, every drop o' blood spilled on the soil we're standin' on—we're gonna make it right. You three and me. For all of us. For our ancestors and for them who will follow us across these hallowed fields in the future."

He looked directly at Livy. "To you, especially, but we'll talk more about that tomorrow. I know I've given you a lot to think about tonight, but I'm finished for now. I need to go back to my bed! You all get to bed now, y'hear?"

And with that, he turned and walked to his house. Together, they stood watching until he disappeared inside. Without much discussion, they all turned and headed to their own beds, hearts and minds full and wondering.

Chapter 24

Trust in the LORD with all thine heart
and lean not unto thine own understanding.
In all thy ways acknowledge him,
and he shall direct thy paths.
PROVERBS 3:5–6

Livy got ready for bed in a daze. This evening had brought reve-
lations she could never have expected. She'd arrived an orphan,
and suddenly she had family. She knew who she was and where she'd
come from. Well, at least in part. The kids had interrupted them as
Wallace was giving her details. She was a Summerton. . . and Wallace
was her cousin. How could that even be?

She was sharing a room with Hattie, and the girl was chattering
on, despite the hour. It was too much.

"Hattie!" Her voice came out rougher than intended, and they
both jumped a little. "I'm sorry. I didn't mean to sound that way, but

this has been a day full of surprises and. . . news. . . and I just need silence. Please. Can we just go to bed?"

"Of course, Miss Livy. I'm sorry. I'm just so excited! I—"

"I know. Me too. But we'll let Wallace explain it all in the morning, okay? Say your prayers and go to sleep." She pulled back the covers on her bed and, ignoring the look of injured puzzlement on her ward's face, climbed in and faced the wall.

But it was a long time before she slept.

The day dawned bright and sunny. Hattie was up as soon as it was light, but Livy would have preferred to stay cocooned under the covers. She didn't know what to do with what she had learned the night before. It didn't matter though, because everyone else was stirring. Time to get up.

Seemed like everyone else had been stewing on the news too. It didn't take long for Hattie and Ezra to find Wallace and start asking questions. Livy tagged along. She wasn't going to ask, but she definitely wanted to know. They were back out by the firepit, Hattie and Wallace on logs, Ezra sprawled on the ground nearby. Livy found her own spot on a wide log and sat down to listen.

"I don't understand, Wallace. I've always assumed you managed this place for someone else. But you said you were going to give it to us. Wouldn't that mean you'd have to own it?"

"Oh, I own it. It's just easier sometimes to look like the caretaker." He laughed. "Keeps me out of trouble."

Hattie smiled but looked like she didn't know what to think of that.

"No, I'm joking." Wallace assured her. "This place—the houses, land, fields—yessuh, it all belongs to me. But it's time to pass it on.

I'm gettin' older, and these things need taken care of." He looked across the firepit to Livy. She felt the warmth of his smile as he continued.

"Me and God—we've been talkin' about this day for a while. Miss Livy, you're the reason for this plan. Hattie, you were the blessing I didn't know I was waitin' for. And Ezra, you're the last piece of this little puzzle of mine. Each of you has your own special place here, and I've been prayin' that you will come to see the potential of that and of this place I call home.

"It is my wish to have you all beside me, yessuh, right alongside the trees and the river. To share the sorrow, yes, but to experience the blessin' that came through it." He stopped, took a breath, then let it out in a long sigh.

"Let me start from the beginning. Generations ago, a great temptation took over the man who owned this place. His sin brought great pain to the slaves who worked for him—'specially to Ned and Chloe. But through that sin, a child was born." He stopped and corrected himself with a laugh. "Well, two, to be exact."

"Twins?" Hattie asked, eyes wide.

"Yes'm. Two beautiful souls. One remained here in captivity. He was my father. The other, his sister, they smuggled away from the plantation, away from Mr. Summerton. He had only seen the boy and didn't know the girl existed."

Hattie nearly leaped out of her skin with questions. Wallace smiled softly. "I will tell you the whole story, Hattie, because I want you to write it down. It's a marvelous story of love and forgiveness and purpose, and I want you to share it with the world. But today, I want to touch only on certain details. You must be patient."

He turned to Livy. "The girlchild was named Hope. Moses, my father, carried his mother's heritage. Green eyes like yours, but dark skin, dark hair. Undeniably Negro. But Hope looked like her father. Fair-skinned. Smooth, dark hair. Green eyes. In fact, she looked remarkably like her half-sister—Miss Julia. Knowing that life would be more difficult for her, livin' between two worlds as she would be if she stayed in slavery, Miss Julia and Ned found a loving family to adopt and raise her as a free White woman. She grew up in northern Virginia; Alexandria, to be exact.

"Hope loved her family, and they loved her very much. When she came of age, her adoptive parents told her the circumstances surrounding her birth and the sacrifice her mother had made. Meanwhile, her parents had another child, a biological daughter. And this"—he stopped and looked at Ezra—"is where you come in. Their daughter's name was Esther. Esther Levine."

Ezra jumped to his feet. "Wait a minute. My mother's family lived in Alexandria for years and. . . yes. . . my mother's family name is Levine. Are you saying that we're related somehow? But my parents were born in Germany."

Wallace smiled. "Yes. Esther is your grandmother. When Mrs. Levine passed away, Esther and her father moved to Germany. Esther got married there and had a daughter; named her Sarah. Sarah met and married Isaac Wolfe while volunteering as a nurse during the last part of the Great War—and eventually they had our friend, Ezra." Everyone's eyes were wide as they absorbed this news. Wallace turned to Ezra as he continued.

"So, yes, in a sense, we are related. I have known of your family my whole life. I didn't meet them until your parents returned to Alexandria in 1938. When they went back to Germany early this year to try to get the rest of your family away from the unrest there, they turned to me for help. It was a risk to go back, but they took that risk."

"So that's how you knew who Ezra was that day we met in the market." Livy mused. "This is incredible. But. . . so. . ." She put a hand to her head. "Okay, but what about Hope?"

"Hope was your mother, Livy. She is the link that connects us, dear cousin."

Hattie and Ezra nearly fell over at that revelation, but Wallace shushed them and continued.

"Hope grew up with the Levines in Alexandria. She and Esther loved each other dearly. She helped take care of Anna, her adoptive mother, while she was ill. Hope was twenty-nine when Anna passed away, and I believe she was engaged to be married. So when the family moved to Germany, Hope stayed here." He stopped and looked at Livy almost apologetically. "This is where things get a little muddy."

"My father and grandparents had been quietly looking for Hope for years. By the time they found the right Levines in Alexandria, the family had moved to Germany. We assumed she had gone with them. Eventually, we learned she had not, and we began searching for her again. But for a long time, we couldn't find the name of the man she had married. To make a long story short, we did finally discover his name—David Marigold. We began looking for Hope under that name, and we discovered that her husband had disappeared. Rumor had it that he worked with the remnants of the Underground and he'd had a target on his back."

Livy's eyes were wide and tearful.

"Then we learned that Hope knew that she was adopted. The friend who told us that said that she had always longed to know who her natural family was. So we widened our search and began looking closer to home as well. Eventually, we found a lovely young woman, Miss Livy Marigold, who had been brought up by the nuns who were with her mother when she died.

"The nuns told us that, yes, the young woman's mother was named Hope, but when her husband disappeared, she had moved south to find her biological family. Unfortunately for all of us, the great earthquake of 1886 that nearly destroyed Charleston also destroyed any records that could have helped her. She became ill toward the end of her pregnancy, and she died in the convent. All the nuns had for the child were a name and a locket."

"And love," Livy said on a sob. "They loved me."

"They did indeed. Like I said, I didn't find you until you were quite the young woman. Everythin' they had to say about you was wonderful. But you were well established in your studies and beginning your career. Our news could have destroyed your life, considerin' the delicate nature of our family line."

Livy's hands went from her head to her hips. "The delicate nature? But I needed family!"

"It was a difficult decision. We have cared for you and watched over you from a distance ever since. When my father died, I continued that care, but keepin' myself a secret became a burden. I introduced myself to you and we became friends. I've wanted to tell you for so long, but have needed to wait for the right time, the right circumstances to tell you all of this."

Livy shook her head again. "I don't understand! How. . . why?"

Wallace took her hand. "We don't write our stories, dear one. Sure, we can change who we are and make decisions based on our circumstances, but it's God who lights the way to our destiny. Chloe and Ned sacrificed everythin' so Hope could be free in a way they would never be. Even when they were given their freedom, they still carried the weight of their past and the color of their skin.

"I ask you, Livy. Can anythin' greater have come from their decision than to have weathered such sorrow and pain, to have walked the path of righteousness without ever knowin' the outcome yet still trustin' that God knows what's best and He has the better plan?"

"So this was God's plan all along?" Livy's eyes flashed both confusion and a growing anger. "What was God's plan, Wallace, what? What good has come of this?"

"You, dear girl." He spread his hands wide. "You, me. This place. The good is here. It's your story. We are family, cousins! I told you last night—Moses Hayes Summerton, my father, was your mother's twin.

"And apparently, you have a gift that runs in the family. You are not the first in our family who's had a love for needy children and orphans. Miss Julia—she cared for every child on this plantation as if they were her own. Despite her father's ire. Your uncle Moses, my dad, opened the first and only orphanage for Blacks in Charleston. Ned and Chloe Hayes, our grandparents, helped create an environment within the establishment where orphans could learn trades, produce items for sale, and learn music." He stopped for a moment, lost in thought.

Livy, too, looked deep in thought, but Hattie had questions.

"But wait," she protested. "Ned and Chloe were slaves! How did they end up doing all that? How did you end up owning this place?"

"Ahh," Wallace said. "That's a good question. I'll skip the long story for now and just tell you that Mr. Summerton died in the quake in 1886. In his will, he left everything he had to Julia and Moses—his children. Despite the past and the sin that had abounded, the two unlikely siblings made good things happen. And when Julia passed on, it all went to Moses. My father used the blessings he'd received to change lives. He gave society's outcasts an education and offered hope to the poorest of all.

"And he's just like someone else I know." He turned and smiled at Livy. "Moses devoted his life to that orphanage. He gave life and hope to the orphaned, the motherless, the fatherless. Just as you do, my dear."

Livy's mouth opened and closed. A tear made its way down her cheek, but no words escaped her lips. Wallace touched her hand gently.

"And now that the time is right, now that I am free to tell you, now that our lives have come full circle"—his eyes swept over his companions, encompassing Hattie and Ezra along with his cousin Livy—"now I can say that you, Livy, as the only child of Hope Summerton Levine *Marigold*, are my next of kin. And everythin' I have belongs to you."

They sat in silence for several minutes. Then Wallace suggested Hattie and Ezra find Clarence and see what might be happening for lunch. When they had gone, he turned to Livy again.

"I know that's a lot of information to get in one day. I'm sure you have questions. I would like to find some coffee and lunch myself. Would you come to the house with me? You can ask me anythin' you'd like."

Livy stood. "I am a bit overwhelmed," she admitted. "Food might help my brain digest everything that's swirling around inside me." They walked in silence. Wallace didn't push, he just waited. At the house, they found a fragrant pot of coffee and some fresh, warm bread.

Livy took the portion he offered, but her eyes were still focused on a distant horizon. Finally, she shook her head. "I'm just confused by it all, Wallace. This place, the history, my part in it. Especially I don't understand, if you knew all along who I was, why didn't you tell me?"

He sighed. "I knew one day you would ask me that question. It began as carryin' forward the torch of Ned and Chloe's sacrifice for Hope. The public outcry that you might have been exposed to—you being White, and we being Black—would have limited your opportunities. We wanted to protect you. So we waited and watched you grow into an amazin' young woman. We waited so that you could be who you were meant to be while God prepared you for this very moment. Your walk was preparin' you to take on something much bigger—to take on the responsibility of managin' this precious place. We did not want to take one moment away from your growth."

He sat down heavily at the table across from her. With a start, Livy realized how gray he was looking, how tired. But when she began to worry aloud, he waved her concern aside.

"All of us on the plantation, we're gettin' old. There's not many of us left to care for it. But I have a plan for this place. One that will honor God as well as the sacrifices that have been made here." He wiped his forehead with his kerchief. "It's been a long day already, and it's only just after noon. I'm going to take a rest now. I think, tomorrow mornin', I'd like to talk more with Hattie. I believe God has brought her into our lives to write our story. This place is rich in history and life lessons, and I think the world needs to hear them."

"Really? You mean, a book? A family history?"

"Mmm hmm. I've seen something special in her since the day she arrived. Her pain is deep, but God is good. And He has blessed her with words. I'm choosin' her to write my story because of the light I see inside her. Her life experiences will make her strong enough to dig deep into truth. They will give her an understanding that not everyone is capable of. We're all different; everyone has a season and a purpose. Her purpose is to write. Her season is beginnin' now. I feel it in my bones. It's all in God's time."

Ezra and Hattie left Wallace and Livy by the firepit, as instructed. Clarence's wife fixed them a picnic lunch and pointed them to the river. "Y'all go have a nice afternoon," she said. "You can go to the river, but Wallace's rules are no one goes in the water without him or Clarence there. That's important to him, so you obey."

They assured her they would and headed off down the path to the water. They were quiet, thinking about who they were in light of all they'd learned that morning. They settled on a grassy hilltop and sat down to eat their lunch.

After a while, Hattie sighed. "I hope you're not still upset with me, Ezra," she began. "You know, at the river. I just. . . You scare me is all. I've been alone for so long. Livy and the kids—they're all I know."

She looked at him shyly. "I never thought I'd meet someone like you. Seems like good things only happen to people in the books I read. You took me by surprise, and sometimes it makes me feel uncomfortable." She set her sandwich aside and pulled her knees up to her chin.

"My daddy was not a very nice man, Ezra. He did things to my mama. It's hard for me to talk about. With his example, it's also hard for me to trust anyone. Your daddy should be someone you can trust. Your home should be a safe place to grow up, but it wasn't like that for me. After a while, it was just easier to keep to myself than let people in." She stopped talking for a minute. "So I stopped trying to be, I don't know, social? I'd rather be alone and just read. Reading takes me away to a whole different place. I feel safe in my books."

She huffed and gave him a comical look that was half frustration and half affection. "Then you come along and boff it all up."

Ezra's quick grin was short-lived as he scooted closer and took her hand. "What happened? What did your father do?"

She hesitated a moment longer, then words tumbled out in a rush. "He was always angry. I don't know why. He drank all the time, then took it out on my mother. It happened almost every night. It got to the point where I just expected it, like a normal person would expect to sit down to dinner or go to school. It was part of my everyday life. Except, the last time he attacked her, he had a knife. I put myself in front of her and he cut me instead."

She put a hand to her face. "You know, it's kind of weird. When I look in the mirror and see my scar, all I see is that everything stopped the minute it happened. All that hell just landed square on my cheek. The drinking, the beatings, everything stopped. I guess when Daddy looked at me after that, it just reminded him every day what kind of man he was."

Ezra squeezed her hand. Hattie shrugged. "I'd do it a hundred more times to save her. A million more times if I could just spend five more minutes with her. She ended up dying of pneumonia a few months later. And that's when Daddy took me to the orphanage. I haven't seen him since."

She fell into pensive silence, and Ezra wrapped his arm around her in a gentle hug. "I'm glad you told me," he whispered in her ear.

Wallace woke the next morning feeling refreshed and surprisingly free of his usual aches and pains. He dressed himself quickly and joined the others who were just sitting down for breakfast. He seated himself between Hattie and Ezra, then looked around the table at all the happy faces. Besides his guests, Clarence's family was present, everyone excited for fresh, blueberry pancakes and a platter heaped with sausage and eggs from the farm.

"Let's join hands," he said and waited as the circle grew complete. He closed his eyes and began to pray. They echoed his amen as he finished, but Wallace stayed still a moment longer, his heart communing with the Father. *Bless them, Lord, every one. Show them who You are.*

Then he opened his eyes, and breakfast began. Food passed, conversation flowed, laughter bubbled. Livy, however, looked a bit harried. It wasn't until she almost poured syrup in her coffee, however, that he intervened.

"What's got you all worked up this morning, Miss Livy?" he asked.

"Hmmm? Oh!" She blushed a bit as she realized what she'd almost done. "Well, that would've been interesting coffee, wouldn't it?"

He smiled and waited. Finally, she sighed. "I do have a lot on my mind," she admitted. "Thinking about everything you told us yesterday. . . And I guess I'm a little worried about Cora at the orphanage. This visit has been full of surprises and wonderful things, but we should be getting back to Charleston after breakfast."

"Pay no mind to the orphanage, dear. We have it covered. Cora will be fine—we made sure of that, didn't we, Clarence?"

Clarence's white teeth shone in a bright smile. "We did, Wallace. We did, indeed. Miss Cora was happy to oblige."

Wallace nodded emphatically. "And I'm thankful that I have another day with my favorite people. I intend on making the most of it, too." He looked at his next of kin and winked. She smiled back, looking reassured.

Ezra had mischief on his face as he spoke up. "What are we doing today, Wallace? Could we go to the river?" The children got excited at that suggestion, but Wallace shook his head.

"We may do that later, Ezra, but right now, I need to talk to Hattie about something. I'd like us to take our time today, all of us, and be, well, just be well." He chuckled at his own play on words. "Miss Hattie, would you do me the honor of going for a walk with me?"

Hattie leaped to her feet, an odd look of relief on her face. "I'd love to go for a walk with you, Wallace. Let's boogie woogie on outta here. I need some air after this wonderful breakfast." Then she stopped and looked at Livy. "Oh! I should help clean up first."

"You may be excused today," Livy said.

"You're a guest, dear girl," Clarence's wife asserted at almost the same moment.

"You go on now," the women said in unison. Then they looked at each other and laughed. Wallace took Hattie's arm and led her out of the house.

They strolled together quietly for several minutes. Finally, Wallace stopped and looked at the girl. "Hattie, why do you think we are here. . . on this walk?"

"I'm not sure but. . . I guess because you want me to write your story. I don't know why, though. . . I mean, I write and all but—" She shrugged.

Wallace smiled. "You're right, but why do you think I've chosen you for the task?"

Hattie's shoulders dropped. "I don't know! Maybe because you know I like to read and write?"

"Oh no, child. That's not why. I would not have chosen you merely because of want or like of something." They started to walk again. "Never because of anything as superficial as that. No, I have watched you—how you read under the tree, how you speak to the other children, and most importantly, how you treated Ezra and helped him improve his English skills. I believe God has gifted you for this job."

At that, Hattie began to fidget. Wallace stopped her and held her hands in his. "Sweet girl, there is no need to question your abilities. I believe in you. Let me explain why." He let go of her hands and began to gesture. "The way you interact with the people around you, your quiet and observant demeanor, your love for the world around you—Hattie, child. To reach the world with what you write, you must experience that which binds us. Real love and. . . sometimes loss of it." They had reached the remains of the mansion, and Wallace again chose a seat outside the old music room.

But Hattie wasn't convinced. "I don't understand. I'm sixteen years old. I'm not a writer!"

"What is a writer but someone who has struggled? Without pain, there is no way to the light or a way to write the words." He reached out to touch her arm. "Let me explain myself. In your case, my sweet girl, without your personal struggle, there would be no artistry in your writing, no push behind your pen, no color in the paintin'. Without pain, there would be no story." The look of confusion did not leave her face.

"Okay, think of it this way. An artist starts with a blank canvas, right?" She nodded.

"Well, that's how we start life—with a blank canvas. How we live—what happens to us and how we respond to it—that's what fills our canvas." He paused and looked out over the horizon. "My canvas is just about complete, but I have an extraordinary story to tell you. It begins right here on this plantation in 1860, right before the Civil War. Yessuh, with a girl named Julia Summerton. And I'd like you to help me share it with the world."

Hattie squared her shoulders and sat tall. "I'd like to try, Mr. Wallace."

And so their humble effort began.

Chapter 25

He hath shewed thee, O man, what is good;
and what doth the Lord require of thee,
but to do justly, and to love mercy,
and to walk humbly with thy God?
MICAH 6:8

September 1861

Julia stood peeking over the Levines' gate. The gardens were slightly overgrown, and hedge clippings were strewn across the piazza and once manicured pathways. It had only been a few weeks since she'd left Hope in the care of Alexander and Anna, but now the mansion looked to be abandoned, save for what appeared to be a gardener working the grounds. She opened the wrought-iron gate and entered the piazza. The door to the mansion was slightly ajar. She placed her hand on the door and poked her head inside. Light filtered through the shutters and lit the dust hovering in the empty room. *Strange.*

"May I help you?"

"Oh!" Julia jumped and turned to find the gardener behind her. She put a hand to her throat. "You gave me quite a fright, sir. I'm here to speak with the Levines—"

"This property has been vacated. The doctor and his wife have recently moved to Alexandria. May I ask who you are?"

"I'm Julia Summerton, from—"

"Ah, yes. From the Summerton plantation, just outside of town?" At her nod, he continued. "Yes, Alexander spoke to me about you. He was concerned that you might be back to look for the family. In fact—" He stepped past her and into the hall. The dust swirled around him as he motioned for her to follow. "If you would come with me, there's an item of great importance he wanted me to be sure you received."

He led her toward the grand hall where she had admired the artwork from all over the world. A single painting still hung, and they stopped before it. It was the one she'd admired on the night they'd heard the cannons over Charleston Harbor.

"This, Miss Summerton, is a family heirloom. I cannot comprehend why he left it for you, but I must imagine you and your family are important to him. I'm happy I happened to be here today to give this to you. I've been keeping an eye on the home."

Julia was stunned. "I. . . I don't understand," she said as the gentleman removed it from the wall.

"Well, my dear, you don't have to understand it, but it's yours." He set the heavy piece next to the doorway.

"I'm sorry," she said, shaking her head. "What is your name?"

"I am Alexander's brother, Ezekiel. I manage the bank on Broad Street. I know your father. William, right?"

"Yes. . . yes, William. He is at my grandfather's home on the Combahee River at the moment."

"Oh, is that so?" He wiped the edges of the painting with his handkerchief.

"Yes, but—" She stopped, and for a moment, worry overcame her features. "I have another matter. . . I was looking for the doctor. But maybe you can help me? I need some medicines, salve, bandages." She stopped. "We've run out of medical supplies. With the war and all, supplies are difficult to come by. I was hoping, I mean, well, it's much less dangerous to travel here than into town. . ."

Ezekiel held up his hand. "No need to tell me the details; the less I know the better. It must be someone important if you came all the way to East Battery for it." He pulled out a Waltham pocket watch. "In fact, we still have time. It happens that I know where we can find such supplies. Come with me." He lifted the painting and carried it out to the carriage. Then he motioned for her to follow him to a small outbuilding. There he loaded a sack with enough medical supplies to more than fill her needs. Julia protested at his generosity, but he insisted she take them.

"Thank you, Mr. Levine, for your kindness. I don't know how to repay you."

"It is no matter. I'm happy to help. I suspect these may be needed to care for a slave who is injured?"

The look he angled her way made her uncomfortable. She hadn't mentioned Ned or his circumstance. Maybe this hadn't been such a great idea. She shifted, and he realized her discomfort.

"Oh, I don't mean to pry, Miss Summerton. My own family has a long history." He looked directly at her. "We believe in the human condition of kindness, in neighbors helping neighbors. Yes, ma'am, my family comes from a long line of shackled sin, and that is why we have devoted our lives to helping those. . . *in need.*" The emphasis he placed on those words somehow made his meaning clear. "What makes my life more important than the life of another? We are all neighbors, and we should treat our neighbors as ourselves—wouldn't you agree? I believe both our treasured books teach us that." He stopped for a moment, looking thoughtful. "The Combahee River, you said? Your family has a place there? Interesting."

' Julia wasn't sure why William's whereabouts would intrigue this man, but she couldn't see any harm in telling him more. "Yes, my grandfather owns a plantation off the river. We have rice fields and slaves to manage so he—"

"How many slaves does he have, do you mind me asking?"

She paused again before answering. "Many. Hundreds across the river basin, not just on my grandfather's plantation." It seemed a private matter to know how many slaves a person claimed, but she felt compelled to tell him.

The Levines background had always been a mystery. There had been talk in town about the family's involvement in the abolitionist movement, but she had seen no real evidence and thus had considered it gossip. But now Ezekiel had confirmed it in his own way. It was obvious to her that they had a common cause. *He is much like his brother*, she thought.

She collected the sack of medicines, climbed into her carriage again, and began the journey home. As her coachman maneuvered the carriage through the streets, she murmured a quiet prayer of thanksgiving. "Oh, dear Lord, there is still good in the world. Thank You for providing." Then her thoughts turned to Hope. "Protect her, Lord. Let her name flourish despite these times of war. I pray, Father, that we have done right by her."

She opened her eyes and turned to look at the painting, perched against the seat beside her. She would hang it in a place of honor, perhaps in the music room. Yes, in the music room, as an homage to Hope. She leaned forward to examine it better. As she wrapped her fingers around the edge of the frame, she discovered an envelope attached there. It was addressed to her, with a return address for Alexandria, Virginia. She read the letter twice, then studied it a moment longer before she carefully tore the paper into bits and tossed the pieces into the street.

No one must ever know where she is.

Chapter 26

The eternal God is thy refuge,
and underneath are the everlasting arms:
he shall thrust out the enemy before thee;
and shall say, Destroy them.
DEUTERONOMY 33:27

June 1, 1863

Spring touched the Combahee River as a fine mist formed along
the shallows. The fowl had been anxious, gathering together in
packs, noisy and restless. Something was in the air. Union navy and
army troops had invaded Port Royal in November 1861, and now
occupied most of Beaufort County and the Sea Islands. Many plant-
ers and overseers had fled the area as Union troops slowly saturated
the region south of Charleston. But not William. *Not only have I vio-*
lated a woman I should have cared for and thus betrayed the ones I loved,
but I am a traitor too. He had made many choices since that day at

Summerton Place, some of which he could be proud to claim—but most days, the guilt he carried outweighed any good he could do in hopes of reparation.

There was talk among the slaves of something impending. Many were traipsing the shores along the edges of this plantation. William spent his days overseeing the rice lands and keeping the Confederacy informed of any unusual activity along the lowlands. The Confederates sought to place torpedoes along the river, as their regiments camped inland at Green Pond. That helped them avoid many Lowcountry diseases, such as malaria, typhoid fever, and smallpox. Yet the Confederates had left smaller detachments in the area, and William was part of one.

But today, he had other things on his mind, and war was not one of them. Together with a man dressed in an impossibly impeccable suit, he strode from the main house to the driveway, where an equally impressive carriage awaited the gentleman.

"Tell my lawyer I want the papers drawn up officially and immediately."

The gentleman shook his head worriedly. "Have you thought this through, sir? It seems so. . . implausible. It might be legal, but it's highly unusual. Are you sure?"

"I've never been more sure of anything in my life. Do it, and do it quickly. This war may be the death of us all, and nothing good will come of it." William handed the gentleman a sheaf of papers. "I want Ezekiel Levine to expedite the transfer. This matter must be taken care of in secrecy. I'm sure you understand." He nodded toward a brooding Negro waiting by the carriage. "And take him with you."

"I don't think I need company, Mr. Summerton. This matter—"

"He's not for company. He has his own job to do." He nodded again at the man, who held the door until the gentleman was seated before he climbed in beside him. They left without further discussion, and William watched as the carriage rumbled down the dusty lane, then turned north for Charleston.

When they were out of sight, William made his way out to the fields where his slaves were singing as they tended to his crops. As he drew near, their voices grew quieter, but he motioned for them to continue. He no longer minded their songs of freedom, especially the one they were singing now. About Moses. He listened to them for a while, watching as they worked. Thoughts of his own son came unbidden to his mind.

Moses. His face the color of his mother's, his eyes as green as new leaves on a tree. He could not escape the memory of his own reflection, staring back at him from Chloe's arms as Ned lay beaten on the ground by his hand. In that instant, everything had changed.

Moses had delivered him from his own hate. He was free.

What a fitting name for that boy. A smile touched his lips as the sun rose high in the sky. It was getting warm, but he stood there a bit longer, thinking about the name and those who wore it. He had a plan, a plan that would be put to action tonight. The risks were high, in fact, they could cost him his life, but his life did not matter anymore. Tonight, on the Combahee River, he would regain the life he was born to claim. He would help fill the boats. He would watermark what was left of himself and cleanse himself from his sin by aligning with the other side.

In the wee hours of the morning, William waited near the bank of the Combahee River. Solomon, the former slave he'd sent to Charleston the day before, had returned and was by his side.

"Everything is in order now," William murmured. "You know what to do if something should happen to me." Solomon nodded, and they both waited. The river remained empty, and their nerves grew more taut.

"They should have all the information! What is taking them so long?" William fussed. A stern look from Solomon had him settling back again in silence. The irony of that wasn't lost on the wealthy slave owner. A while later, he looked over at Solomon again.

"You will return to your unit when this is over?" The man nodded. "Is everyone ready?"

"Yessir." He smiled, but his gaze never left the river. "Y'know, they say that when the Spaniards came up this river, they named it after the river Jordan. 'Tis an interestin' coincidence, no? It being like a barrier between bondage and freedom an' all."

They were quiet again, then Solomon looked over at William. "There's somethin' I need to tell you, Mr. Summerton. Somethin' you need to know before we part." William straightened, intrigued by an odd tone in his companion's voice.

Solomon cleared his throat. "Your son, Moses, has a twin. Her name is Hope. She's alive and in Alexandria. We smuggled her out not long after Miss Julia brought her to us. She lives as a member of the family." William's mouth worked, but no sound came out. "What you're doin' tonight—'tis the right thing. And it's why you deserve to know. I will tell our friends in Virginia what you done. Your daughter will be proud. I will tell her, I promise, about the risk her father took."

William was stunned. *She's alive? But I thought—* Then he remembered the risk Julia and Ned had taken, and a familiar shame washed over him. The weight of his past actions was never far from heart and mind. He kept his gaze on the river and swallowed hard before replying.

"Thank you, Solomon, for telling me. I have wronged my whole family. They were right and justified for keeping her from me. She is safe and that's what matters. As for me? My life will be judged just like everyone else's, no matter what transpires here tonight. What I do, I do not for myself. I will pay for my sins—"

"Your sin was nailed to the cross, Mr. Summerton. We're all washed clean by the blood of it. Your sin ain't no greater than mine or the next person. I don't know what caused you to come to this place and do this deed tonight, but a greater hand is involved in all this. He means for you to do right by it." Even in the moonlight, William could see the compassion in the Black man's eyes as he continued thoughtfully. "You know, she looks like you. She has your eyes, your hair."

Suddenly, there was movement on the river. The men watched as two Union ships approached the riverbank and anchored along the rice fields of William's plantation.

"It's time," William said. "Let's go."

In a sudden burst of controlled chaos, the gunship set fire to the temporary pontoon bridge that spanned the river a short distance from where they were. The few Confederate troops stationed along the riverbank fled across it as it burned. Union troops from the Second South Carolina, an all-Black infantry regiment, deployed onto William's fields. As planned, slaves appeared in droves, carrying belongings and food and even livestock, as they hurried to the hope of freedom. In the rush of activity, William and Solomon informed the Union soldiers of vital information regarding the location of Rebel torpedoes along the riverbanks.

A Black woman approached the bow of the ship just as the last slaves tumbled out of the fields and scrambled to get on board. She wore a kerchief around her head and a dark shawl draped over her shoulders. William could hear the murmurs, fugitives whispering the name *Moses* again and again as they boarded.

She looked toward shore. "Solomon," she called, "'Tis time to go."

William shoved his rifle into the Black man's hands. "You must do this." His voice was firm. If he felt fear or trepidation, he kept it inside.

"We will be waiting for you in heaven one day," Solomon said. "Your Moses and your Hope. But Mr. Summerton, for your own freedom, you need to forgive yourself."

William closed his eyes for a brief moment, then said, "When you see my daughter, tell her that her father will not forget her. Thank you. . . thank you for telling me. It gives me peace knowing that she's out there, free and away from all this. Now do it. It's the only way."

A shotgun blast echoed through the air, and William tumbled to the ground. Solomon turned and fled to join the others on the gunboats.

Within minutes, the Union ships with their cargo of enslaved men, women, and children were churning their way downriver. William, bleeding from his wounds, would swear he could see Solomon watching from the bow of the boat until it disappeared completely into the fog.

Chapter 27

There is therefore now no condemnation
to them which are in Christ Jesus,
who walk not after the flesh, but after the Spirit.
For the law of the Spirit of life in Christ Jesus
hath made me free from the law of sin and death.
ROMANS 8:1–2

December 1939

"Wait!" Hattie sat forward in excitement. "So, you're telling me William aligned himself with Harriet Tubman?"

Wallace nodded, and the grin on his face threatened to reach both ears. They'd been sharing time together—him talking and reminiscing, her listening and writing—for weeks now. Some days, she did well, while others, she struggled beneath the burden of the tale and her own insecurities. He most loved the days when Hattie fully engaged in the stories he was telling.

"I just can't believe it! So did he do it out of guilt or to redeem himself somehow?" She shook her head. "Harriet Tubman! I gotta say, Wallace, this story is unbelievable. It's so powerful. William was an important part of Charleston history. Shoot, *American* history! I can't remember the exact number but weren't more than seven hundred slaves freed after that raid? Yes, I'm sure of it—I remember studying it in history class." She was quiet for a moment, and when she spoke again, the animation was gone.

She dropped her head to her hand and moaned. "Oh, goodness. I just don't think I should be the one to write it. You sure you shouldn't just hire someone else to do it? Someone who. . . I don't know, who's qualified. This is just so much bigger than me!"

Wallace looked lovingly at the young woman before him who was struggling to find her confidence. The ghosts behind her scar had stolen it away. "It is indeed an undertaking," he agreed. "But you are the one to do it. You *are* the qualified one." But how could he convince her of the truth he felt at the very core of his being?

He thought for a moment, then asked, "Is it possible to put back the pieces of a fallen world? Have time and circumstance negated the will of the good, or can we destroy the bitter root that firmly plants itself in the soil?"

She looked at him blankly. He had to make her understand. "We can weave those threads back together again. Me and you—my story, your words." He reached for her hand and they stood together silently. "Let God be your guide, dear one. Trust that He will give you the words."

"I don't even know where to begin." She traced the sand with her foot, moving it back and forth with a certain anxiousness. She looked up at Wallace, squinting with the sun in her eyes.

"Trust Him," Wallace repeated. "Let Him peel away those layers that unkind circumstance developed. The insecurities, childhood memories, the vicissitude of fortune and loss. . ." His voice became a

200

whisper. "Take off the chains that hold you back. What you are left with is a sweet, beautiful girl." He put his finger on her heart. "There you will find your soul, the light within you that believes and makes you shine. That is who you are meant to be."

Hattie's hair blew across her face as the wind picked up across the Ashley River. Wallace closed his eyes and savored the cool breeze. But he wasn't finished talking. "You are an artist, and I believe in you. God believes in you. He made you for this purpose. *You* can do this."

Anxiety still clouded her features. "What about Livy or Ezra, can they help me? I mean, do I have to do this alone?"

"Alone? You'll never be alone." He brushed his fingers across her face. "Have you been readin' the Bible I gave you?"

"Yes."

"Okay. D'you know the story of Joseph in the Old Testament?" She nodded, and he continued. "His brothers were jealous because his father let everyone know that Joseph was his favorite son. When the opportunity arose, they sold him into slavery. But was Joseph's life over when that happened?"

"No. He ended up a ruler, didn't he?"

"Yes! God used Joseph's brothers' betrayal to place him in Egypt where he would become prime minister of a powerful nation. Life wasn't easy—he even had to spend time in prison first, but when the time was right, God put him in the palace. And when famine struck Egypt and Canaan, Joseph's position allowed him to provide food for his brothers—and that preserved the nucleus of what would become the nation of Israel. The nation from which the Savior of the world would be born."

"Yes, I remember. It was like God used Joseph's brothers' selfish, hateful actions for the greater good."

"Exactly, child. But could Joseph see that good while he was stuck in slavery? Or in the depths of that prison?"

"No."

"You're right. It wasn't until decades later that Joseph could look back and see how God had used an inherently evil action to achieve His purpose," Wallace said. "It's the same today. It's the same with you and with me. Our world is defined by how we emerge from our tunnels of despair to arrive at a just and righteous light. Every pain you or I ever suffer, God can change over to good. We must surrender those hurts and injustices to Him, but when we do, He turns every-thin' meant for evil into good."

She was quiet, but he could see he had touched something within her, a spark that had helped her understand.

"You are young. I know it's hard to understand, but faith is grown in the fires of affliction. If the world were perfect, would we choose to seek Him?"

"Probably not."

He nodded approvingly. "When you're sufferin', it's hard to find any purpose in it for good. You just have to trust that you are being prepared for your journey." She was reluctant, Wallace could sense it. He stood abruptly, then staggered a bit as he straightened. "Just believe, Hattie. Trust your instinct about people—that's a gift God has given you. It's also part of why I chose you to do this. Believe in your abilities. Know your weaknesses, yes, but do not accept the lies of the deceiver who will try to defeat you. You were perfectly made for this. Use your heartache to fuel you, use your circumstances to refine you, and trust that in this life, everythin' is as it should be." He held out a hand and she took it.

"Follow me," he said. "I have something to show you."

They walked until they reached the old gravestones of Wallace's forefathers. Here he paused to listen. The beat of African drums thrummed the air as they had his whole life, faintly at first but gain-ing strength as each day passed. It was a song that only Wallace could hear, and every day it drew him closer to home. His heart quickened in anticipation. Bessany and Ida were waiting for him on the other side. Just a little while longer, he knew. For now, the scarred little girl he'd spotted at the orphanage years ago was soaking in the words of his story. *Finally, Lord.*

He could see the ruins of the plantation home through the trees, and he placed himself there as he told her the story. He imagined himself a bystander, watching the events unfold as his father before him had shared the story when he was a young man. He told her of the atrocity that had unfolded in the music room and the blessing born of it.

They stopped by his father's gravestone, and she read the inscription there. "Here lies Moses, who, despite it all, believed in the contradiction of fate, of love and war, and of his holy path that would guide his people home to freedom." She looked up, puzzled.

"What does that mean, contradiction of fate?"

"Ah. Good question. Well, we battle against good and evil every day. Towers fall on the righteous and unrighteous. When they do, we are left with questions. We want justice against those who wronged us. The struggle of right versus wrong continues, but sin will not have the final word." His voice was confident as he touched Moses's headstone.

Hattie's curious gaze caught the light from another stone, an older one, and she walked over to it.

"Ned Hayes," she read. "Your grandfather. But that's all it says for him."

Wallace's heart was touched by the gentle tone of her voice. "Yessuh, Ned Hayes." A tear touched his cheek. "There's nothin' on his gravestone because no words could express who he was. What can you say for a man who looked evil in the face, yet turned away so humbly?" He looked off into the distance. "He was my grandfather, in a godly sense at least. Not by blood, but deeper. A biblical sense."

He walked to the gravestone and kneeled before it. "It's because he turned from evil and thought more of humanity that I am here today, that Livy is here, and even Ezra, in a way. He stood whipped by the man who raped his wife. He raised that man's child as his own—and *he forgave him*. What Ned did for his enemy is beyond belief." He stopped and shook his head in wonder.

He turned to Hattie. "Only God's angels have the right to write his eulogy, child. The Lord Himself must have paved the way for him, with trumpets and song. Yessuh, I can only imagine how the heavens welcomed such a man."

Tears flooded his eyes, and he stumbled to a nearby bench. Hattie followed and put her arm around him. Together, they sat quietly as Wallace mourned for a man who was greater than this world.

Hattie fumbled in her pocket and withdrew the tiny piece of brick he'd given her all those weeks ago. He was surprised to see it. She held his weathered hands tightly in hers and looked him straight in the eyes.

"I understand now," she said. "I'll do it, Wallace. I'll write your story for all the people it represents—for you and us and for all of 'em up in heaven looking down on us. For everyone who ever lived in those slave homes." Her eyes shone as she spoke, and Wallace was captured by the beauty of her soul. "It's about sacrifice, isn't it? That's what these bricks represent. That's why you gave them to us."

"Yes, child, yes. . . the sacrifice. God took away the sins of man by staking them to the cross. We are clean because of Him. God will right the wrongs of this world, but only in His time. He is in control. We must trust in Him, even when our human nature causes us to do horrible things to each other.

"Ned understood that. It's only now that I can put in motion what God wanted to happen, generations later. I wish my grandfather was here to see the man that my father became, who I am, what Livy has become. As a result of his actions, Hope lived most of her life beyond the boundaries of a society that would have shunned her. She gave birth to a child who has grown into a woman who gives life and shelter to the innocent. Livy gives hope to the orphaned and the unwanted she cares for." He smiled at the irony. "Hope, born of Hope."

Hattie and Wallace walked among the gravestones for a long while that afternoon. As the hours passed, she remained immersed in his words, listening to every detail of the people behind the stones. Finally, Wallace stopped. He walked to the edge of the cemetery and picked a few fresh tiger lilies. Hattie picked some wildflowers as well. Then together, they laid the flowers on Ida's and Bessany's graves.

Wallace was quiet, a look of firm contentment on his face. Gone was the heartache he had carried so long. In its place, there was an air almost of excitement about him. But he was not finished.

"I have one more story to tell you today, Hattie," he said. "You won't believe it, but it is the very essence of forgiveness. It happened in 1863, right here on this very plantation." Then he laughed and corrected himself. "Well, actually in the river."

Hattie held Wallace's hand in hers. "I can't wait to hear it, Wallace. You know what? I think I'll title this story *Wallace's Wish*. Would you like that?"

Wallace laughed. "Indeed, my girl. Indeed I do." He squeezed her hand. "Now, where were we? Ah yes. . . William Summerton. I can't wait to tell you what happened to him, it was nothin' short of a miracle. But where God is concerned, it shouldn't be surprising. God can make everythin' right, especially for the sinner who repents. Yessuh. . . in His mercy, He takes all their guilty stains."

Chapter 28

What? Know ye not that your body
is the temple of the Holy Ghost
which is in you, which ye have of God,
and ye are not your own?
For ye are bought with a price:
therefore glorify God in your body
and in your spirit, which are God's.
1 CORINTHIANS 6:19–20

September 20, 1863

William stopped short of the oak-lined road that would lead him home. He closed his eyes and asked for strength. War had changed him and left him weary. As he stood there, his heart uplifted, a warm breeze circled him as if to hold him up. He opened his eyes to find the way ahead warmly lit with afternoon sun. He took a deep breath, hitched his wooden leg, and with his walking stick in hand, started slowly down the dusty road.

Chloe was outside, hanging clothes to dry. He was sure she would not recognize him. He had aged significantly in the years since he'd last been here, most notably while recuperating at the field hospital. His wounds had become infected more than once, and for a time, he had not thought he would survive. It had been three months since the Union raid on the Combahee River, yet infection clung to him, an almost constant companion. *Just get me home, Lord.*

It wasn't until he reached the plot where Ned's cabin stood that Chloe recognized him. She dropped the basket she was holding and ran into the cabin. *No, don't be scared. I'm not going to hurt you ever again.*

"He's here. Ned, he's here!" William could hear the terror in her voice from where he stood.

"Who?" Ned's voice boomed out the window. "I don't see no one." He walked outside, but he was not alone. William stood still, struck at what he saw. A boy, no more than two years old, marched out with purpose in his stride. Confident, even at his young age. William smiled. *Moses.* He leaned over and held out his hand for the curious and precocious little boy to take. Ned recognized him immediately.

"Moses." His voice was stern. "Leave the man alone and go back inside. Go help yo' mama."

William continued walking toward the cabin. Ned positioned himself defiantly in front of the doorway.

"I mean no harm. I just have something to ask of you and Chloe." William was breathless. "I need to speak with you, Ned." *I need to sit down.*

Ned crossed his arms but otherwise didn't move. "Chloe," he said over his shoulder, "take Moses and go let Miz Julia know her father is back."

When they were gone, Ned stepped aside. "You look rough from the road," he said. "Come, have a seat."

Even now, he is a gentleman. William tried to find the words he needed, but he didn't know where to start. He shifted forward to take the weight off his wooden leg. A pressure point was forming on his stump. He began to scratch along the edges of his pants. Ned watched, his expression unreadable.

"I still feel it, you know, my leg. Like it's there. I lie down at night and reach for it, but it's gone," William said, nearly whispering. He looked at Ned, who stood quietly next to him.

"Do you think that makes sense? It's like a phantom in the night, always tapping, but when you light the lamp, nothing's there. It's like something else I'm missing too. I feel it around every corner, on every street, in the sky, in the wind. Something is there. But when I reach for it—it's gone. I would like for once just to see it, to feel it. To know that no matter what sin I've committed, there is still love for me. . . forgiveness." He stopped, his eyes on the horizon. After a minute he shook his head and looked back at Ned.

"But I look for it, and it's not there. It's never there. Why is that, Ned? Can someone like me ever be forgiven for the sins I've committed? Against you? Against Chloe? I took your wife. I nearly killed you. I know the evil I've done. And I'm sorry!" His voice broke. "I know that Jesus died for sin. But maybe my sin cannot be redeemed. Maybe forgiveness is not meant for me."

Ned's posture softened. He sat down next to William and put a hand on his shoulder. Still, he towered over his former oppressor. "I don't know why God done brought you back here, Massah Summerton, but I do know one thing for sure. We ain't promised a perfect life on this earth, and we is always gon' fall short of the glory of God. Ain't no man ever gon' be deservin' of His forgivin'. Not even the most righteous. But it be there for the takin'. Jesus loves you as much as He loves me. Mebbe He be scratchin' away at you 'cause He want you to take what He done give you. So take it. Reach for it."

"I've tried!" William's distress broke free from his body in a wail. "Why won't He show Himself? I feel Him there, but I can't see Him." He turned and reached desperately for Ned. "I need *you* to forgive me, Ned. I need to hear you say it to me. And I need you to. . . to plunge me in the river. I don't deserve it, but I have to ask—baptize me, Ned, and release me from this torment. Please, do this for me."

Ned rose the next morning as he always did, before the sunrise and before the rooster's crow. Chloe had prepared his clothes and left them neatly folded beside his Bible. Now she stood next to him and ran her fingers across his bare back. . . across the scars that remained.

"I need to go up there, help him get ready."

Chloe kissed his shoulder and handed him the cleaned and pressed shirt. "I know. An' I got his shirt ready too."

He took the shirt, shrugged into it, then took her in his arms. They stood motionless for a long while before Chloe spoke again.

"You doin' a good thing today, Ned. The Lord, He really do work miracles. You's a fine, blessed man to do this."

Ned picked up his Bible, straightened his shoulders, and headed out toward the mansion.

William was sitting on the edge of the bed when Julia knocked at the door. "Daddy, do you need me?" she asked.

"No, but come in. Sit with me for a moment."

Julia sat next to him, then reached for his wooden leg by the window. Ned appeared in the doorway.

"I'll take care of that, Miz Julia," he said.

"I'll go finish morning preparations, then," Julia said. With a quick squeeze of her father's hand and a smile for Ned, she left the room.

"I brung you a clean shirt, suh," Ned said, holding out the garment. "Chloe done washed and pressed it for you." He helped William into his clothes, then reached for the wooden leg and helped him strap it on.

William grabbed Ned's hand and looked at him with sorrowful eyes. Ned grasped that hand and helped him stand. Then he looked straight into William's eyes. "They's no need to look at me with such great sadness and pain. Today, you lose all your guilty stains. Besides. . . I forgave you long ago. God sent His Son, done nailed your sins and mine to the same cross. Today, you become who you was always meant to be—a child of the Most High. Your sins are washed away. It is a gift. Don't never forget that."

"Will Chloe be there? And Moses. . . I'd like them both to be there, if you don't mind."

"They's already there. We's all waitin' for you, Massah Summerton." He handed William his cane.

The two men made their way through the house and outside. There, William stopped at the edge of the front porch. He shaded his eyes against the early morning sun and looked out at the river in the distance. *Close enough to touch, yet so far.*

Julia stepped up and placed a quick kiss on his cheek. "Are you ready, Daddy?"

He nodded. Then, with Ned and Julia at his side, he began the trek to the river. The familiar hum of harvest celebrations filled the air as the plantation came to life. The slaves knew he was back—several lined the path as they passed. They seemed transfixed on him.

His senses were especially alert this morning. The leaves were beginning to change, and a few crunched beneath his feet. He could smell a touch of cinnamon in the air—but that couldn't be, it wasn't

Christmas yet. Then again, that's what it felt like to him. As the wind swept through the ancient oaks, a newfound sense of belonging washed over him. He was almost there.

They cleared the last bend before the riverbank, and William stumbled at the sight of Chloe standing there. *She's here.* The hem of her dress fluttered with the breeze as she waited for him to pass. But he couldn't. He stopped in front of her.

I don't have the words. He held out both hands. "Chloe. Forgive me. I am not worthy of your forgiveness, but I ask it of you as a man who desires to cleanse himself of his sin."

She looked deeply into his eyes for a moment, then took his hands and smiled. "I do forgive you, and God does too. He makes all things good. Today," she said, "you hold your head high."

The men stepped into the river together, then Ned held William against the current as the cattails swayed. Slaves gathered along the edges of the river and listened to Ned speak.

"God's Book tells us it ain't by anythin' we can do that we are saved. It's only by His mercy He saves us. Jesus Hisself said, 'he that believeth and is baptized shall be saved.' Massah William Summerton, does you believe that Jesus be the Son of God and that He taketh away the sin of the world?"

With trembling lips, William declared, "I do believe. I want to be Yours, God. Take away my evil and my sin!"

As Ned plunged him into the cool waters of the Ashley River, William's sin washed away with the current, and Ned's reason to hate gave way to forgiveness.

Chapter 29

For by grace are ye saved through faith;
and that not of yourselves: it is the gift of God:
not of works, lest any man should boast.
For we are his workmanship, created in Christ Jesus
unto good works, which God hath before
ordained that we should walk in them.
EPHESIANS 2:8–10

December 1939

"I s that how the story ends, Wallace? Ned baptized William? My word! It's so beautiful!" Hattie's eyes shone as she erased a word and blew the residue off the paper.

"How it ends is entirely up to you. I gave you my story. You'll write it, but then you'll write your own too. And Ezra's and Livy's, of course. Because you are *all* a part of this testimony to God's grace."

"Oh." That was a new thought, and her face filled with wonder and perhaps trepidation as she processed it. Wallace was quick to reassure her.

"You write your story by livin' life, child. Live it well. Live it to His glory." They sat quietly for a few moments, reflecting on all that had transpired. But Wallace had more to say, and this part would be hard. He cleared his throat.

"We need to speak of Ezra, child."

"Ezra? Why?"

"His love for you is strong; I see it in his eyes when he is with you." A shy smile grew on her face, and he lifted a cautionary finger. "But the day is coming when you will have to let him go."

"Let him go?" She jumped to her feet, her eyes wide. "What do you mean?"

"Oh, my sweet girl, you are still so very young. . . . Our boy must follow the path God has for him, so he can become who he was meant to be. When all is said and done, I believe he will find his way back to you. Come, sit down. There's more I need to tell you."

She perched nervously next to him, unsure of what was coming. Wallace's heart ached, but he forged ahead.

"Ezra's father is coming back from Europe. He should be here by tomorrow noon, when the train comes in. I haven't spoken yet to Ezra, but I'd like for you and Livy to come with us to the station." He took her hand. "Tomorrow, your friend will leave the orphanage and return to his father. That is his rightful place. For now."

Wallace's eyes glazed over, and his mind wandered. "Praise be to God that his father survived. There is no one else left in his family. They were taken from their homes in the dead of night, shipped off in trains to nowhere. Women, children. . . everyone. His father is the only one who escaped."

After an initial gasp, Hattie sat silent, tears in her eyes.

"We are burdened by circumstances beyond our control," Wallace continued. "But who we are in the midst of it is what will define us. The true measure of a man is determined when he decides whether to take up his sword and look evil in the eye or to look the other way, leaving it to fester and grow. When he does that, it manifests itself at his core and spreads itself to the ends of the earth." He shook his head. "Why do we so often choose the latter?"

The question hung in the air as they stood and began walking back to the house. After a minute, Hattie, who was trying hard to understand, said, "Is it because we are selfish? Because we are weak?"

"Yes, because we are selfish. We desire apathy over the work needed to change what we know is wrong."

"But how do we change it? Why are people so mean to each other? Why does God allow evil to happen?"

"Ah, ultimate questions from such a young heart. Why would He? Well, that is the question." He scratched his chin. "I reckon it's because God uses it for good in the end. Yessuh, just as we've seen from my story."

Livy and Ezra were waiting when they reached the house. Hattie couldn't help the thrill that shivered through her as she caught Ezra's eye. She actually felt his demeanor change as she grew closer. It was as if somehow his soul had leaped inside her and set up camp. Even when they stood far apart, their hearts reached for each other, past the barricades each had built because of their circumstances. She loved him completely, yet she understood that with his father's return, her time with him would come to an abrupt end.

Wallace called everyone to the front room. Hattie held Ezra's hand as Wallace broke the news as gently as he could. Ezra was emotionless as Wallace relayed the events that had led to his father's return—his family taken to concentration camps, the attempts they'd made to escape.

"Your father was the only one from your family who made it out safely," he concluded.

"But. . . Mother?" Ezra's voice was rough. He got to his feet and strode to the window. Anger stiffened his form when he turned to Wallace. "You want to talk about God?" he raged. "There was no one more faithful than my mother! She lived every day the way it is written in the Torah." Hattie reached for him, but he shrugged her away.

Livy looked at Wallace, her face tight with emotion. Then she caught Ezra's arms in hers. "Ezra, I'm so sorry," she said. "There's no way to make this easy. But your father is alive, and he's coming home. I think that's the best way to look at it right now." He huffed and tried to pull away, but she kept her grip.

"It's hard to understand why we live in such a hateful world but we do, and there's not much we can do about it. We grieve, and then we move forward. It won't be easy, for you or your father. But you know what? You will always have us, all of us. We cannot control what life puts in our path, but we can choose to pick up the pieces and trust that no matter what, we will always have each other." She tried to wrap her arms around him, but he shrugged loose.

"We're your family, too, Ezra, and we're not going anywhere. Tomorrow, we will all go with you to meet your daddy at the station. He's going to need you to be strong. Imagine what he must have gone through. From what I've heard, it's a miracle that he is here." Ezra gave her a dark look, and Livy subsided.

"But my mother. . . why would God let this happen?" Ezra collapsed on a chair at the table and dropped his head on his arms. "I don't know what to believe in anymore."

Wallace put a hand on the boy's shoulder. "God gives us opportunities to find Him. We are all on borrowed time." He smiled at Hattie and Livy. "Let's sit down again, please. I'm an old man and I'm tired."

They did as he asked, settling close to Ezra at the table. Wallace continued, "My time is spent, dear ones." He held up a hand to hush them as they protested. "No, I know this. But I foresee what's beyond the marshes, beyond the ocean, above the sky. It helps to know what's beyond the naked eye. The Bible says, 'We look not at the things which are seen, but at the things which are not seen: for the things which are seen are temporal; but the things which are not seen are eternal.'"

"What does that even mean, Wallace? What is unseen? And how do you know?" Ezra's voice was tight.

"How do I know? I know that David stood against Goliath and won. I know that courage is contagious, and taking on the giants that life puts in our way builds and develops us and prepares us to meet in His mighty kingdom. Humility is what takes us there. Every event in your life can change the tide for the good or for the bad—you choose! You can allow the bad to defeat you and lead you astray, or you can take up your shield and stand against the giant. One act of courage can impact an entire nation; one act of kindness can change the world for the better. Pick up your sword; let your faith be your shield, my boy! God has already won the vict'ry."

Wallace stopped speaking and looked out to the fields. They were moving again, as if dancing to his words. In a quieter voice, he assured them, "Our God is in control, even as we suffer the consequences of man's actions. God sees everythin'. But it's important that we understand it is Christ who wins our battles. Christ who died for our sins, who nailed them to the cross. We are only strong in Him." Beads of sweat formed along his brow as he put his hand over his heart.

"We have life because He died for us, we need only to depend on that. Our destinies are fixed—we need not live in shame, hate, or remorse. Instead, we live in repentance and certainty that we are saved from the shackles of life's circumstances. We are free, my beautiful children, we are all free. This is what I know—and this is my gift to you, so that you can share with others what it means to be a child of God."

"Wallace," Ezra said, "I am Jewish. My God is Jehovah."

"Jehovah is the one true God," Wallace agreed. "And Jesus is His only begotten Son. Because of Him, we are all children of God, Ezra. All of us, in every denomination, church or synagogue, every walk of life. . . we are all equally His.

"You know in your heart what to believe. He's already written the answer on your soul. Acceptin' Christ as your Lord and Savior does not change who you are. It does not change your heritage or your loyalties. You are Judah, and you will always be God's chosen. Your change comes from God himself. It does not alienate you from your background; it enriches it with hope. One day, every eye will look to the heavens and see. Because of what Jesus—God's only begotten Son—did for us, sin and its devastatin' consequences will not be the final word in human history."

They continued the discussion through the afternoon, asking questions and getting answers, each gaining a clearer understanding of what they believed. And then they made their way to the river, where Wallace baptized them that very day.

One by one, by their own choice, he led them into the cool waters of the Ashley. First Livy, then Hattie. Ezra stood at the edge of the marsh until Livy and Hattie came and took his hands. Together, the three stepped into the river, then Ezra made his way to Wallace.

"There is no need for fear, my boy," the old man said. "We gather here today as one believer. We believe in the Messiah and His teachings. The love you feel here, the love we have for one another, the unity—it comes from our Lord, from Jesus, the Messiah Himself. Our God is the God of Abraham, Isaac, and Jacob! Come to Him, child, and take your inheritance. It is yours."

The afternoon sun slanted through the trees as Ezra surrendered. When he rose from the river with his sins washed away, water cascaded from his body like diamonds spilling across the current before disappearing back into the flow.

It was quiet in the truck that evening as they headed back to the orphanage where Cora again awaited their return. Upon their arrival, the children tumbled out to greet their favorite benefactor. Ezra and Hattie wandered off to her big tree, but Livy stayed close.

"Tomorrow, Wallace," Livy said. "Will we see you at the train station?"

"Of course." He turned from watching the children. "I will be there, Livy. Yessuh, no place I'd rather be." His eyes tracked across the yard to where Hattie sat. Ezra was on his knees beside her, and they were deep in conversation. He nodded their way. "Make sure they have some time together. Tomorrow will be hard on them, but in time they'll understand that this is only the beginnin' of their story. And when he's gone, I'd like for Hattie to spend more time with me at the plantation."

"Do you really think she can write your story, Wallace? I know she's agreed and she's been taking notes, but don't you think she's a little young to take on such a responsibility?"

"I've been watchin' her since the day her daddy left her, Livy. God placed her on my heart. He has given her the tools she needs, and she will use them all to make it work. Yes, I believe in her." He opened the truck door and put a foot on the running board.

"But wouldn't it make more sense if I wrote it?" Livy asked. "I mean, they're my ancestors. I've always felt a connection to you and the plantation—now I know why. I feel so free, Wallace. I've always questioned my faith, but over the last few weeks, learning how God has worked through your story, no, *our* story"—Her smile was brilliant—"Thanks to you, I can sing 'Amazing Grace' with my whole heart. 'I once was lost, but now I'm found.' But I do wonder if this should be my job."

"Nah, dear one. You will have your hands full with what I have in store for you."

"In store for me?"

He grinned. "Yes'm, but I'm savin' that for another day." He couldn't help the groan that came as he lifted himself into the truck.

"Wallace! Are you okay?"

"Oh, I'm feelin' mighty fine, Livy. I'm achy and hurtin', but nothin's gonna take me away till I know that all of you are safe and sound. You are my last livin' descendant—everything I have is yours. But don't you fret; I'll leave you instructions!" He pulled the door shut and cranked down the window. "I'll see you tomorrow at the station, but I'll be back in two days to pick up Hattie." And with that, he was off.

Livy walked toward the back of the house where Ezra and Hattie were sitting. She watched them in silence, not wanting to disturb them. There was love between them, she could see it. But tomorrow, there would be heartache and questions. *One child gone from the roost.* Her heart ached for Hattie, but soon enough she would busy herself with Wallace. Besides, who was to say it would be over between them. *Not me.* She watched them for a moment longer, then turned back to the house.

Hattie put her hand in his as they watched the sunset together. "You know where to find me, Ezra," she said. "I'll either be here or at the plantation. Maybe you and your daddy can visit."

But Ezra did not know what the future held for him. He didn't even know if his father planned to stay in Charleston or if they would go back to Alexandria. There was so much going on in his mind that it was hard to think. The only thing he knew for sure was that tomorrow, everything would change. Again. With a start, he realized Hattie was still talking.

"Let's do something," she said. "Let's close our eyes and always remember how we felt at the river. Not just today. . . other times. Though today was important, of course! Oh, you know what I mean." She stopped and laughed at herself, her cheeks a pretty pink. "If we remember that, it will bring us back together again. You make me feel so many things, Ezra. Just by being you. I feel like I can breathe again.

"You know, it's the strangest thing, how you've felt so familiar to me, even from the day we met. I can't explain it. It's like I've known you forever, like we've had a million years of knowing each other's soul."

Ezra agreed. "The minute I saw you, Hattie, I knew. You, sitting in that room with your hair covering your face. I was scared, then I saw you. It's like God placed you there at just the right time. I'll never forget you, no matter what happens tomorrow."

Hattie thought for a moment as they stood together. "Wallace said that God makes no mistakes, no matter what. Look at Joseph in the Bible! But I need to hear you say it, Ezra."

He stepped closer, put his hand behind her neck, and looked straight into her eyes. Their foreheads touched lightly.

"God never makes mistakes. Never. We'll see each other again, I promise."

They stood in silence, allowing the Charleston breeze to embrace who they were and were yet to become.

Wallace had ignited the flame, but it would be up to them to find their middle and end.

The next morning, Hattie helped Ezra pack his things, and then they were off to the train station. Ezra was deep in thought. She could feel him watching her and sensed the pain radiating from him.

She wanted to shield him from it but knew it was something he needed to go through on his own. It was probably better for both of them not to try to make sense of things.

Wallace was sitting on a bench as they approached. When they arrived, Wallace pressed a package into Ezra's hand.

"This is for you, my boy. I want you to have my Bible. I want you to read it. The answers to all life's questions are inside." Ezra thanked him and tucked the package into his suitcase. His decision from yesterday was still so new, he wasn't quite sure what to think about having a Bible, but it was a piece of Wallace he could take with him. He wasn't going to turn it away.

They waited for what seemed like hours before the train arrived. Steam filled the air as Ezra peered at each person who stepped off the train, but his father wasn't there. At long last, a frail old man reached for the rail and stepped down to the ground. When Wallace stood, Ezra took another look at the broken man coming their way. A moment of shocked silence ended as he rushed to the man's side.

The man looked up and fixed his eyes on Ezra. He swayed as he stopped to pull something from his pocket. "From your mother," he said as he wrapped Ezra's fingers around it. "She found it at the family home, before they took her."

Emotion overcame them and they collapsed together onto a nearby bench. Mr. Wolfe held his son for several minutes before he spoke to Wallace. "Thank you, my friend," he said. "Thank you for watching over my son." He tried to put something in Wallace's hand, but Wallace turned it away.

"No need for that—we are family. I am grateful that after all these years, our families remain connected."

"The Levine and Wolfe families will always be indebted to you," Wolfe declared. "Ezra is the last from his mother's side. Thank you for watching over him. And we are so pleased that you have found the last of yours."

"Just as your family took in our Hope so many years ago," Wallace said, "we were happy to watch over Ezra. He is a part of our story now, and we are eternally grateful. Now, go and be with your son. You know where to find me if you need anything."

There was a quick flurry of goodbyes, then they went their separate ways. Hattie turned at the corner just in time to see Ezra look back. Their eyes locked, they exchanged waves, and then he was gone.

Days became weeks and weeks became months with no word from Ezra. The new year came, and Hattie entered her final year of high school. Soon she'd be too old to stay at the orphanage. Livy had promised to keep her on as an employee if she wanted. It was tempting, but she was also thinking about college or maybe a newspaper job. Wouldn't it be neat if she could be like Nellie Bly and travel the world?

So many things pulled at her young heart, but she remained determined to be strong. When she wasn't at school or helping Livy with the children, she immersed herself in researching the Civil War and spending time with Wallace. She knew that Ezra and his father had gone to Alexandria to take care of business, but she didn't know if they had stayed there or where they might be.

As time stretched on, Ezra featured less in Hattie's thoughts, but there were days when loneliness and sadness threatened to overcome her. She tried to face those times with courage, firm in her pursuit of her own dreams. Her obstacles became welcomed challenges, pushing and changing her for the better. She used everything that came her way to refine her craft and to build for herself an identity that would meet the expectations of a waiting world. Writing became who she was. Her time with Wallace was a welcomed distraction. She spent every possible day with him, living and learning by way of his story. Hattie was most intrigued by Julia, who despite everything, had remained strong in her loyalty to a people in bondage.

"It is the measure of a greater plan that defines us," Wallace liked to say. "Who is to say that life in its toil and depravity doesn't have a place in God's bigger picture? We need only wait to see it bear its fruit."

Hattie was amazed by Wallace's wisdom as he told her of the events that had unfolded over the years at Summerton Place. She was impressed, too, with his ability to teach with a loving heart and not an embittered one. She couldn't comprehend the evil of what had happened between William and Chloe or William and Ned, and she was in awe that the story could end in a miracle, despite the deeds that formed it.

She voiced that wonder for the hundredth time, one fine spring day as they sat at a makeshift table in the old music room. Wallace was happy to respond.

"My dear," he said, "the world conspires against us. History teaches us that. We pit ourselves against each other, neighbors fighting neighbors, brother against sister, nation against nation. As a society, we accept distortions of the truth that make it easier to look the other way. But all we have to do is dig deeper within ourselves to fight against the travesty of the day. And when we put on God's armor, we find true peace."

"But you always say that God is in control, Wallace," Hattie protested after a moment of thought. "Why does He allow us to suffer?"

He stood up and took her hand. Together, they walked toward the slave cabins, still standing strong against the Charleston sky. "Refinement comes from within, child. Use your circumstances, the good and the bad, to guide you. We suffer, yes'm, we do. But purpose is born in sufferin'. It's up to us to discover who we are in the midst of it."

That night at the orphanage, Hattie wrote diligently, hastily, and without looking back. Finally, she laid down her pen and stretched.

She let her eyes read back through the manuscript as she sifted through the lessons of the day.

Each was given a personal purgatory, each with seeds to sow. Together they stood on the ramparts, waiting for their time to place the seeds in the soil. Truth would grow from the seedlings until, hand in hand, they would learn that their crossed paths were inevitable; their love for one another was true in its complexities, and in the end, good would grow from their despair.

She was getting it. She was understanding everything! Her path had been predestined by a greater power. Before the dawn of time, He had anointed her head for a cause greater than she. *Wallace's Wish* had always been God's will, but in its execution, it had in essence become *God's* wish for her.

Chapter 30

A seed shall serve him;
it shall be accounted to the Lord for a generation.
They shall come, and shall declare his righteousness
unto a people that shall be born, that he hath done this.
Psalm 22:30–31

November 1940

Wallace stood at the window, watching the gentle wisps of snow fall from the sky. The ground was too warm for it to stick, but it was still beautiful. Anytime his father had told the story of the night that Ned and Chloe were married, he'd always remembered the snow. Wallace had described the night for Hattie as best he could, just the way his father told him, not missing any detail. And Hattie, who was writing every word as if her life depended on it, had portrayed it faithfully in her manuscript as well. Wallace smiled. *I'm so proud of her.*

Clarence, who was straightening things in the room, paused to pick up a framed photograph of Moses Hayes, standing in front of the orphanage he had founded in Charleston.

"I do wish your father was here to see the fruits of your labor, Wallace. He'd be proud. I bet him, Ned, and Julia are all standing here right now, pushin' you forward. You've done a good thing by these kids; they will turn this place into somethin' special, like it was always meant to be. Think of all the lives they will save." Clarence set the photo on the table, then turned to Wallace. "Speakin' of which, your estate attorney has sent the final papers, makin' sure that everything is in order for you to pass on the plantation to Livy."

Wallace had settled himself into an overstuffed chair by the fireplace and pulled a blanket over his legs. He closed his eyes and hummed an old Gullah song.

"Wallace?" Clarence asked. "You still here?"

"Hmmm? Oh, yes. I'm still here. Thank you for takin' care of that. You've been such a good friend to me. It's important that we make good from the past." He moved restlessly, a sure sign that his body was in pain. "We've been given a solid foundation on which to build, but we must be sure we use it well. If we make our home in a prison of resentment, we will fail to thrive as a people. The past can be like a ball and chain, making us unable to put one foot in front of the other. The weight can be heavy on us, the burden unbearable. But we will not trap ourselves in bitterness, will we, Clarence? No suh. We have released our burdens at the cross. Our hearts are free."

"Yes, they are. Thanks be to God." He straightened a sheaf of papers covered in neatly written prose. Hattie's latest work, left for Wallace to read. "Can I ask you something, Wallace? Why Hattie? How did you know she was the one?"

A contented laugh rumbled out of the depths of his being. "Oh, old souls recognize each other, and that girl's soul runs deep. She thinks much, and she feels everything. The weight of the scar on her face, the way she observes life, the way she looked readin' her stories under the oak tree, the way she carries herself . . . but mostly, the way she loves. And the obvious talent she has for expressin' herself through words, of course."

"And what about Ezra? You orchestrated their meetin'; we both know that. Did you know she would love him when you suggested the orphanage to the Wolfes? He coulda 'bout raised himself given his age, or you coulda brought him here, but you didn't."

"Well, I had a hunch them two would have an effect on each other. They are the same, yet different. . . where it matters." He chuckled. "Yessuh, that's where the magic happens. It's one thing to bring two people who are alike together, but it's where they are different that they will have the greatest impact on the other. I brought him to help her. She needed someone. He needed someone."

"Except now he's gone. He hasn't contacted her once, has he?"

"It's not their time yet. Ezra's place is with his father right now. That boy has much to accomplish before he can be what he needs to be for her. They'll find their way back to each other. The hardest thing in life is knowin' when to put aside your own happiness for a greater purpose. I suppose it was almost cruel to expose her to him in the first place. But you'll see, what comes out of her will be perfection."

Hattie turned out the light and lay in her bed. Her thoughts lingered on Ezra. She missed him. In the year since he'd left, he'd not written or visited the orphanage, even though she'd heard rumors he was back in town. There were days when she was angry and days when she told herself she didn't care. Yet she sensed him everywhere.

She got up again and pulled aside the shade on her window. Clouds rolled in from the west, making the moon barely visible.

Snowflakes drifted lazily past. *The first snow is always the best.* With a wistful smile, she gathered her writing paper and began to compose a poem. Wallace was right. Her gift was a blessing *and* a curse.

She drew the words from her core. From everywhere, from everything. She stole the sunrise and chased the sunset as it ran from her across the sky. She imagined herself by the ocean with her feet buried deep in damp sand, on a mountaintop gazing out onto nature's glorious expanse. She placed herself everywhere but where she was.

As the snow fell and the moon lit the frost in the sky, Hattie wrote until the night had passed and she fell asleep. And though she traveled alone in her imagination, Ezra still went with her in her dreams.

Chapter 31

The Lord is my shepherd, I shall not want.
Psalm 23:1

December 1940

Livy and Hattie were back at the plantation for the weekend. Christmas was around the corner, but Hattie had no interest in holiday celebrations. Wallace occasionally received word on Ezra and shared it with Hattie, but she never asked for information. She told herself it was easier to accept that he was gone than to dwell on the uncertainty of his whereabouts and a very real sense of desertion.

"Hattie, I've got news!" Wallace came barreling through the door with a poinsettia and a fresh-baked cinnamon something in the paper bag he was holding. He took a big whiff of the bag, then placed it on the kitchen counter. Hattie couldn't help herself but smile as she sniffed the air and voiced an appreciative *mmmm*.

"What news, Wallace?"

"I hear he graduated early from school and was accepted into the Citadel. It's not far from here." Wallace said as he pulled out a cinnamon roll.

"Wallace, I know where the Citadel is, for Pete's sakes." *So he's been in town since the school year started?* She took firm hold of her emotions but kept her eyes averted as she lifted the poinsettia from the table and placed it by the window. She would not allow herself to start wondering, longing, and thinking about him again. It was difficult to write when thoughts of him permeated her soul. *It is?* A voice inside mocked her. If she were honest, she was beginning to think it helped, although she wasn't ready to admit it. She picked a dead leaf off the Christmas plant. She wasn't sure of anything, just that she needed to get back to writing, and Wallace was getting on her last nerve, eating all the rolls in the bag.

"Hey!" She exclaimed as he reached in for yet another roll. "Maybe save one for me?" She grabbed the bag and grinned. "Can we get back to work, Wallace, please? I'm sure he's off and happy, blah blah. . . but I need to stay focused on this and not be wondering about what he's doing." She plopped down at her desk and pulled out a cinnamon roll. Before she knew it, that one was gone and she'd started on another. *Jeepers.*

The afternoon music program on the radio faded into the somber tones that indicated the beginning of the evening news. Livy stepped into the room to listen, and the mood changed as they listened to reports about more bombing raids between Germany and England. The whole world was at war around them, but theirs was a tiny peaceful niche centered on stories, writing, and taking care of the children. America wasn't fully engaged yet, but it wasn't hard to imagine it happening.

Hattie's heart fluttered suddenly as she realized that Ezra wasn't just in college. He was studying at the country's leading military academy. Before long, he would be a soldier.

Livy clicked her tongue. "It's getting quite worrisome, this war. So many men volunteering for service. If we get involved. . ." She sighed. "Do you think things will ever straighten out again?"

"It always does, Livy, dear," Wallace replied. "God is still in control, no matter what men choose to do."

"It doesn't always seem like that's true," Hattie interjected. "All I know is, this old war had better be finished before Ezra graduates from the Citadel."

"The Citadel?" Livy's voice showed her surprise.

Wallace nodded. "I told Hattie just a few minutes ago. I learned this week that he's matriculated there." Observing wide eyes and worried expressions on both women, he hurried to reassure them. "We needn't fret. He'll come out ready—both for life and for war if need be. And like I said, God is in control."

"My head knows that," Hattie muttered, "but my heart doesn't always believe it."

Wallace nodded. "In God's time, child. Remember, everythin' has a time, a place, a season. We might feel like we're hangin' on to the edge of a cliff with our fingertips, but even then, we can trust that God is right there waitin' to catch us. We can't fix everythin' that's gonna happen, but when we let go, He'll give us rest in His grasp."

He reached over and turned off the radio. "You know what, Hattie? Let's go down by that river of ours. I want to show you somethin'."

"Now? It's cold and it'll be dark soon."

"This won't take long," he assured her.

Hattie couldn't figure out what was so important that they'd go out there on such an unpleasant evening, but she didn't argue. They bundled up and headed down the familiar path to the river. Wallace stopped next to a big old tree that overhung the water.

"Look at this," he said, pointing to the trunk. Hattie stepped closer and was surprised to find some letters carved into the bark.

"I-L-Y," she read. "What is this?"

Wallace cocked an eyebrow at her. "Remember that day, last summer. You and Ezra stayed here after the rest of us went back to the house. You sat right here, actually. But then, you had a big fight."

Hattie's eyes widened. She did remember, all too well. Wallace continued. "That day meant a lot to Ezra. He gave you his heart, but I don't think you realized that."

"He wrote this?"

"Mmm hmm. About you."

She swallowed hard.

"These are uncertain times, and the news has a way of makin' things worse." He shook his head and pursed his lips. "I know you feel deserted. I don't know why he's not contacted you either, but I want you to know how that young man felt about you. I saw it every time he looked at you."

She didn't look at him, but she listened.

"I want you to trust that no matter what life throws your way—or his way—good always wins. *Love* always wins. That boy loved you then, and I believe he loves you still. Time and circumstance won't take that away. War won't change it. Absence won't change it. Love is eternal, child. Ezra's body might not be here with you right now, but I believe his heart is." He squeezed her shoulders, then stepped away. He pulled a flashlight from his coat pocket and handed it to her. "I'm going to head back to the house. You stay as long as you need to."

Tears trembled on Hattie's lashes as her fingers traced the letters on the tree. *How did I not see this?* Time had weathered the letters, but the message remained. She wished she could go back to that afternoon, erase the stiffness of the days that followed. If only she'd known. . .

But what would she have done differently? It didn't matter now. She could only move forward.

She straightened her shoulders, then reached down and picked up a sharp-edged rock. "I love you, too, Ezra," she said aloud. With care, she etched the letters L-Y-T into the tree and drew a heart around both declarations. "And I'll trust God to bring you back to me."

It was a brave declaration, but one that proved hard to stick to. Wallace had brought her other news of Ezra and of his father, who now lived in the old Levine mansion. He was so close, but as far as she knew, he'd made no effort to see or call or even write to her. The days passed, and as they did, her thoughts grew darker.

New Year's Day came, and she was scheduled to help Wallace with his booth at a celebration in the market downtown. She awoke grumpy and tired. She hadn't even made it to midnight last night, but who cared?

Livy stuck her head in the door. "Hattie! Why are you still in bed? Come on, girl. It's a new day—a new year!"

Hattie groaned and pulled the covers over her head.

Livy crossed the room and pulled them down. "Seriously," she said. "Wallace will be waiting for you."

He doesn't need me. Just let me sleep. But grudgingly, she swung her legs over the side of the bed. "Okay. I'm up."

Livy looked sideways at her, then stepped to the door. "I don't know what's going on with you, but cheer up, girlie. It's going to be a good day. Now, come on. Cora's got breakfast ready."

I don't know what's going on with me either, Hattie thought miserably. She got dressed, then picked up her brush and began attacking the tangles in her hair. Then she made the mistake of looking in the mirror. *What in the world?!* She was a mess—frizzy hair, dark circles under her eyes, clothes hanging too loose on her body. Obviously, her sleepless nights were catching up with her.

She reached for the makeup Livy had recently allowed her to begin wearing. Livy insisted she didn't need it, but Hattie liked the way it covered her scar. Except today, it just seemed to lay on her skin like . . . like lard. "Ugh, forget it," she muttered. "Who are you trying to impress, anyway?" She grabbed her coat, ran out of her room, skipped breakfast, and headed straight to Market Street.

She made her way through Marion Square, glancing at the old Citadel buildings there. The school had moved to its current location near the Ashley River years ago, but for some reason, every time she passed this place, she thought of Ezra. Of course, she always thought of him. Every minute of every stinkin' hour of every day.

Here we go again. Can't I just get through one day without thinking of him?

Meeting Street was crowded as she meandered through the people to get to the market where Wallace was waiting. *All these people out celebrating the new year. Big whoop. Me, I'm just going to work.* The noisy commotion coming out of the buildings nearby was so loud, she stopped. At the same time, a door swung open and several handsomely uniformed young men stepped out. Jazzy dance music followed them, but not as quickly as a bevy of giddy girls, running to catch up.

Hattie watched as one of the girls slung an arm around the tallest of the men. She laughed as the man tried unsuccessfully to swat the girl off like a fly. She rolled her eyes. Girls seemed to come out of the woodwork these days when there were boys in uniform around. She stood still, watching as they laughed and carried on. *My, how different my life is.*

Another boy stopped, turned around, and headed back to the restaurant as if he'd forgotten something. Her breath caught in her throat. *It's him!*

He wasn't paying attention as he whisked by, but then he stopped abruptly and turned around. Their eyes met. They stood on the side-

236

walk, neither knowing what to say. She wanted to run to him, but something kept her standing still. The boy who had captured her heart so completely had changed somehow. He was different. The way he carried himself, the way he'd been acting. . . This was not the same Ezra.

His blue eyes drove a stake right through her as he moved toward her, cautiously, as if he already knew of her disappointment in him.

"Hattie? I—" He cleared his throat, his eyes still glued to her face. Her heart stopped. He was unbearably handsome. He was in his element, like a bright shining star she could never have. He was pure torture.

A girl suddenly appeared and wrapped her hands around his arm. "Who's this?" she asked with her nose in the air. Then she snapped and cracked her gum. The rest of the gang gathered around, peering at Hattie.

Immediately, she could feel her scar, like fire blazing on her cheek. Her hand went to her face as Ezra reached out to her. He tried to say something, but she backed away, then turned and ran toward the market. Laughter seemed to fill the street behind her.

Why did I come out, today of all days? I should have stayed home. Not knowing where he was, was better than. . . than knowing. Until today, she'd been able to create her own reality. Now she knew—the whole time he'd *chosen* to stay away. *What did you expect, Hattie?* she asked herself bitterly. *He's a college man now. You're nothing but an ugly little schoolgirl.*

She found Wallace at the market and ran into his arms.

"What on earth? Tell me," he said as she clung to him.

"I saw him, Wallace, I saw him."

"Who?" He held her at arm's length and looked at her. "Saw who?"

"Ezra." She could hardly get the name out. "He was with his friends and some—*some girl.*"

"Oh, child." He pulled her hands from her face and held them tightly.

"This whole time he's been here," she wailed. "So close, but he never comes to see me. I told myself they kept those boys at the military college, that they weren't allowed to go out. Oh, I don't know what I thought. I'm so stupid! I kept telling myself there was a good reason he never came to visit." Her voice became hard. "I guess I know the truth now—there's someone else in his life."

"Now, Hattie, you don't know that. There could be an easy explanation. Did you talk to him?"

"No! How could I with that horse-faced girl chomping her gum at me? He has a girlfriend, Wallace. I didn't expect that. I could have taken anything but that."

Wallace shook his head. "Nah. I bet she's nothin', just a friend, Hattie. I'm sure he's just been busy with all of his obligations, with being a cadet, with helping his father—"

"You didn't see him," she replied. Then she stepped to the back of the truck, effectively ending the conversation.

She spent the remainder of the day quiet, busying herself with Wallace's stand. When it was time to shut things down, she left Wallace to load the truck while she went for a walk on the riverfront.

She hadn't been gone but minutes when a group of young men appeared on the corner. Wallace recognized Ezra probably the same instant the boy saw him. He watched as Ezra separated himself from the crowd and headed his way. He shook his head.

"Hello, boy," he said. "Where've you been keepin' yourself?"

"Wallace! It's so good to see you!" Ezra exclaimed. His face flushed a bit at his next question. "Was Hattie here with you? I saw her earlier, but— Do you know where she is?" He looked anxiously around the marketplace, but she was nowhere to be found.

Wallace raised his brows. "She's here, but I don't think she wants to see you. I don't know what transpired between the two o' you today, but she's been nursing a mighty sore heart these last few hours. Or longer."

"It was a misunderstanding, that's all," Ezra said. "Look, I'm not supposed to be here. I don't have a lot of time, but could you give her this?" He handed Wallace a note. "I've been meaning to visit her, but—ugh! My life is *not* my own anymore, Wallace. But it's all in there. Just give it to her when you see her, please."

"Wolfe!" At the sound of his name, both Ezra and Wallace turned. His friends were still waiting for him at the corner.

"I've got to go. Please give it to her, sir," he begged. "It's important." Then he turned and ran off.

Wallace finished loading his truck as the sun was setting. *Hattie must still be at the riverfront,* he thought. *I'll just sit here and wait for her.* He stumbled to a nearby bench.

A familiar sound filled the air. He felt dizzy. Drums sounded in the distance. The voice of a beloved little girl tickled his ears.

"Daddy. . ."

Hattie returned to find him slouched over on the bench. Frantically, she screamed for help. The note he'd clutched in his hand fell to the street as a curious crowd formed around them.

Chapter 32

Whom have I in heaven but you?
And there is none upon earth that I desire beside thee.
My flesh and my heart faileth:
but God is the strength of my heart
and my portion forever.
PSALM 73:25–26

January 1941

"I think he's trying to wake up. Wallace. . . Wallace. . ." Livy leaned close over the bed, her eyes locked on the old man's face. Across from her, Hattie stood up and took his hand. It was cold like everything else in this dismal hospital ward. "Wallace," Livy said again. "Can you hear me? You gave us such a fright!" A nurse stepped over to investigate, shooing them back from the bed.

"I think his fever has broken," she said. "He is out of the woods for now, don't y'all worry. Once he's cleared by the doctor, he can go home. We'll send some medicine home with him." The nurse looked them both over for an uncomfortable second. "Make sure he stays warm. Give him some good old-fashioned chicken soup for a few days. Make sure he stays in bed. He needs a lot of rest, or the pneumonia will come back." She pulled the covers up over him and tucked the sheets under. "Now, will someone be coming by to pick him up when he's ready?"

Livy and Hattie looked at each other. "We'll be here."

The look the nurse gave them rankled in Livy's soul. She stood tall. "I'm his next of kin, so I'll be taking him home *and* providing his care." She'd been a bit surprised at the looks she and Hattie had gotten in this all-Black hospital on Cannon Street. Very few White folk entered this building, apparently, but that wasn't going to stop her.

The nurse shrugged. "Well, he will need someone to watch over him for a while—a few weeks, maybe—until he has fully recovered. Pneumonia makes you too weak to do much of anything."

Wallace stirred again, then opened his eyes. "Nope. No suh," he said weakly. "Ain't nobody takin' care of me." A fit of coughing overcame him. When he could speak again, he asserted, "I'll be fine on my own, plus I've got Clarence to help in case I need anything." He tried to push himself up in the bed, but he couldn't seem to get his breath. The nurse quickly adjusted the head of his bed, raising him to a more upright position. Another fit of coughing overtook him, and he nearly choked.

"You'll have to spit that out, Mr. Hayes," the nurse said matter-of-factly. "That stuff needs to be in the trash, not in your lungs." An orderly came in bearing a bowl of soup and set up to feed it to him. When Livy asked to feed him, Wallace protested as strongly as he was able. Livy ignored him.

Suddenly, Hattie was in tears. Wallace noticed and pushed the spoon away. "Child, what is it?" He held out his hand, and she laid her head on his chest.

"Oh, Wallace," she cried. "What if something had happened to you? We didn't even know you were sick. You shouldn't have been out in the weather, much less working in the market."

The old man waved his hand dismissively. "T'ain't my time, child. I'm not goin' nowhere till I've finished the work God has for me here."

A feeling of foreboding rushed over Hattie. She sat back and looked at him earnestly. "I don't want to finish this book, Wallace. I don't want to do it. God's going to call you home when you're done with me. I just know it!"

Wallace patted her hand gently. "Hey, hey now," he murmured. "I will always be here, Hattie. Even when I'm gone, I'll still be close by. You'll feel me, just like *I* feel *them*. Just like we've talked about."

"How can we go on without you, Wallace? How? I've lost everyone in my life. I don't want to lose you too, and I know it's coming."

Livy was quiet as Hattie cried. In her own pain and uncertainty, she was unable to offer any advice or comfort. She had questions of her own. The girl was right. How would they cope without Wallace to guide them? They needed him. He was a tower of strength. For years, he had supplied their needs from the plantation. He'd watched over them diligently. Who would do that when he was gone? The burden of responsibility hit her shoulders, heavier than ever, and she drew a shaky breath. Whatever did happen, she'd need to be strong for the children. Especially for Hattie.

Wallace wasn't unaware of her struggle. He reached out and caught her hand as well. "Listen here, you two," he said. "We're gonna make the most of the time we have together. We'll learn from each other. We'll make each other strong, and we'll strengthen our foundation of faith together. God is our fortress—the place we can take all our sorrows and fears, our questions, and our doubts." He tried to laugh. "God ain't done with any of us yet. We still have somethin' very important to build. Leastways, now we have a place to jump from. Let all eyes look upon His grace and see that His is the best way. . . the only way." His eyes closed. Just before he fell asleep, he whispered, "Glory be to God that He has brought us together."

The doctor didn't release him as quickly as the nurse thought he would. Wallace spent the next two weeks at the hospital. He was weak, and his fever came and went. Livy and Hattie took turns visiting him when he was well enough for visitors. Together with Clarence, they planned for his return. When he was discharged, they would accompany him to the plantation to assist with his care. Wallace continued to insist he would not need the women, but they moved ahead despite his protests. Livy requested a leave from the orphanage, and with the increasing absence of both her and Hattie, the board put Cora in charge of the day-to-day details there and hired two new employees to help.

On his last night at the hospital, Wallace insisted both Hattie and Livy go home to rest before they moved into the guest cottage the next day. The women complied with his wish, but not before making it clear that they would be the ones giving the orders once he got home.

That evening, after they had finished packing up their things, Livy and Hattie sat for a while on the front porch in silence. There were no words spoken between them, just an understanding that things were going to change.

Finally, Hattie stirred and looked at Livy. "You know," she said, "you don't have to come. I can take care of him."

"You can't do it alone, dear. You have school to finish, for one thing." She sat quietly for another minute, her eyes on a distant horizon. There was an odd note in her voice when she spoke again. "I think I'll be putting in my resignation here, Hattie. Wallace is my cousin, and he needs me now."

"Oh, Livy!" Hattie couldn't imagine the orphanage without its sweet, loving director. "Oh my goodness. But. . . you don't have to do that. I can take care of him, I can. And Clarence will help when I'm at school. It's just a couple more months. Wallace wants me there as much as possible to write anyway. If I live there, I can just be there for everything. Or. . ." She gulped. "If I have to, I can just quit. School's not that impor—"

"You will *not* quit!" Livy exclaimed. "You're four months from graduating with honors. Wallace would not want you to do that, and I will not allow it. No, my place is with him for now." She took a sip of her sweet tea. "We'll figure this out. Don't worry. There's still so much I need to know about my background, my heritage. This might be my last chance—no, *our* chance—to fill in the blanks and figure out our plan for down the line." She chuckled and slipped an arm around Hattie. "Guess I'd better *plan* to read your book when it comes out, huh? How are your talks with Wallace coming, anyway? You writing everything down?"

Hattie took a deep breath. "Yeah, I'm trying to. I get so nervous sometimes though. He believes in me so much. It's a lot of pressure, you know? But it is what I'm supposed to do." A soft smile lit her face. "That much I know. And when I'm with him, I know it's where I'm supposed to be, too. I can't explain it better than that." She shrugged.

Livy smiled. "I understand. He's so sure of what God wants him—us—to do. But it's a nice feeling when you know your own purpose, isn't it?" Hattie nodded. "Most people just live their lives, day in and day out, and never know. You're unique. He told me from the start that there was something about you, something special. He knew God had a plan for you the day he met you."

Hattie shook her head wonderingly. "But who am I? I'm just a know-nothing girl with a pitiful past."

Livy had been leaning forward, observing the stars as they illuminated the night sky. Now she turned to look at Hattie almost incredulously. "Who are you? Oh, my sweet girl! You might have been broken, but your soul is as deep as the deepest ocean. Your mind is so sharp, you see things that others don't." She caught Hattie in a huge hug. "I've never known Wallace to be wrong about anything, but even if I had, I *know* he's right about you. If he says it, I'm pretty sure we can count on it to be true. And you know what the best part is?"

Hattie shook her head, and Livy pushed a strand of hair away from the girl's face, tucking it behind her ear. "God has your back, and that, my dear, is worth more than anything else. Wallace isn't the only one who saw something different in you, way back when your daddy left you here. You were a frightened little girl, but your spirit was so strong. I always knew you were going to be someone special." She laughed and added in a whisper, "Don't tell anybody, but you've always been my favorite."

Hattie rested her head on Livy's shoulder. "I was afraid of everything back then. I thought this scar was the first thing people saw when they met me. Maybe the only thing. And for a while, I was right. I mean, look—no one adopted me. I was passed over so many times."

"Maybe, but Wallace would say that was part of God's plan. That He uses everything we go through for good. That everything happens for a reason. . . and now look at you! You aren't even eighteen, and you're writing a book. What an accomplishment that will be!"

Hattie pulled her arms tight around herself. "But what about my mama? How does losing her the way I did help me? It just brings heartache. I miss her every day, Livy."

Livy looked up at the sky. The wind had picked up and the clouds were moving swiftly across the moon. A bluish mist covered the ground as far as the eye could see. "I bet your mama is here somewhere right now, cheering you on. Did you feel that cool kiss on your cheek just now? I bet that was her telling you to believe. We all have our troubles, our sorrows. And we choose the path we let those things take us down."

"Now you sound like Wallace." Hattie rolled her eyes and giggled. "I guess that's only natural, seeing you're related and all." They sat for a moment, just looking at the stars beyond the clouds.

"You know," Livy said eventually, "I can't help it, but I'm a little excited for what's to come, aren't you?"

"Really? What do you think is coming?" Hattie sounded worried again. "I mean, what's going to happen to us when he goes to heaven? That's what I'm worried about."

"Well, that I don't know." Her voice was soft. "But no matter what, we will be strong, you and I. God already has a plan. I can feel it, and I trust that, when He is good and ready to take Wallace, we will be prepared for what's next."

Hattie was quiet, but Livy knew where her head was.

Weeks passed while Livy and Hattie remained in the guest house on Wallace's plantation. When Hattie wasn't researching or learning from Wallace's words, she was writing. Meanwhile, Livy worked closely with Clarence, visiting with Wallace's attorneys, learning the daily affairs of the plantation, and caring for her cousin.

Spring had sprung again when Wallace took Livy aside. Together, they walked to the ruins of the old plantation house. They spent an hour there, wandering the grounds as Wallace detailed his vision for the place. When he finished outlining his plan, they were sitting on that wall at his favorite spot.

"I don't know how much time I have left," he said, "but that's what I want to have done. I want it all built on top of this place. Oh! There's something else, Livy, and this is important to me. I want this to be the music room, right here like it used to be, and I want you to take the room directly over it. Will you do that?"

Livy had been puzzled many times by Wallace's fixation with the old music room. This time she had to know. "Why is that so important to you, Wallace? It seems such a small thing."

Wallace's face was somber when he finally put together the words to answer her. "Because of what God did for us here. You and me, Livy." Her brow furrowed. "Terrible things happened in this room—you know that. But good came from them. And *we* came from them."

He squeezed her hand. "But God keeps no record of the sins of man. Love keeps no record of wrongs. When God's Son died on the cross, He took away our sins and made us new. He nailed all of our evil to the cross. You and I—we will lead by God's example. Forgiveness means forgetting, yes. But it doesn't mean we force the awful events from our minds. No, it means we learn from them."

He stood up and looked out over what was left of the crumbling foundation. "Life in its toil and depravity has a place in the bigger picture. It is the measure of the greater plan that defines our lives—we need only wait to see it bear its fruit." He turned to look at Livy. "You are the fruit. That's why I want you there. *You* are the blessing."

He swept a hand toward the remaining row of slave cabins. "Forgiveness means refusing to dwell on the wrongs of man." A tear formed and ran down his weathered face as he looked up at the sky and smiled. "This—all of it—has been reconciled through the blood of Jesus, God's one and only Son. Good wins in the end. *Love* wins in the end. And your love will bless so many for generations to come." He pulled out his Bible. "Psalm 103 is one of my favorite passages of Scripture, Livy. Listen:

> "The Lord executeth righteousness and judgment
> for all that are oppressed. . . The Lord is merciful and
> gracious, slow to anger, and plenteous in mercy. He
> will not always chide: neither will he keep his anger

for ever. He hath not dealt with us after our sins; nor rewarded us according to our iniquities. For as the heaven is high above the earth, so great is his mercy toward them that fear him. As far as the east is from the west, so far hath he removed our transgressions from us. Like as a father pitieth his children, so the Lord pitieth them that fear him. For he knoweth our frame; he remembereth that we are dust."

He closed the book and looked up. "I'm so glad God doesn't hold our sins against us. When we surrender to Him, He forgives and uses our lives for good. Our grandparents, they surrendered. They forgave. God is using them and their choices to bless us and He will continue to do so as we surrender our lives to Him as well. Oh, Livy. He has such great things planned for this place. I just know He does. The Bible says He purifies us like gold. He puts us through the fire and—" He walked over and rested a hand on the crumbling music room wall.

"It's just like this ol' house, Livy. All the beauty and prideful things of man that were here—paintin's, fancy china and tapestries, all the trappin's of the Summerton wealth—it all burned up. There wasn't much of anything they could save after the fire here. Just a couple sticks of furniture and the plantation itself. We're the same. When we turn ourselves over to Him, all that's old and bad and not of Him gets burned up. And then He builds His new creation on the gold that's left."

Livy understood. Hers was a legacy. A story that the world needed to right itself. As Wallace had outlined that day, they would turn the plantation into a place much larger than anything she had ever imagined or seen. An orphanage for the innocent, a church along the river that opened its doors for every person, no matter the denomination, a place where the hopeless could find peace. And she would be the one to bring it to fruition.

It was late, but Hattie couldn't sleep. So many changes had happened lately. And for some reason, she was missing Ezra terribly this week. It didn't matter how many times she told herself he had moved on or that theirs had been a childhood infatuation, he still haunted her dreams. Well, he would if she ever slept. So instead, she was writing.

> *Unfortunate circumstance or a faultless possibility? Would they endure the test of time and discernment. . . and end in a union more beautiful than they could ever imagine?*

Hattie put down her pen and flexed her fingers. *Wishful thinking,* she thought. But when she thought about him, it was easy to write; the words flowed from her. She picked up her pen and continued.

> *In the end they would see that in all things inevitable, theirs was a path preordained before the dawn of time.*

She understood it now. She did. Wallace had told her to be patient and to use her pain to fuel her gift, and she was. She thought for a moment, then smiled and wrote one final sentence.

> *Their hold on each other would grow from the darkness to the light, and they would learn that they were, in fact, not the ones in control of their destiny.*

She reread her words, then put down her pen and stacked her papers. She felt different. Peaceful, even. She climbed into bed and turned out the light. And for maybe the first time since Ezra left the orphanage, Hattie slept soundly through the night.

Chapter 33

Give instruction to a wise man, and he will be yet wiser:
teach a just man, and he will increase in learning.
The fear of the LORD is the beginning of wisdom:
and the knowledge of the holy is understanding.
For by me thy days shall be multiplied,
and the years of thy life shall be increased.
PROVERBS 9:9–11

May 1941

A candle stood on the old Chippendale desk in Wallace's front room. Hattie struck a match and held it to the wick till the flame caught. She pulled out the matching chair and settled herself behind the desk, running her fingertips across its venerable surface. This desk had belonged to the Summerton family for generations, one of the few items that had escaped the devastating fire, yet here it was in Wallace's humble home.

Staring into the candle's flame, she could picture William here, signing off on the deeds of the day, running the plantation, and immersing himself in the human sin that came with the bondage of a race. The irony of that image made her heart stop, as this was often where she sat to hear Wallace's story. It was here where her telling of the story had begun and where the souls of the past could rest easy as they pushed her pen forward with their blessings.

"There you are!" Livy stepped into the room from the kitchen. "Supper's just about ready. Goodness, you look solemn. What are you thinkin' about, child?"

Hattie sighed. "Oh, I don't know. Just trying to get a feel for what happened here. This desk, this home—it just feels familiar and scary and wonderful, all at the same time. I can't believe how ugly the world can be, and yet, somehow it's perfect."

"Yes, it is." Wallace shuffled in from his room. "But think about that—the complexity of life, the shackles we bear that keep us from growin'. If we only learned to wait patiently, we would see that everythin' is carefully woven together over time." He looked over at Hattie.

"If only that desk could talk. . ." He shook his head wistfully. "It holds so many memories. When I knew her, Julia used to sit and read there. Before that, from this very desk, she and her father argued politics. From its platform, he bought and sold slaves. And from this desk, he freed Ned after he resolved himself to the glory of a good and just God." He touched the top of the desk lightly, almost reverently.

"Grandpa Ned always told us that William was a different man after fightin' that war. But some say it was when he looked at his son's face in Chloe's arms that he changed. He came back badly injured after the Combahee River raid in 1863, but his mind was as clear as day. Different, but clear as day."

"How was he different?" Livy asked.

Wallace leaned heavily on his cane as he walked to the window and looked out. "The war got to him. His guilt ate at him. Seeing death all around him every day. Many things affected him. He made a difficult choice. He knew both sides—he'd enjoyed the benefits of a people in bondage, yet when he met the Savior, he found a need to set them free. Which side would you have chosen if you'd have been in his place?"

"Well, I know which side I'd choose!" Livy said.

"Me too, no question—I'd have been fighting to free a human race. Even if it did mean fighting for the North." Hattie was enough of a South Carolina girl that she had to add that.

Wallace smiled at them, but there was an odd look on his face. "You both are so innocent and your hearts are filled with love. I don't think it was an easy choice for anyone. Beyond the slavery issue, there was a whole way of life under siege. Family against family." He shook his head. "William's heart was filled with pride and doubt and hate for a time, but God was already at work, slowly changing him. Do you think it was coincidence that while his compatriots fought for their way of life, William ultimately decided to fight for the other side? Or had it always been a part of God's perfect plan?

"Until his grievous sin, William didn't see keeping us Black folk in bondage as anything against God. It was just his way of life. And then his own sinful actions changed him. For the first time, when he saw his son in Chloe's arms, he saw his slaves as people. And God used his sin for good." Wallace chuckled. "Yessuh, our vile sinner became a part of an abolitionist movement that saved hundreds of slaves. And he did it in partnership with a former slave named Solomon—a caretaker for the Levines before they moved up North. Was that merely a coincidence, or was it, too, always in the threads that God had weaved together before the dawn of time?"

Hattie looked up from the desk in awe. "The whole story is just so unbelievable, Wallace." She flipped through the pages of the manuscript that were piled in front of her. "Let me read the part about Solomon to you. His part is so small in the whole story, yet so large. Do you mind?"

"Not at all," Wallace assured her. "You go right ahead, little miss writer. Let's hear what you've got."

Hattie cleared her throat. She hadn't shared much of the manuscript with anyone but Wallace yet, but she was gaining confidence in her storytelling abilities. She took a deep breath.

> *"Solomon became a free man and volunteered to join one of the first all-Black Union regiments. In fact, his regiment, the Second South Carolina, had a hand in the raid that Harriett Tubman led off the Combahee River. From his plantation there, William worked hand in hand with Solomon the night of the raid in 1863. Many slaves escaped because of what those men did that night."*

As she read, Wallace began to hum. When she paused, he sang a few words, then said, "God showed up to take the sinner's heart and make him whole again. Glory be to God!"

"What happened to Solomon after the war?" Livy asked. "Did anyone try to locate Hope when the war was over?"

"Ooo!" Hattie sat up straight in her chair and began flipping through the pages again. "I have that answer, Livy. Hold on now. . . Yes! Here it is—1865.

> *"When the war ended, there was a big parade down Meeting Street. Slaves from everywhere went to meet the soldiers as they marched through town. Members of the Fifty-Second Massachusetts Infantry and Solomon's regiment marched together. It was a fine day. William had joined Ned and Chloe in downtown Charleston to greet them. And he recognized Solomon as he marched past."*

Hattie looked at Livy, then set the pages down. "Ned and Chloe remembered Solomon from their visit to the Levines' home when she first learned she was pregnant. William had told them of Solomon's involvement in the raid.

"By that time, William knew that Hope was with the Levines in Alexandria, but together with Chloe and Ned, they had decided to leave her where she was instead of disturbing the life of freedom God had given her. Anyway, after the parade, they found Solomon in the crowd, and Chloe gave him her locket—the same one that Julia had given her the night of William's attack. And Chloe asked Solomon to give the locket to Hope when she was old enough to understand."

Wallace nodded in agreement. "Yep. Charleston was a disaster after the war. It took years to rebuild. Social graces and tensions were still high." He cleared his throat. "They did the best thing for her. They did not want to tear Hope from her family and bring her into an unsafe environment." Wallace put his hand on Livy's shoulder. "And we know that Hope received the gift and news of her true family, because the locket you have is the Summerton heirloom."

Livy's smile was tremulous. "Yes. As she was dying, she gave it to the nuns to give it to me."

"Glory to God," Wallace said as he gathered her hand in his. "It wasn't until after Bessany and Ida died that my father and Ezra's uncle found you. We knew to begin our search in Alexandria, but for so long we'd found no trace of where Hope had gone after the Levines traveled to Germany. We didn't know she'd come here, looking for us. And we didn't know we were looking for you. We were still looking for Hope. It took a long time, but finally, we found you. And you were a young lady about to embark on a career as a social worker."

Livy smiled. "And I know where the story goes from there," she said, "but what happened to Chloe? And to Julia?"

"Those wonderful ladies lived out the remainder of their lives serving in the orphanage and school that my father, Moses, and my grandfather, Ned, founded in Charleston with the money they inherited after William Summerton's untimely death. That's what happened to the house, you know. The great earthquake in 1886 caused great damage to the property and started a raging fire that trapped both women. William died saving them. Oh, but I already told you that, didn't I?"

Wallace looked out the window toward the ruins of the mansion. He was quiet for a long moment. Livy and Hattie sat silent, watching him, waiting to hear more. Finally, he turned back to them.

"I knew that God had plans for this place, but I didn't know what they were, so I left it the way it was. It was only after I met you that I understood what belongs here. Our legacy, Livy, will be built on top of it. It will be a fine place that welcomes the orphaned, the unwanted, and the innocent. The fatherless, motherless, the needy, and the victims of war-torn sacrifice."

He stopped for a moment as resolve washed over him. "It will be for all people, regardless of origin, because there is neither color nor race when it comes to need. Of course, you know the school that Moses built still stands to this day. His name is on the plaque in front of the building."

"You mean the Hayes School on Broad Street, of course."

"Yes'm. Part of my father's legacy. Like him, what I have inherited will be given back to the community, a hundred times over. Together, we will continue what God started—what our family began after the Civil War. We will bring it all back here, to our home, to our land. Here we can expand and do great and wondrous things with the blessings that God has given us." He gazed out over the fields again. "And we will do it where it all began."

Livy shook her head. "Wallace, all this time, why didn't you ever say anything to me? You've been coming to the orphanage for years. It's because of you, isn't it, that Palmetto Manor has been able to stay afloat, even during the leanest years. Oh, I wish you could have told me."

Wallace smiled. "I was tempted so many times," he said. "But I wanted all the pieces to fall together first. I waited for a clear word from God so it would happen in His timing, not my own. And you were doing so well on your own, growing and learning. I didn't want to disturb the life you'd made for yourself and the kids. I'm so proud of you and what you've become. What a series of events God weaved together, to lead us here. To perpetrate the mighty fine things we are goin' to do. God is goin' to make miracles happen right here, in this very special place. I know He is. He already has."

Chapter 34

Surely goodness and mercy shall follow me
all the days of my life:
and I will dwell in the house of the Lord for ever.
PSALM 23:6

August 1941

In the days that followed, Wallace continued to weaken. He was only in his fifties, but his many health issues were taking a significant toll on his body. Hattie and Livy had moved permanently into the guesthouse next door to Wallace's home, where they could care for him easily. Repeated bouts of pneumonia had become almost routine since his collapse in the marketplace, but even so, a diminished Wallace was not an incapacitated one. His mind was sharp as a tack. An urgency to finish telling his story had overtaken him, and Hattie often found herself working late into the night to finish some new anecdote for his approval. They had moved her work area to just outside Wallace's bedroom so they could talk even on days when Wallace didn't feel well. He wasn't bedridden, but he certainly wasn't as mobile as he used to be.

This morning, Hattie had been at her desk for more than an hour before she heard Wallace stirring. She looked up when his voice came through the doorway.

"Good morning, child. What are you thinking about? You're over there scribbling away without me saying a word." His bed creaked and he grunted as he shifted his body weight, trying to get comfortable. Hattie grabbed the morning's newspaper from atop her desk and hurried to help him with his pillows.

"Good morning, sleepyhead. I have something for you," she said, waving the paper. "It just came this morning."

"Something for me in the paper? Clarence and Livy take care of the business these days."

"Oh, it's not business. It's especially for you. I wrote it."

"And it's in the paper?" A grin grew on his face. "Well, read it to me, girl. What are you waiting for?" Wallace wasn't like most people. He never feigned interest in anything she wrote.

She grinned back, then cleared her throat. "It's a poem. I think it will be part of the book. I've named it 'Wallace's Wish,' to match. Listen." She lifted the paper and began to read.

"Reach for me, sweet child of time, and take my wearied hand."

Wallace reached out and held her hand. "Mmm, I like it already," he said.

Hattie squeezed his hand and continued. "Follow you must, down cobblestoned roads, past listless moss and rubble. Come hear my tale of love long lost, of steadfast hope despite the cost." She risked a glance at Wallace, who was beaming from ear to ear. "'Mid huckster's cries and bondaged hope, from bless-ed grounds I call."

"Yes, Jesus," Wallace whispered. "Life is such a paradox."

Hattie swallowed against the rush of sudden emotion that pushed against the back of her throat. "Rebuild, I whisper; refine, I beg! Let not your heart be troubled. The grasp of sin has lost its hold; God's grace has overcome. Take heed, sweet child, glean hope in all, our souls have been set free."

The room was silent for a long moment. Hattie didn't quite have the courage to look up until Wallace cleared his throat.

"Oh, Miss Hattie." She raised her eyes to find a tear making its way slowly down his cheek. "My sweet girl, you were born for this. So powerful, that was."

"Do you really think so?"

"Oh, yes, child." Another tear made its way downward.

She swallowed hard. "Well, it's because of you. I wouldn't be writing otherwise, I'm sure."

"Nonsense." He wiped his eyes and said firmly, "God planted that seed, not me. He gave me the privilege of watering it, of caring for it. Nurturing it out of the ground, you might say. But the gift is from Him."

Hattie ducked her head. "Well, I thank you for that. This poem— it just kind of happened. It. . . sums it all up, you know? How I feel about our story and about you. It's like, your whole being is inter- mixed with my words. You're like a beautiful song, Wallace, with beats and meaning, sound and rhythm." She stopped, embarrassed that she had shared these innermost thoughts. She'd grown comfort- able with Livy and Wallace reading her manuscript, but her poetry she usually kept to herself. Of course, most of her poems were about Ezra and weren't meant to be shared. But this one—this one she'd chosen to share. With the world. Because it was time to celebrate.

Livy's voice from the doorway startled them both. "I thought I heard voices in here. I've brought you some tea, Wallace. And, Hat- tie, That was beautiful."

"You heard?"

"Some of it. But I read it early this morning, before you came in.

I'm so proud of you!"

"Me too, child," Wallace chimed in. "How did you get it in the paper, anyway?"

Hattie shrugged. "They take submissions from time to time. I sent it in last week. I'm surprised they used it so quickly, but I'm glad they did. It's a good way to introduce my announcement today."

"Your announcement?" Livy set the tea tray on the table next to Wallace's bed and turned to Hattie, curiosity on her face.

"Mmm hmm. It's a big one, too."

"Well, now," Wallace rumbled. "I wonder what you've got stirrin' in that head of yours."

"Oh, it's not in my head anymore." Hattie giggled. "It's on my desk." She got up and stepped out of the room. When she came back in, she had a stack of papers in her hands, pages and pages of neatly typed words. The top sheet proudly proclaimed, "Wallace's Wish, by Hattie Whitfield with Wallace Hayes."

Eyes shining brightly, she handed the stack to Wallace. "It's finished."

In the days that followed, Hattie and Wallace worked back through the manuscript, polishing and fine-tuning the story till they were both happy with it. In October, Hattie took a part-time job at the *Charleston Daily Mail*, and with help from the editor there, she sent out queries to two publishers.

Chapter 35

For God hath not given us a spirit of fear;
but of power, and of love, and of a sound mind.
2 Timothy 1:7

November 1941

It was the Monday before Thanksgiving and Hattie, who now drove herself to work and back in Wallace's old pickup truck, had stopped at a grocery store in town to pick up some essentials for the coming holiday. She was loading the bags into the back of the truck when someone behind her said her name. She froze.

"Hattie? It is you, I know."

Ezra. For an instant, Hattie's heart stopped. She set the last bag carefully in the bed of the truck, then turned. As their eyes connected, her heart reengaged. . . at a full gallop. With an effort, she pulled herself together, closed her mouth, then opened it again.

"Ezra. Are you still in town?" The icy tone of her voice belied the heat flooding through her veins.

He stepped back. "Of course I am. I'm at the Citadel."

"Oh. We hadn't heard from you, so I thought you must have moved on."

"I haven't heard from you either." His tone was slightly defensive.

"A lady doesn't initiate the conversation, sir."

"I—uh—" He fumbled for words, and Hattie relented. Slightly.

"Yes, well. You look. . . good. *Healthy.* The Citadel must be treating you well?"

"Aww, Hattie." He had the grace to look ashamed. "I'm sorry. I know I should have kept in touch. Everything went crazy when my father returned. We went to Alexandria, then we came back here, and I enrolled. There are a lot of responsibilities there. I—"

"You were in the same town. You couldn't write a letter or use a telephone?"

He didn't answer, just looked at the ground.

"It's not like the Citadel is a prison. But it's okay. You found a new life. It's fine."

"But it's not the same."

Hattie held on to her temper. Barely. "Well, that was your choice. Meanwhile, I'm doing well. Thanks for asking." She tossed her hair over her shoulder.

He looked up, and their eyes connected. She'd forgotten the depth of those blue eyes. The fight left her spirit, and she sighed.

"I'm sorry too, Ezra. I shouldn't have attacked you just now. I know life can get crazy. But I've missed you. We all have."

"I did give Wallace a note for you one day."

"You did?"

"Yes. That day I saw you in town. I saw him in the market, too. New Year's?"

"But I—" Hattie's eyes went wide. "Oh! Oh, no."

"What?"

"Oh, you don't know. Wallace almost died that day. He was in the hospital for weeks."

"What?!"

"Yes. He had pneumonia. He hasn't been well since. In fact, Livy resigned from the orphanage, and she and I are both living on the farm now. He's really not doing well at all, Ezra. I worry about him."

They spoke a while longer, catching up on each other's lives. He told her about college and she told him about the farm and her job and life outside the orphanage. She didn't mention the book, and neither did he. He'd probably forgotten. Why should he remember?

While the distance between them lessened, Hattie didn't let down her wall entirely. There was no reason to—all too soon he looked at his watch and said he had to be running. He had a commitment that evening. She didn't ask if it was another girl.

He opened the truck door for her and she climbed in. Before he closed it, he took her hand. Her brows lifted and she looked at him questioningly.

"I am sorry I haven't been back to see you, Hattie. I haven't forgotten you. I couldn't if I tried." That was followed by a small huff of a laugh. She wasn't sure how to interpret it. "I don't deserve for you to say yes, but would it be okay if I called or wrote to you now?"

She pulled her hand from his and reached to start the engine. "We would all love to hear from you, Ezra. Like I said, I'm at the farm now. You can find me there."

"Thank you." He closed the door, then leaned down to peer through the window. "I'll be in touch, I promise."

She nodded and put the truck in gear. The drive home was a tempestuous one as Hattie's emotions bounded back and forth between anger and hurt and happiness and confusion and. . . not love. Nope. Not love.

It was the first Sunday in December. Wallace had felt unusually well that morning, so they had driven into town for church, then made a quick visit to the children at the orphanage. After that, they had all come home and spent a lazy afternoon relaxing. Now, Hattie was curled in a chair in Wallace's living room, reading a book. Livy and Wallace were seated near the radio, ready to listen to their usual Sunday evening programs. They got comfortable as the signature music announcing the beginning of Eleanor Roosevelt's weekly program filled the air. And then the world changed.

"Good evening, ladies and gentlemen." The first lady cleared her throat. "I am speaking to you tonight at a very serious moment in our history. The Cabinet is convening, and the leaders in Congress are meeting with the president."

Hattie looked up from her book. The first lady sounded strange. Livy sat forward, frowning. Wallace held up a hand to keep them from speaking.

"The state department and army and navy officials have been with the president all afternoon. In fact, the Japanese ambassador was talking to the president at the very time that Japan's airships were bombing our citizens in Hawaii and the Philippines and sinking one of our transports loaded with lumber on its way to Hawaii. By tomorrow morning, the members of Congress will have a full report, and be ready for action. In the meantime, we the people are already prepared for action."

They listened to the rest of the broadcast in stunned silence, mouths open and fear on their faces. The first lady's voice, however, was firm and confident as she finished her address: "We are the free and unconquerable people of the United States of America. To the young people of the nation, I must speak a word tonight. You are going to have a great opportunity. There will be high moments in which your strength and your ability will be tested. I have faith in you. I feel as though I was standing upon a rock. That rock is my faith in my fellow citizens. Now, we will go back to the program which we had arranged for tonight."

Whatever programming followed fell on deaf ears. The three of them looked at each other in silence as they digested the first lady's message. Hattie was the first to speak.

"The Japanese bombed *us*? But how? I mean—" She stopped, shaking her head.

"Hawaii isn't that far from Japan, and they've got troops on the ocean just like the allies do." Wallace scratched his chin. "How they got all the way through to Hawaii, though. . . that's beyond me."

"Wallace." Livy was hesitant. "There have already been rumors that the Citadel cadets could be inducted into the armed forces and be sent overseas if we join the war. I've heard training is at an all-time high—like they're preparing them. I thought it was just talk, but now I'm really worried. What if Ezra is called up?"

Hattie didn't move. She'd been worrying about this too. It had been almost three weeks since she and Ezra had met in town and he still hadn't called or written her, but she'd been listening to the news and talking to the reporters at work. Details about a recent Jewish uprising in Warsaw had been especially worrisome. Ezra was at the Citadel—of course there was a possibility of him going to war. She knew that, but her heart could not wrap itself around the added fact that he was Jewish and the whole other dimension that added to the situation.

When she tuned back in to the discussion in the room, Wallace was speaking. "I know," he said. "I'm concerned about him too. As difficult as it is to understand, though, I'm convinced that Ezra is right where he should be. All we can do is pray that he will be safe, and this war will end. We won't always understand the whys, but we can trust that God is workin' within every soul involved in this catastrophe."

On the radio, a comedy show began, as if this were any old Sunday. Wallace reached over and turned it off. "All I know is we must pray for our leaders and our allies. And for the souls of every man, woman, and child who is lost. We are fightin' for the survival of God's own people—and for that, we must let Ezra go."

He looked over at Hattie, compassion on his face. She had told him about their meeting. "But only for a time, my child. There is a place for everythin'. . . . a time for everythin'. Not always by our will, but always within the will and grace of a good and just God."

Americans spent the next day glued to the radio as reports filtered in. Somber voices recounted the nature of the casualties and the catastrophic damages incurred, both in Hawaii and on the island of Manila. Other islands, too, had been attacked. The number of dead continued to rise. By the time the president addressed a joint session of Congress—and the nation, via live broadcast—everyone knew war was inevitable. Still, they gathered around their radios as the president prepared to speak.

Wallace's house was no exception. Clarence and his family joined the three of them in the living room at 12:30 that afternoon. Even the children stood in silence as the broadcast began.

"Yesterday, December 7th, 1941—a date which will live in infamy—the United States of America was suddenly and deliberately attacked by naval and air forces of the Empire of Japan. The United States was at peace with that nation and, at the solicitation of Japan, was still in conversation with its government and its emperor looking toward the maintenance of peace in the Pacific."

Hattie listened as President Roosevelt pressed on, outlining the events of the day before. Her heart pounded in her chest, in her ears, almost drowning out the sound of his voice.

". . . There is no blinking at the fact that our people, our territory, and our interests are in grave danger. With confidence in our armed forces, with the unbounding determination of our people, we will gain the inevitable triumph—so help us God." He paused for a moment as applause broke out in the chamber. Then he spoke the words she had been dreading. "I ask that the Congress declare that since the unprovoked and dastardly attack by Japan on Sunday, December 7th, 1941, a state of war has existed between the United States and the Japanese empire." The raucous applause that followed seemed out of place to Hattie, and as the broadcast ended, she stumbled from the living room.

Late that afternoon, the sound of an engine in the driveway caught her attention. It didn't sound like the truck. Wallace had retired to his bedroom, his body overcome with aches and pains. Hattie had seated herself beside his bed and was reading aloud from the Psalms to comfort him. They both looked up when they heard a knock on the front door. Within minutes, Livy was ushering a uniform-clad Ezra into the room.

Reveille had sounded at 6:15 that morning, just as it always did. Ezra, however, had been awake for hours. Japan's actions the previous day had solidified the convictions that had been hounding him for weeks. He arose quietly and readied himself for the day. Around him, everyone was somber, sober, and serious. If they were anxious or afraid, the men around him hid those feelings well. Ezra was not afraid. He was resolute. He would speak to his superiors today, and when the semester ended, he would leave the Citadel to join the army. He might have better prospects in the navy or the marines because of his training here, but Ezra wanted his feet on the ground where his people were. It seemed the army would give him the best chance for that.

The schedule that day was shortened. The brass were all in meetings. The cadets gathered together at lunchtime and listened to President Roosevelt address the nation. As the address came to an end, speculation began around him. He was startled, however, to hear his name called out loudly.

"Wolfe!" He turned to see his immediate superior in the doorway. The man motioned for him to come, and Ezra did so with alacrity.

"Sir?" His salute was ready and properly executed.

"General Summerall has asked me to escort you to his office. Now."

"General Sum—Yessir!" Heart pounding, Ezra followed the lieutenant to the office of the Citadel's president. After appropriate introduction and salutes, the officer left and General Summerall motioned for Ezra to take a seat before his desk. The general wasted no time on niceties.

"Wolfe. I hear you're German."

"I was born in Germany, yessir. My mother was an American."

"You're also Jewish?"

"Yessir."

"You speak German?"

"I lived in Germany the first sixteen years of my life, sir."

"And you know the country and its people."

"Yessir."

"I've been reviewing your records and speaking with your superiors. You appear to be a loyal citizen of the United States, a good and dedicated student, and an honorable and trustworthy cadet. I, uh, I also knew your family, and I know the sacrifices they made, both your mother and your father." The general stopped, cleared his throat, and looked Ezra over for a moment, as if taking his measure and making a decision. With a brisk nod, he continued.

"The United States of America has a job for you, son."

The hour that followed was beyond anything Ezra had imagined. It was jarring but fulfilling. Terrifying but exciting. An end and a beginning. His time at the Citadel was officially over. His time as an authorized representative of the United States government was about to begin. There were moments he could hardly breathe.

And as soon as he was free, he borrowed a car from a friend and drove out to Wallace's farm.

Livy met him at the door. Tears filled her eyes, and she hugged him as if his unexplained absence had never happened.

"Ezra," she said. "We've been worried about you."

He acknowledged her concern with a nod. "I'm sorry," he said. "I know I should have come around."

She shook her head. "No. You were doing what needed to be done." His heart swelled at her generous response.

"May I see Wallace?"

Her gaze flickered. "He's not well today," she responded. "He's in bed, but I'll take you to him."

His heart sank as he followed her into what was obviously a sickroom, not just the bedroom of a man he admired.

Hattie stood as he entered, almost dropping the Bible she'd been reading from. Wallace sat up straight and began to swing his legs to the side of the bed. A fit of coughing overtook him, and he lay back against the pillows. Hattie grabbed a tube of salve from the bedside table. Ezra stepped forward and took it from her.

"May I?" he asked. "I'd like to talk to Wallace for a while."

Hattie opened her mouth to protest, but Livy moved closer and put an arm around her. "Let them talk, Hattie," she murmured. "We'll be in the living room, Ezra, when you're finished. We'd like to see you too, if you have time."

Hattie allowed herself to be led from the room, but Ezra would not soon forget the look in her eyes as Livy closed the door between them. *Now is not the time*, he told himself sternly. Then he turned to the old man he so admired.

"Well, look at you, mister military man!" Wallace held out his hand and, as Ezra took it, pulled him to his chest. "We are all so proud of you." After a long embrace, Ezra took a seat in the chair Hattie had been using. Wallace continued to look him over, eyes shining.

"Mmm *mmm*," he said, almost crowing. "Just look at you now— you are a fine young man with a world of responsibilities. But what brings you here tonight?"

Ezra took a deep breath, then looked Wallace straight in the eyes. "I'm leaving the Citadel. I have orders to report to Washington on Monday next."

"Before the end of the semester?"

"Yes. My family history has been brought to the attention of. . . a certain agency. I am not at liberty to say anything more."

Wallace nodded gravely. "I have wondered how you would fare in this new world," he said.

Ezra opened his mouth, then closed it. He did it again, then shook his head.

Wallace looked at him quizzically. "What?"

Words burst forth in a rush. "I'm honored, but at the same time, I'm torn. I don't really want to go, Wallace. I know I have to. I can't *not* go. I have to, for this country and for my family. But I don't want to fight this war. My whole life has been about obligation and hon- or and tradition. And that's fine, but this—this is war. And I don't want to die. When do I get to live my life?" Heat flooded his cheeks. What kind of man was he, that he would admit something like that? "I mean, what's happening over there isn't right. I know that. And I have family who have disappeared or died because of it. I know others who are caught in the thick of it. Many of my friends from growing up are on the other side of this. I know where I stand, but it isn't easy. I don't know if I—" He caught his breath. "I don't know if I can do this. Or if I even *want* to." He was afraid to look up, but Wal- lace reached over and lifted his chin. And he didn't look a bit upset.

"Ahh, my brave military man. I don't think anyone wakes up in the morning *wantin'* to go to war, but throughout history we've fought so many wars, on the home front and abroad. We can discuss all day whether it's right or wrong; we can make our own opinions on it, but it doesn't change anythin'. Only God knows our hearts and the reasons we do the things we do. But there is a time and a place for war, just as there is a time and a place for peace. Your own Scriptures say so." He patted the worn black Bible that lay beside him on the bed. "Read Ecclesiastes chapter 3. And you know what? There's even a time for tradition and obligation. God doesn't leave anythin' out. There's a time and a season for *every activity* under heaven. That includes the good and the bad."

"Yessir, I know." But still, he struggled.

Wallace looked at him wisely. "God will bring judgment on both the righteous and the wicked. Your job is to play your part in the unknown, Ezra. To be honorable. To be faithful. And to trust that this, too, shall pass." Then he smiled. "And when it does—because it will—when you have done God's work for your people, you'll come back home to us. That's how I see it, boy. You were meant for greater things than what you can do in the here and now. You will fulfill your purpose, and God will do great things through you. He's not anywhere near finished with you. He will give you the strength, the resolve you need."

"Yessir."

But Wallace wasn't done. "You come back to our girl, too."

Ezra gave a half-laugh, a rueful look on his face. "She doesn't want me, Wallace. I don't know what I was thinking, but I left her too long."

Wallace shook his head wisely. "No, son. You have things to work out, but she loves you very much. There's a will not our own at work here, but just because the timin' is off, it shouldn't lessen or hinder the love that you share."

"I do love her, Wallace. I don't have any right to, but I want to ask her to wait for me. I don't know how long I'll be gone, but I know one thing. If she'll have me, she's the reason I'll come home."

"Well, if that's true, it's time to talk. If you love her, tell her. Don't let the questions fester any longer or the bitter root will take hold. She has been waitin' for you this whole time, waitin' for you to reach out to her. When the timin' is right, God'll bring you back together."

"Yessir. I hope you're right, sir."

"Oh, I am," Wallace said confidently. "Now, go open that door, and let's call them ladies back in here. We'll be careful what we say, but they've been missin' you something awful."

They visited for a good hour, recounting what had happened since they'd seen each other last—Ezra's accomplishments as a student, Livy's leaving the orphanage and joining Clarence in managing this estate, Hattie's graduation from high school with honors, and her triumphant completion of Wallace's story. Finally, Ezra explained he'd been called to service and would be leaving the Citadel earlier than planned. With Wallace's help, he managed to deflect the questions he could not answer.

The grandfather clock in the living room chimed the six o'clock hour, and Ezra stood reluctantly and announced he had to leave. "I've got to get back before curfew, or I won't even have a chance to enlist," he joked.

Livy scribbled something on a piece of paper that she pressed into his hand. Then she gave him another hug. "Here's our address and some stamps. Now that you've been back, you'd better write to us, young man," she admonished. "You let us know where you are. And if there's ever any way we can help you, speak up."

"I will," he replied.

Wallace reached up and took his hand. "Do not be afraid, son," he said. "Be wise. Learn all you can before you go. Trust your trainin' and your instincts, and most importantly, trust your God. He will not let you down." Then he reached out to Livy who stood at the other side of the bed. "Let's pray."

Ezra reached out his free hand to Hattie, who took it, then reached her free hand across the bed to Livy. The old man nodded in approval.

"A circle tightly woven will not be undone," Wallace said. He raised his eyes to the heavens. "Our hearts are joined as one before You, Lord. You know the fears and the worry, the hopes and regrets we bear. We put them before You now, and we trust You to bring us back together. You know the days of our lives; You've counted all our moments. Whether here on earth or with You in glory, we know we will meet again. Bind us together in Your love and Your strength and Your mercy. Bring an end to the evil we face. Carry us forth, from this day forward, as soldiers in Your army, even as Ezra leaves us as a soldier for our great land. Protect us, protect him, and bring him home again. We know You are able, our great God. Amen."

A quiet chorus of amens followed as the women wiped surreptitious tears. Wallace lay back in the bed, his eyes still closed, the stress and weariness of the day written on his face. It was time to go.

Ezra had kept Hattie's hand in his, and now he squeezed it gently. She looked up at him, and the beauty in her face caught at his heart.

"Walk me to the car?" he asked. She nodded and led the way. At the door, he turned back. "Thank you, Wallace," he said. "For everything."

The old man nodded. "You'll be fine, my boy. Go with God."

Hand in hand, Ezra and Hattie walked out to his borrowed car. She was struggling to contain her tears, and Ezra couldn't blame her.

"When do you leave?" she asked.

"Umm, before Christmas," he said vaguely. "I don't know where they'll send me, but I'll have several weeks of, uh, basic training, you know. After that. . ." He shrugged. "I don't know."

"Will you be back to see us before you go?"

"If I can. I don't know."

"I don't know how much longer Wallace will be with us. His doctor says one more bad bout with pneumonia or if he gets the flu—" Hattie's voice shook as she spoke the dreadful words. "We're trying to keep him here and inside as much as possible, but he's pretty determined to get out when he can. We went to town yesterday, but then with the news and all the stress from today, he's just wiped out again. If you can come back, you should."

He was silent, standing beside the car, her hand still in his.

"Or you should write, at least." A sob caught the last word.

He turned and held out his other hand. She turned at the same moment and stepped into his arms. They closed around her with neither permission nor protest. For a long time, they held each other. The contact brought Ezra bittersweet memories. Why *had* he stayed away? He'd been busy, then he'd found new friends. It'd been easy to pretend he was too grown-up for her. Or had he avoided her because of all the grown-up things she made him feel? He didn't know. But being with her now left him without a doubt. He loved her. He did.

"I'm sorry, Hattie." He squeezed her tightly, then stepped back. "I have to go, but I'll be back. Somehow, someday, I'll be back. And I have the address now. I'll write. I promise."

Chapter 36

Casting all your care upon him;
for he careth for you.
1 PETER 5:7

The weeks passed quickly. Christmas 1941 was different from any other Hattie had experienced. It was her first in many years outside the orphanage, though she and Livy visited and took gifts to the children, but it was different for other reasons too. Wallace's strength was low, and through concern that he'd catch the flu or some other bug from the children, the women insisted he stay home. Instead, he spoke to the children on the telephone.

The atmosphere in town had changed. Always a military town, Charleston was experiencing a level of patriotism it had not seen before. Scores of men, young and old, had enlisted and were heading off to do their duty as American citizens in a great war against the evil of the Axis countries. Women were looking for ways they, too, could serve their country.

As the new year came and went, life settled into new norms, and Hattie's heart was full. Her boss and several of the reporters at the *Charleston Daily Mail* had enlisted, and she now found herself a full-time beat reporter. This gave her quick access to both reports and rumors from the war. It was exciting and exhausting and, oftentimes, frightening. She kept her eyes on Ezra's class at the Citadel. He was gone, but they were still there. That was a bit of a puzzle, so she kept her eyes open for anything that might give her a clue as to his whereabouts or activities.

She arrived home one day in early February to find a stack of mail on the table beside the door in Wallace's home. Her name was neatly typed on the top envelope. The name of a leading publisher announced itself from the corner. She snatched it up, hope warring with caution inside her heart. She'd already experienced one rejection. She bit her lip, weighing her chances with this one. Then another envelope caught her eye. Thin paper. Official postmarks. Her name. Ezra's handwriting.

Finally!

She caught both letters to her pounding heart, debating whether to run to her room to read them in peace or to share them with the others. The decision was made when Livy stuck her head around the corner.

"There you are! We've been waiting for you. We've got a letter from Ezra! Come, see."

Hattie glanced down at the letter in her hand. It was unopened. Maybe he'd sent another? She slipped out of her coat, hung it on the rack, and kicked her shoes to the rug. Then she followed Livy into the living room.

"Ah, our lovely newspaper woman," Wallace greeted her cheerily from his favorite spot near the fireplace. "Look what I've got!" He waved a couple sheets of onionskin paper in the air. "Our boy was finally free to write. I'd like to say we waited till you got home to read it, but. . . we didn't." He grinned as he handed her the missive. "Read it aloud."

She tucked her own letters inside her handbag, then perched next to her friend on the overstuffed sofa.

Dearest family,

Oh, how I wish I could spend this day with you on the riverbank, enjoying the sunshine and some nice home cooking. As you can see from the post-mark, they've got me here in Virginia. Let me tell you, February is not nearly as nice here as it would be in Charleston.

Days here are long and full of training, but I won't bore you with details. I've been up to my eyes in work—I thought the Citadel kept me busy. Ha!

Our world is so different now. I still don't know where I'll be going or what part I'm to play. All I do know is, it will be somewhere far from you.

I have something important to ask. I've been given a 48-hour leave to take care of family and Citadel business before I ship out. I'll be back in Charleston on the 20th of February. They're planning a parade on the 21st to honor the new servicemen shipping out. Since I'll be there, my superiors are letting me join them in formation. I would very much like for all of you to be there as I march with my brothers-in-arms to the train station.

Wallace, I hope you're feeling better. I know you've been in touch with my father over the years. Since I left, his health has declined. Would it be too much to ask if you all could bring him to the parade as well? I'm required to be at the Citadel that day, so I won't be able to do it. Plus, I'd love for Hattie and Livy to meet him. I so hope to see all of you before I leave. Please come if you can.

Yours, Ezra"

Hattie looked up from the letter and over to the calendar hanging on the wall beside her desk.

"The twenty-first?" she said. "That's next weekend! Do you think he'll come here?"

"I don't think so," Livy said. "It sounds like he's got a lot to do and not much time to do it in."

Wallace nodded. "We can make sure his father gets to the parade though. That won't be a problem. I've already spoken to him on the telephone."

"You know where he lives?"

"Yep. Been there a few times. The parade might go right past the house, actually. Well, no, not from the school to the train station. . ." His voice trailed off. When he didn't say more, Hattie looked at him carefully.

"Wallace? You feeling okay?"

"I'm fine. Just a mite tired today, that's all."

Livy's lips quirked downward a bit as she looked at him, then she turned to smile at Hattie. "I saw another envelope in the mail. From a publisher?"

"I haven't opened it yet." Carefully, she pulled the letter from her handbag, leaving the one from Ezra untouched. She'd read that one in private.

Wallace's eyes brightened. "Open it, girl, open it!"

Hattie grinned and slid her finger under the flap. She pulled several sheets of heavy stationery from the envelope and unfolded them carefully. Then she let her eyes skim the top page. The letter was short, but her heart raced as she read aloud.

> Dear Miss Whitfield:
>
> We have read your manuscript and find it fascinating. We would like to discuss with you the possibility of our publishing your story. We understand that it

is an account of true events of historical importance. We have included in this packet some information and forms that you will need to complete before we meet.

There was more, but she had to stop to catch her breath. Livy crossed the room and threw her arms around her in a hug, while Wallace reached out for her hand.

"We did it, girl!" he crowed. "*You* did it! Yes, indeedy, you did it."

"Well, they just want to talk. It's not a contract or anything," Hattie demurred.

"Maybe not yet," Wallace said. "But it will be. Yessuh, it will be!"

<hr />

By the time Hattie got to her room that evening, she'd almost forgotten about the other letter waiting to be read. Almost, but not quite. She laid the letter on her nightstand, then made herself finish her evening routine. She changed into her nightclothes, washed her face, chose her outfit for the next day, and read a selection from her Bible. All the while, excitement bubbled within her. Finally, she could wait no longer.

Leaving only a small bedside lamp on, she climbed into bed, propped herself against the pillows, and reached over to pick up the envelope. Oh! She hadn't noticed it this afternoon, but it smelled like him. Was it her imagination? No, that was definitely Old Spice. She sniffed the envelope appreciatively as she sliced it open.

He really did have nice handwriting.

She pulled up her knees and smoothed the pages over them.

My dearest Hattie,

Seeing you again in December was such a strange thing. Wonderful but confusing. I can't tell you why I stayed away so long. I don't really know. My life of tradition and obligation would seem so restrictive for someone like you. You are a butterfly I wanted to set free because, my sweetest Hattie, you were meant to fly and do the greatest of things. I didn't want to burden you with my life.

I loved you then, but who was I to think that someone as amazing as you would even want someone like me? I might have stayed away, but I've missed you every day since I left. And now. . . I find I love you more.

There isn't much time here for longing or for remembering, but still, I find myself doing it. I have been missing home in the most unimaginable way. And you. This last week, especially, I've been fighting this feeling. I wake up having had only a few hours of sleep, and all I can think about is all the time I wasted trying to forget you while I was at the Citadel. Oh, Hattie. I thought I was doing the right thing, but I wasn't.

The sun is coming up soon. I look out of my window waiting for it because, in some way, it makes me feel closer to you. The world has changed, and so have I. I understand now where I belong. I'm shipping out very soon and I don't know where I'm going, but I do know this. I want to sit beside you at the river again just like we did not so long ago. That memory of us will be what keeps me warm at night, wherever strange place it is I lay my head.

I don't deserve you, my beautiful girl, but I hope you'll wait for me. I want to come home to your arms after all this war is over.

He'd signed the letter with love and a flourish of *X*s and *O*s. She wasn't quite sure what to think. She didn't understand his ever wanting to forget her or wanting to set her free. She hadn't tried to lay any claims on him when they were kids. Theirs had been a simple love. They'd been but children.

Of course, there hadn't been anything childish about the way she'd felt when she'd seen him in December either, and he had apologized—then and now. And he'd said he loved her. Maybe she didn't need to understand everything. She couldn't help the thrill that went through her as she reread the letter. She folded the pages thoughtfully.

The scent of his cologne wafted over her again, and she held the letter close as she snuggled deep into her bed. She'd see him next weekend. Maybe they'd have time to talk. Meanwhile, she'd have to think up an answer to his letter. She drifted off to sleep, a smile on her lips.

Chapter 37

Blessed are they that mourn,
for they shall be comforted.
MATTHEW 5:4

On Wednesday, February 18, Wallace could resist the early call of spring no longer. The sun was shining, birds were singing, and the camellias had opened their faces wide to the sky. While Livy and Clarence took care of the business of the day, Wallace donned a light jacket, gathered a few things, and went out for a walk by the river. He could hear the whispers in the tall grass and budding trees, and soon he paid the day and time no mind.

Livy returned to the house at noon to find him nowhere around. She waited awhile, sure he would show up for lunch. At 12:30, she walked down to the manor house and back but didn't find him. Truly worried then, she called for Clarence. Together, they set out to look for him.

They found him on the ground between Ida and Bessany's graves, a bouquet of wilted spring flowers in one hand and a white lace dress in the other. He was shivering violently, feverish with a bluish tinge around his lips. They picked him up and got him back to the house, but the damage had been done. The pneumonia that had plagued him over the years was back with a vengeance.

Hattie arrived home from work just as Wallace's doctor was driving away. The sight of his car sent a bolt of fear through her being. She jerked the truck to a stop, pulled on the parking brake, and ran inside. One look at Livy's tearstained face, and Hattie knew.

"Is he okay? What happened?"

"He went for a walk. Lost track of time or maybe passed out, we don't know for sure. We found him on the ground, wet from the dew and shivering. He must have been there for hours. He says he went out about ten. We didn't find him till almost one."

Hattie dropped her things and tossed her coat to a chair. Livy stopped her with a hand on her arm.

"It's not good, honey. He's really sick. He's awake, though, and he's wanting to see you."

Hattie swallowed hard and stepped through the doorway to Wallace's room. He looked asleep, but at her soft footfall, his eyes flew open.

"Child, you're home," he breathed.

"Wallace!" She dropped to her knees beside the bed. She couldn't stop the tears as he reached out and brushed back her hair with an unsteady hand. She caught that hand in both of hers and kissed it.

"Oh, Wallace, you were doing so well."

"I was, wasn't I?" He coughed, and she reached for a cloth beside the bed. "It was so pretty today, I thought I could go for a walk." His voice was so weak, she could barely hear him.

"It's okay, child. I'm not afraid." But the words struck fear in her heart.

"Afraid? You don't need to be afraid anyway. The doctor was here. You'll be better in no time—"

"I'll be better by the weekend," he agreed. "Ezra will be here." His hand fell to the coverlet and he closed his eyes.

After a minute, Hattie shifted, thinking he was asleep. She stood, moved the chair closer to the bed, and sat down. The late afternoon sun shone through the window, lighting the dust in the air, forming a cocoon around them. She looked up to find Livy in the doorway. Their eyes met and their hearts mourned.

Wallace took a labored breath, and Hattie caressed his forehead. His eyes fluttered open and he opened his mouth to speak but only a whisper emerged. He shook his head slightly, cleared his throat, and once again, he spoke in his powerful voice.

"Delight thyself in the Lord, sweet child, and He shall give thee the desires of thine heart. . . . Commit thy way unto the Lord; trust. . . in Him. He shall bring it to pass."

Hattie knew these words well; they were from Psalm 37, one of Wallace's favorite passages. She leaned close again and joined her voice with his as he continued. "And He shall bring forth thy righteousness as the light, and thy judgment as the noon day."

He paused to catch his breath, then he reached out his hand to her face. "Our cause. . . yours and mine, sweet Hattie. . . like the noonday sun." His finger traced the line of her scar. "Let it all go, my love. Let it all go, and your blessings will come."

Blessings, indeed.

Saturday morning, the house was in an uproar. It was the day of Ezra's parade, and Wallace was determined to go. Livy was just as determined to keep him at home. He sat on the side of his bed, winded but not backing down. And his window was open again!

With a huff, she stormed into the room. As she reached to pull the window to the frame, something strange caught her eye. The fields were moving with the wind, and the trees swayed as a breeze lifted the moss and danced it around the branches of the ancient oaks. Everything appeared to be in motion, but not just any motion. It was as if it were all dancing in unison, a partnered waltz of nature. She paused to watch.

Wallace's voice came from behind her. "Keep it open, please. It's warm today. They're callin' for me, and I want to hear them."

She sighed and left the window open part way. "I don't know if there's a storm coming or what, but it's pretty breezy out there. Seems kind of strange, it being so warm and not a cloud in the sky."

"Perfect day for a parade, if you ask me," Wallace said smugly. And promptly broke into a violent coughing spasm.

Livy's exasperation boiled over. "Wallace! Just look at yourself, will you? You can barely walk from here to the bathroom, and you want to go to a parade?"

"I don't care what you say, Livy. I'm goin'!" Wallace's voice was downright belligerent as he struggled to his feet and reached for his shirt.

"No!" She yanked the shirt away. "Wallace, we all want you there, but you are still sick. I don't think you can afford to take that chance."

Hattie stuck her head in the doorway. "What is going on in here?" she asked. "I could hear you two outside!"

"Wallace is determined to go—"

"I'm goin' to town with you—"

They spoke at the same time, their frustration obvious.

"Oh. Umm. Look, I understand, Livy, but. . ." She shook her head. "I think he should go."

"Well, at least someone around here has some sense," Wallace growled.

Livy's mouth dropped open. Her hands went to her hips and she looked at Hattie in disbelief. "Are you crazy? He can hardly make it from here to there and—" She looked back and forth between them. The expression on Hattie's face brought her to a stop. "Well, I guess everyone has lost their minds then. Okay. C'mon, old man. Let's get you dressed."

"Yessuh. So much love in this room, so *much* love." Wallace buried a cough in his handkerchief, then grinned at Livy. She couldn't help but smile back.

They walked Wallace outside and put him safely in Clarence's car. He fussed while they wrapped a blanket over his shoulders and another across his legs.

"You two are a bunch of old hens," he protested. "It's 'most seventy degrees, and you're actin' like it's gonna snow."

"It's not that warm, and you know it," Livy replied. "Keep them on. We'll be right back."

She and Hattie placed two chairs in the back of the car and went in to gather their own jackets. She was almost in tears as she went, muttering to herself.

Hattie stopped her in the hallway. "I know it makes more sense to keep him home, Liv, but I–I just have a feeling about this. I know he's sick, but we need to let him go." She began to cry. "I just. . . I just. . . Livy, Ezra needs to see him. We *all* need this. Trust me, it's for all of us. I don't know how much longer Wallace has, but to take this from him when Ezra is leaving to go God knows where—" She couldn't speak anymore.

With a sob of her own, Livy wrapped her arms around her and for a moment, every emotion they'd been holding back to be strong for each other came pouring out.

Maybe Hattie was right. Maybe they needed this just as much as Wallace did.

Ezra's heart was heavy. He'd arrived later than expected last night and had spent the evening with his father, who'd told him of Wallace's grave illness. He'd been hoping for time to run out to the estate, but that wasn't going to happen. They might have called this a leave, but obligation still ruled.

He'd risen with the dawn, as the sunrise touched the misty sea, visible from his father's windows. He'd dressed himself in his crisply pressed uniform and packed a remaining few things into his bag. Lastly, he'd picked up the Bible Wallace had given him that last day at the train station. It had caused his father some concern, but it had brought Ezra great comfort, especially in the last few months. It was time to head to the school.

The Citadel had become more than an education for him; it had introduced him to his destiny. He thought about the irony of the fear that now mixed with excitement. Being at the Citadel, he'd always known a soldier's road was the one he would travel, but with recent training, the direction of that path had changed. Regardless, he would take up his armor and his sword and immerse himself in God's will.

Wallace had taught him well.

Ezra looked at his reflection in the mirror and he was happy with what he saw. He was a man of God now, and he would stand tall in his calling.

He marched in rank with his brothers, through town to the Charleston station. Full honors accompanied them as they went. Boys who would become men and men who would become American heroes proudly strode behind the Citadel's marching band. What trials that lay ahead, they had only vague knowledge of, but they stood tall in their brave fortitude.

Charleston had come out in full force, it seemed. Crowds lined the street and roared with favor as they marched past. Girls he had known called his name, but he heard them not. He was looking for one girl only.

He searched for her along the way. His beautiful impossibility, his weakness. . . his love. Where was she? He knew she'd still been planning to come. She'd promised his father to be sure he made it as well, even if Wallace couldn't. Finally, he spotted them at the end of the street. His father, and yes, Wallace. Both were seated in chairs at the side of the road, Livy and Hattie standing behind them.

Marching as he was in formation, he couldn't physically acknowledge them, but once he'd seen them, he didn't look away. Wallace was the first to react, to point him out. As Ezra drew near, Wallace struggled to his feet. Beside him, his father did the same. Two old men, paying homage to the young.

The one who had given him life and the one who had taught him to live.

Wallace swayed as he stood, but brushed away Livy's arm, refusing her assistance As the regiment passed, he saluted and nodded his affirmation. Ezra's eyes burned. Still in formation, he turned the corner. He could see them no longer. They reached the station and at the command, stopped. They stood still, stiff, until they heard an "at ease!"

At the same moment, he heard her voice. He turned to see Hattie running toward him through the crowd. All around them, women—mothers, sisters, girlfriends, wives—were clamoring for attention, for one last touch, one kiss, a final goodbye.

She pushed her way past the last few people between them, and he caught her in his arms. For a moment, neither of them moved or spoke. Then he leaned back and looked down into her beautiful eyes. They reached deep into his soul, just as they had done that first day they met.

Everything and nothing had changed.

She raised her arms and wrapped them around his neck. He drew her closer, and then put his lips on hers.

The conductor began calling for them to board. She dropped her head to his chest and he closed his eyes. They stood for a moment, maybe longer, till the movement of the crowd pulled them apart.

"You'd better come back to me," she said fiercely.

The final call came, and around them, men surged toward the train. He kept hold of her hand as long as he could, but he couldn't resist the force of the crowd.

As their contact broke, he found his voice. "Hattie Whitfield, you're a beautiful mess, you know that? I love you! Wait for me—I'm coming back! I promise you!"

And with that, he was swept into the gleaming body of the train.

Chapter 38

For to me to live is Christ, and to die is gain.
PHILIPPIANS 1:21

Hattie sat next to Wallace that very same night with her writing pad. She was distracted, Wallace could tell. Whatever she was writing was not coming to her easily. Finally, she gave a heavy sigh and tossed her pen to the table.

The day had taken a bigger toll than he wanted to admit, but there was something he needed to say before time ran out. He gathered his strength and boosted himself up on one elbow. Then he reached for her hand and wrapped his around hers. He looked at her so intently that she stopped breathing for a moment. When he spoke, his voice was barely above a whisper.

"You have greatness in you, Hattie. Don't just write the words. Believe in them and then write them down. You have such passion for good, my sweet child." He closed his eyes briefly, then continued.

"Believe that in all things, there is a greater good, a purpose. . . . What greater gift is there than to love and to forgive the sins of the past? What greater gift is there. . . than to know. . . we have a just God who will right all paths? Let the fruit of the Spirit lead you, child, and know that no matter where you are. . . I will be there too." He squeezed her hands, then let them go. "Now, write."

"I'm trying, Wallace. It's just *today*. And. . . I don't know." She sighed.

Livy stepped into the room, carrying a tray of medicines. Wallace's heart swelled as he surveyed the two beautiful women he loved. God had blessed him so richly. He sighed with satisfaction.

"Yessuh, now you're both here. Good. Livy, my girl, sit next to me." He patted the far side of the bed.

"I've got your med—"

"No. I want to talk first." She set the tray down and walked around to the other side. She perched gingerly beside him so she could look in his face, careful of his comfort.

He took her hand, then reached again for Hattie's. "I want to ask you both a question and I want you to really think about the answer." A cough interrupted him. When he could speak again, he looked first at one, then the other. Keeping a tight control on his throat, he pushed the words out in a rush.

"What would you do if you had the power in you to right the wrongs of the past?"

Livy reached across the bed for Hattie's other hand. Neither answered, they just waited for him to speak again, as if what he would reveal to them would have the power to change everything.

The curtains in the room danced to the weight of the breeze flowing in from the fields outside. All of nature seemed to pause, to listen. A blessing was about to happen.

Wallace closed his eyes in a quick prayer. He knew what God would have him to say. He just needed the strength to say it.

"When William came back from the war a changed man, he asked Ned to baptize him in the Ashley River. God makes no mistakes. You see, God worked a miracle between two men that day. Not only for William's redemption, but for Ned's as well. Yessuh." His breath came quicker, shallower. "What did Jesus say after He was nailed to the cross by his enemies? He said, 'Father, forgive them; for they know not what they do.' Forgiveness, yessuh. Ned was cleansed of the bitter root. It washed away in the Ashley River, right along with William's sin."

He stopped. Hattie's eyes were wide as she watched him. Livy wiped tears from hers. He drew another shaky breath. "My story—the one you've written, Hattie, and the one you inherit, Livy—it's all about forgiveness. Forgive them as He forgives you. It's only through forgiveness that we can piece back the bricks that humanity tears apart. Only forgiveness gives us the power to right the wrongs done to us."

Hattie's breath caught on a sob, and he squeezed her hand close. He was almost finished. "If you can look your enemy in the eye an' forgive him, you have the power to change the world." He stopped again to catch his breath.

"I'm so tired," he murmured. Every word was more difficult to speak than the last. "Our Ezra today. . . he was so handsome in his uniform, wasn't he?"

Hattie reached over and kissed his cheek. "You don't need to talk anymore, Wallace. I understand. I'll read back through and make sure it's all clear in your book. It's your wish, right? *Wallace's Wish?*"

She understood. Wallace let himself relax as Livy tucked the blankets neatly around him. *She understood.* Relief made his next breath easier.

"*Wallace's Wish,*" he repeated. "Yessuh, I like it. 'Deed I do. Now, I'm just goin' to close my eyes for a bit and rest." He took a shallow breath. Suddenly, he sat forward.

"Livy, I see 'em! All of them, they're waitin' for me—do you hear 'em? They're singin'." His voice was filled with awe. "Sweetest. . . song. . . I've ever heard."

"Then it's time, Wallace." Livy's voice caught on a sob. "Go to them."

She kissed his hand and whispered goodbye in his ear. Tears soaked through his shirt as Hattie laid her head on his chest, but Wallace didn't know. He was already gone.

The soughing trees stood still as a wistful hush came over the fields. Just beyond, somewhere above the darkest Charleston sky, a single heavenly flame shone in the depths of the night as if to light the way. Wallace was home.

The End

A Purposed Path

Time expelled its sand, disbursed itself amongst the many.
They hid themselves within its likeness,
obscured themselves from His view.
Stubborn, they fastened their footing deeper
and welcomed its soft consume.
Yet still, their Creator would find them.
Regardless, His will would have its just due.

—Patty Mullins-Elson—

Acknowledgments†

There are not adequate words to express all that I hold in my heart for those who have helped me get to this point, but I will try. To the first person who called me an artist and to the editors without whose encouragement this story would have sat in my heart and not on these pages—I thank God for you. To Kim and Gail, who read my first draft and still pushed me to completion, thank you. To those who supported and encouraged me along the way, thank you. And to my children, Alex and Anna, my husband, Steve, and the rest of my family—this is what I've been working on all these years. I love you.

When I began writing this book, I knew I wanted to begin each chapter with scripture. I asked my friends to contribute their favorite Scriptures and promised I would pull from them as the chapters developed. I am so grateful for those who contributed; you are every bit a part of this story as I am because your chosen scriptures helped express what was in my heart. As promised, I am only including your initials here, but your names are in my heart.

I used the King James Version in the body of the story because that's what would have been available to the characters, but I wanted to include them as you gave them to me as well, so here they are, your contributions to *Dancing on Fields of Sorrow and Blessing*.

Between all of you, myself, and God, thank you from the bottom of my heart.

Patty Mullins-Elson

†The following scripture versions were used in this publication:

ESV—The English Standard Version.
ESV® Text Edition: 2016. Copyright © 2001 by Crossway Bibles, a publishing ministry of Good News Publishers.
ISV—The International Standard Version.
Copyright © 1995–2014 by ISV Foundation. All rights reserved internationally. Used by permission of Davidson Press, LLC.
KJV—The King James Version of the Bible. Public domain.
NET—The New English Translation. NET Bible® copyright ©1996-2017 by Biblical Studies Press, L.L.C. http://netbible.com All rights reserved.
NIV—The New International Version®, NIV® Copyright ©1973, 1978, 1984, 2011 by Biblica, Inc.® Used by permission. All rights reserved worldwide.
NKJV—The New King James Version®. Copyright © 1982 by Thomas Nelson. Used by permission. All rights reserved.
NLT—The New Living Translation, copyright © 1996, 2004, 2015 by Tyndale House Foundation. Used by permission of Tyndale House Publishers, Inc., Carol Stream, Illinois 60188. All rights reserved.

Prologue (AE, BCWS)
But those who hope in the LORD will renew their strength. They will soar on wings like eagles; they will run and not grow weary, they will walk and not be faint.

ISAIAH 40:31 NIV

Chapter 1 (LB)
And now these three remain: faith, hope and love. But the greatest of these is love.

1 CORINTHIANS 13:13 NIV

Chapter 2 (JW)
And we know that in all things God works for the good of those who love him, who have been called according to his purpose.

ROMANS 8:28 NIV

Chapter 3 (TM)
Be still before the LORD and wait patiently for him; do not fret when people succeed in their ways, when they carry out their wicked schemes.

PSALM 37:7 NIV

Chapter 4 (PE)
Delight yourself in the LORD, and he will give you the desires of your heart.

PSALM 37:4 ESV

Chapter 5 (GS)
Now faith is being sure of what we hope for, being convinced of what we do not see.

HEBREWS 11:1 NET

Chapter 6 (BK, KG, MT, SC)
So do not fear, for I am with you; do not be dismayed, for I am your God. I will strengthen you and help you; I will uphold you with my righteous right hand.

ISAIAH 41:10 NIV

Chapter 7 (LS, PE)
Be strong and courageous. Do not be afraid; do not be discouraged, for the LORD your God will be with you wherever you go.

JOSHUA 1:9 NIV

Chapter 8 (SE)

Commit to the LORD whatever you do, and he will establish your plans.

PROVERBS 16:3 NIV

Chapter 9 (CS, DD)

"For I know the plans I have for you," declares the LORD, "plans to prosper you and not to harm you, plans to give you hope and a future. Then you will call upon me and come and pray to me, and I will listen to you. You will seek me and find me when you seek me with all your heart. I will be found by you," declares the LORD, "and will bring you back from captivity."

JEREMIAH 29:11–14 NIV

Chapter 10 (JM)

Be strong and courageous. Do not be afraid or terrified because of them, for the LORD your God goes with you; he will never leave nor forsake you.

DEUTERONOMY 31:6 NIV

Chapter 11 (LWD, GKJ)

For you created my inmost being, you knit me together in my mother's womb. I praise you because I am fearfully and wonderfully made; your works are wonderful, I know that full well. My frame was not hidden from you when I was made in the secret place, when I was woven together in the depths of the earth. Your eyes saw my unformed body; all the days ordained for me were written in your book before one of them came to be. How precious to me are your thoughts, God! How vast is the sum of them! Were I to count them, they would outnumber the grains of sand—when I awake, I am still with you.

PSALM 139:13–18 NIV

Chapter 12 (TG)

For he has said, "I will never leave you and I will never abandon you."

HEBREWS 13:5 NET

Chapter 13 (DD)

For everything that was written in the past was written to teach us, so that through the endurance taught in the Scriptures and the encouragement they provide we might have hope.

ROMANS 15:4 NIV

Chapter 14 (CG)

Wait on the LORD; be of good courage, and He shall strengthen your heart; wait, I say on the LORD.

PSALM 27:14 NKJV

Chapter 15 (JA)

Even though I walk through the valley of the shadow of death, I will fear no evil, for you are with me; your rod and your staff, they comfort me.

PSALM 23:4 ESV

Chapter 16 (M&AM, DA)

For God so loved the world that he gave his one and only Son, that whoever believes in him shall not perish, but have eternal life.

JOHN 3:16 NIV

Chapter 17 (FM)

Being confident of this, that he who began a good work in you will carry it on to completion until the day of Christ Jesus.

PHILIPPIANS 1:6 NIV

Chapter 18 (AM)

Finally, be strong in the Lord and in his mighty power. Put on the full armor of God, so that you can take your stand against the devil's schemes. For our struggle is not against flesh and blood, but against the rulers, against the authorities, against the powers of this dark world and against the spiritual forces of evil in the heavenly realms. Therefore put on the full armor of God, so that when the day of evil comes, you may be able to stand your ground, and after you have done everything, to stand. Stand firm then, with the belt of truth buckled around your waist, with the breastplate of righteousness in place, and with your feet fitted with the readiness that comes from the gospel of peace. In addition to all this, take up the shield of faith, with which you can extinguish all the flaming arrows of the evil one. Take the helmet of salvation and the sword of the Spirit, which is the word of God. And pray in the Spirit on all occasions with all kinds of prayers and requests. With this in mind, be alert and always keep on praying for all the Lord's people.

EPHESIANS 6:10–18 NIV

Chapter 19 (EC)

Be still, and know that I am God.

PSALM 46:10 NIV

Chapter 20 (HC)

But he said to me, "My grace is sufficient for you, for my power is made perfect in weakness."

2 CORINTHIANS 12:9 NIV

Chapter 21 (SF)

Call to me and I will answer you and tell you great and unsearchable things that you do not know.

JEREMIAH 33:3 NIV

Chapter 22 (AB, MB)

For am convinced that neither death nor life, neither angels nor demons, neither the present nor the future, nor any powers, neither height nor depth, nor anything else in all creation, will be able to separate us from the love of God that is in Christ Jesus, our Lord.

ROMANS 8:38–39 NIV

Chapter 23 (RO)

"For my thoughts are not your thoughts, neither are your ways my ways," declares the LORD. "As the heavens are higher than the earth, so are my ways higher than your ways and my thoughts than your thoughts."

ISAIAH 55:8–9 NIV

Chapter 24 (JC)

Trust in the LORD with all your heart and lean not on your own understanding; in all your ways submit to him, and he will make your paths straight.

PROVERBS 3:5–6 NIV

Chapter 25 (KB, SW)

He has shown you, O mortal, what is good. And what does the LORD require of you? To act justly and to love mercy and to walk humbly with your God.

MICAH 6:8 NIV

Chapter 26 (AO)

The eternal God is your refuge, and underneath are the ever-lasting arms. He will drive out your enemies before you, saying, "Destroy them!"

DEUTERONOMY 33:27 NIV

Chapter 27 (BC)

Therefore, there is now no condemnation for those who are in Christ Jesus, because through Christ Jesus the law of the Spirit who gives life has set you free from the law of sin and death.

ROMANS 8:1–2 NIV

Chapter 28 (AE) (MD)

Do you not know that you are God's temple and that God's Spirit dwells in you? If anyone destroys God's temple, God will destroy him. For God's temple is holy, and you are that temple. . . . You are not your own, for you were bought with a price. So glorify God in your body.

1 CORINTHIANS 3:16–17, 6:19–20 ESV

Chapter 29 (KK)

For it is by grace you have been saved, through faith—and this is not from yourselves, it is the gift of God—not by works, so that no one can boast. For we are God's handiwork, created in Christ Jesus to do good works, which God prepared in advance for us to do.

EPHESIANS 2:8–10 NIV

Chapter 30 (PE)

Posterity will serve him; future generations will be told about the LORD. They will proclaim his righteousness, declaring to a people yet unborn: He has done it!

PSALM 22:30–31 NIV

Chapter 31 (CR)

The LORD is my shepherd, I shall not want.

PSALM 23:1 KJV

Chapter 32 (GTP)

Whom have I in heaven but you? And earth has nothing I desire besides you. My flesh and my heart may fail, but God is the strength of my heart and my portion forever.

PSALM 73:25–26 NIV

Chapter 33 (JMH)

Instruct the wise and they will be wiser still; teach the righteous and they will add to their learning. The fear of the LORD is the beginning of wisdom, and knowledge of the Holy One is understanding. For through wisdom your days will be many, and years will be added to your life.

PROVERBS 9:9–11 NIV

Chapter 34 (SW)

Surely your goodness and love will follow me all the days of my life, and I will dwell in the house of the Lord forever.

PSALM 23:6 NIV

Chapter 35 (LS)

For God did not give us a spirit of timidity, but one of power, love, and self-discipline.

2 TIMOTHY 1:7 ISV

Chapter 36 (LWD)

Cast all your anxiety on him because he cares for you.

1 PETER 5:7 NIV

Chapter 37 (CS)

"Blessed are the poor in spirit, for theirs is the kingdom of heaven. Blessed are those who mourn, for they will be comforted. Blessed are the meek, for they will inherit the earth. Blessed are those who hunger and thirst for righteousness, for they will be filled. Blessed are the merciful, for they will be shown mercy. Blessed are the pure in heart, for they will see God. Blessed are the peacemakers, for they will be called children of God. Blessed are those who are persecuted because of righteousness, for theirs is the kingdom of heaven. Blessed are you when people insult you, persecute you and falsely say all kinds of evil against you because of me."

MATTHEW 5:3–11 NIV

Chapter 38 (RO)

For to me, to live is Christ and to die is gain.

PHILIPPIANS 1:21 KJV

Extra Scriptures That Inspired Me

From JB:

A friend loves at all times, and a brother is born for adversity.

PROVERBS 17:17 ESV

From MB:

There is a time for everything, and a season for every activity under the heavens: a time to be born and a time to die, a time to plant and a time to uproot, a time to kill and a time to heal, a time to tear down and a time to build, a time to weep and a time to laugh, a time to mourn and a time to dance, a time to scatter stones and a time to gather them, a time to embrace and a time to refrain from embracing, a time to search and a time to give up, a time to keep and a time to throw away, a time to tear and a time to mend, a time to be silent and a time to speak, a time to love and a time to hate, a time for war and a time for peace.

ECCLESIASTES 3:1–8 NIV

From CC:

Rise up; this matter is in your hands. We will support you, so take courage and do it.

EZRA 10:4 NIV

From EC:

I can do all things through Christ who strengthens me.

PHILIPPIANS 4:13 NKJV

From LWD:

Train up a child in the way he should go, and when he is old, he will not depart from it.

PROVERBS 22:6 NIV

From MD:

And why do you worry about clothes? See how the lilies of the field grow. They do not labor or spin.

MATTHEW 6:28 NIV

From RF:

When pride comes, then comes disgrace, but with humility comes wisdom.

PROVERBS 11:2 NIV

From CG:

And he said to them all, "If anyone would come after me, let him deny himself and take up his cross daily and follow me."

LUKE 9:23 ESV

From JM:

Do not judge, or you too will be judged.

MATTHEW 7:1 NIV

From CVO:

"But me she forgot," says the LORD. "Therefore, behold, I will allure her, will bring her into the wilderness, and speak comfort to her. . . . And she shall sing there, as in the days of her youth."

HOSEA 2:13–15 NKJV

From RO:

May these words of my mouth and this meditation of my heart be pleasing in your sight, LORD, my Rock and my Redeemer.

PSALM 19:14 NIV

From LW:

Finally brothers and sisters, whatever is true, whatever is noble, whatever is right, whatever is pure, whatever is lovely, whatever is admirable—if anything is excellent or praiseworthy—think about such things.

PHILIPPIANS 4:8 NIV

From SW:

Do you not know that in a race all the runners run, but only one gets the prize? Run in such a way as to get the prize.

1 Corinthians 9:24 NIV

Order Information

REDEMPTION PRESS

To order additional copies of this book, please visit
www.redemption-press.com.
Also available on Amazon.com and BarnesandNoble.com
or by calling toll-free 1-844-2REDEEM.

CPSIA information can be obtained
at www.ICGtesting.com
Printed in the USA
BVHW071002131221
623912BV00009B/345